To Kiss a Wallflower

TIMELESS *Regency* COLLECTION

To Kiss a Wallflower

Jen Geigle Johnson
Heather B. Moore
Anneka R. Walker

Mirror Press

Copyright © 2022 Mirror Press
Paperback edition
All rights reserved

No part of this book may be reproduced or distributed in any form whatsoever without prior written permission of the publisher, except in the case of brief passages embodied in critical reviews and articles. These novels are works of fiction. The characters, names, incidents, places, and dialog are products of the authors' imaginations and are not to be construed as real.

Interior Design by Cora Johnson
Edited by Meghan Hoesch, Lisa Shepherd, and Lorie Humpherys
Cover design by Rachael Anderson
Cover Photo Credit: Abigail Miles / Arcangel

Published by Mirror Press, LLC

To Kiss a Wallflower is a Timeless Romance Anthology® book.

Timeless Romance Anthology® is a registered trademark of Mirror Press, LLC.

ISBN: 978-1-952611-26-1

TIMELESS REGENCY COLLECTIONS:

Autumn Masquerade
A Midwinter Ball
Spring in Hyde Park
Summer House Party
A Country Christmas
A Season in London
A Holiday in Bath
A Night in Grosvenor Square
Road to Gretna Green
Wedding Wagers
An Evening at Almack's
A Week in Brighton
To Love a Governess
Widows of Somerset
A Christmas Promise
A Seaside Summer
The Inns of Devonshire
To Kiss a Wallflower

TABLE OF CONTENTS

The Wallflower's Dance
By Jen Geigle Johnson _____ 1

Letters to a Wallflower
By Heather B. Moore _____ 109

To Marry a Wallflower
By Anneka R. Walker _____ 217

The Wallflower's Dance

Jen Geigle Johnson

Dedication

We're all wallflowers sometimes.

One

DESPITE LOTTIE'S MOTHER, WHO wished to know and be known by all and sundry, Lottie was still of the opinion that few people were required for happiness. Three things were needed: her closest friends, a good book, and lovely walks in the park.

And perhaps a husband.

Someday.

If he too preferred little company, books, and walks in the park.

She brought her brush, thick with paint, over the wood of a new table. She'd found a particular shade of lavender and knew it would go well in her sitting room. The lovely rich color covered the white beneath it completely.

Lottie smiled. Once this coat dried, she could add embellishments, flowers, a trailing vine of green, whatever she liked.

Her mother peeked her head in the door to her art room. "Lottie." The higher-pitched energy that exuded from her mother any time of day only felt companionable when Lottie too was full of energy. Which was usually reserved for the late hours of a ball. Something about the middle of the night filled Lottie with adventure. By then, her mother was typically nodding off in a corner somewhere.

"I'm painting, Mother. Come see this shade of purple. It's like nothing I've ever used before."

To her credit, she stepped into the room and glanced at the painting. "Very nice. Now. If you could take a break, we need to be stunning, absolutely beautiful for a walk in the park."

Lottie perked up at *walk*, but when the gleam in her mother's eyes sharpened and Lottie paid attention to *stunning* and *beautiful* as requirements, she knew this was going to be less about walking and more about being seen. "Perhaps you and your friends could go without me this morning? I'm hoping to finish up this coat." She knew her excuse sounded weak and her mother did too, judging by the dismissive wave of her fingers.

"Oh come, word has it that Prinny will make an appearance, which suddenly turns a casual walk in the park into a major event of the Season. This is your chance for more introductions, more doors opened to you. Who knows, you may even meet a duke!" The wide, hopeful eyes at the doorway were evidence that Lottie was not going to be able to avoid the park. She left her brush in water and stood, wiping fingers on her apron.

"Should I wear the violet?"

Mother was about to give Lottie's maid very detailed instructions as to her appearance anyway, so she might as well ask her before choosing a dress herself.

"No, too dark and bold for a walk in the park. Wear a pastel. But a colorful bonnet. Don't worry, I've instructed Dorothea in all the particulars."

Dorothea, Lottie's maid, very obviously worked for her mother. She could never be convinced to alter the prearranged instructions on Lottie's presentation. But no matter. Lottie moved obediently to her bedroom and the preparations began, starting with an intricate hairstyle that would be hidden underneath her bonnet. But Lottie knew better than to discuss her opinion on the particulars. She watched Dorothea in the mirror. Perhaps they would be able to have some entertainment to enliven them both. Entertainment in the form of another maid, reading aloud their latest favorite novel. Lottie's eyes met Dorothea's. "Will Penny be able to slip away?"

"I believe so, miss." Dorothea smiled. She enjoyed the books as much as Lottie, and if Lottie was to be sitting in this chair for hours, they may as well be entertained.

Lottie had discovered the rare occurrence of a servant who knew how to read. Even though she sometimes stumbled, she did less so now that she'd been tasked with the very important assignment of reading to Lottie while she prepared for the day. Penny slipped in through the servants' entrance. "I've just come from the kitchen." Her mischievous smile made Lottie laugh.

"Are they missing you?"

She waved a hand. "Not at all. Cook has an army of people in there, helping. I've finished all my other chores."

"Excellent and, of course, I called for you. That should help."

Both servants shared a look, which she took to mean that she had little clout in the servants' eyes. Well, no matter. "Please start at the beginning."

Penny nodded, her eyes gleaming with the same hopeful expectation Lottie herself felt. And then she began to read.

"The Family of Dashwood had long been settled in Sussex."

On and on she read, and the endless preparations for her promenade in the park faded away as the story took light. Until Penny regrettably closed the book, and Lottie stood before them, surely as stunning and beautiful as her mother had hoped. Too much time had been spent for her to be anything but.

Her mother's shining eyes at the base of the stairs were proof enough. Well, at least Lottie would not be asked to change anything, which often happened.

They exited their front door together, servants in tow. Lottie opened the pristine white parasol, rested it on her shoulder, and twirled it in between her fingers.

"Lottie, the parasol remains still. Keep it just so." Mother demonstrated the perfect angle at which to block the sun. Lottie imitated her out of habit. The woman would not be denied. Their townhome rested across the street from the park. Their row of homes stood tall and stately. She knew the families who owned each one. Sometimes they came to town, and sometimes they didn't. Her family had owned the property for a long time, generations of Hugheses, the very first of which had the great foresight to invest in the property because of its lovely situation and the trees across the way. When in London, a bit of green was always welcome, even back then.

But now they were on the most sought-after place in all of London, surrounded by the *ton's* most elite. Lottie, at times, wished to be somewhere else, somewhere less conspicuous. But then she'd have to give up the trees, and it turned out that Lottie was much like the very first Hughes. She admired the park and trees above all other inconveniences. Even though she might, at any moment, run into someone her mother would like to impress, with a thrown-together dress and hair only rapidly tied in a knot at the base of her neck. Before the Season had begun, her mother had allowed such a thing, leaving the house less than well presented. Now a step outside required several hours of preparation. And many books from the library.

Her mother walked with crisp hurried steps. "We are the slightest bit early because I felt it important to beat the rush. Once the others get here, I don't know how much of a chance you'll get."

"Others?"

"Your competition, my dear. They come with much more fanfare than you, I'm afraid. Dowries, glittering clothing, beauty that far surpasses anything we can offer." Her mother's appraising eye was obviously all business, so Lottie attempted to not be insulted by the assessment. But the tiny tears of hurt widened. Going up against the other ladies of the *ton* was intimidating enough without her mother finding her wanting.

Lottie knew she must marry. Certainly, her mother would absolutely demand such a thing, as she talked of it so often. But since Lottie had not yet attracted anyone, she was fairly certain her banns would not be read anytime soon.

They stood exposed, in the middle of the park, walking toward a well-used intersection of walking paths. People were starting to arrive in greater numbers. Lottie searched the area for her friend Denny, or his sister, Grace, particularly. Surely they would come if this was the event of the Season. She stood taller. They would come.

But unfortunately, all she saw were more of her mother's set. They curtseyed in front of the first of such.

"Mrs. Gladstone." Lottie smiled.

"Oh, Miss Hughes. You are going to be so enchanted. Today will be the day of all days to be at the park, just you wait and see. Come, we must position ourselves." She fluttered about, being as caught up in Lottie's Season as her mother. Perhaps that is just what friends did, or perhaps she loved it all as much as Lottie's mother appeared to.

The two walked in front of her, chattering and gossiping

and making plans. Names flew into the air—this duke, that earl, even a marquis who had been missing but had now returned. And Lottie could not keep up with it all.

But the day was beautiful. The sun shone gently; the breeze tickled her skin in a refreshing manner. The trees towered high against a rare blue sky. The light hint of roses wafted in her direction from the gardens up ahead. "Perhaps we could stand at the head of the fountain?" She braved a suggestion to the chattering duo.

But they didn't hear.

And so she followed along.

They paused at the crossway between paths. "Come, child." Her mother gestured as though they were in the greatest hurry. "You must stand here, with the flowers as your backdrop." She pointed to an exact spot on the ground.

Lottie would have preferred looking at the flowers, but the trees off on the other side of the path seemed interesting as well. Perhaps she could imagine lurkers in the shade.

"Now, Lottie"—her mother smiled—"you are lovely. With any luck, you will make every advantageous introduction today. Just think." She fanned herself. "To begin your Season with such a boon. I am greatly optimistic. Good things are in store. I feel it in all my bones. Good things."

Mrs. Gladstone nodded emphatically through her mother's speech. "They are, indeed, my dear girl. For are you not the most deserving, as well as the loveliest? Surely good things are in store." Their chatter took on a new energy.

Lottie squinted into the trees. Something, or someone, was wandering about in the shadows.

But she didn't have time to explore further. Mother's hand squeezed her arm, and an exuberant whisper filled her ear. "Smile."

"Of course." She breathed out and pasted on her smile.

Mother assessed her with one long appraising eye. "Perhaps if you could look happy while you smile—"

"Mrs. Hughes, Miss Hughes, Mrs. Gladstone," a deep rumbling voice interrupted.

They curtseyed, and Lottie lifted her gaze to a smart man sitting atop his horse. "I hear we are to have quite the crush this afternoon." His hair looked positively stuck to his head in a certain way. Lottie thought him clipped and pressed and rigid.

"Are we? That's lovely." Mrs. Hughes pressed a foot against Lottie's.

She jumped. "Oh, my lord. It is good to see you." Her greeting sounded more like an exclamation.

He eyed her a moment and then dipped his head. "You as well. You're looking quite fetching in that bonnet."

"Thank you," Lottie murmured. And then had nothing else to say. She panicked, searching her blank mind, then clenched her hands together. She could feel all eyes on her. She didn't know much about this man. Did he have a sister? A mother? At a nudge from her mother, she stammered out, "You too."

Could awkwardness actually pull her down into a sinking abyss to hide? At first, she daren't look at her mother.

The earl nodded his head, gave a quick small bow and then moved on. She didn't even remember his name, just that he was an earl. That's how her mother referred to him, at any rate.

Lottie held up a hand to an exasperated-looking Mother. "I know."

A group of laughing ladies, all on the arms of handsome gentlemen, walked by next. And then Lottie regretted immensely that they were standing in so public a location. Everyone in the group eyed her from toe to bonnet and seemed moderately friendly, but since none were introduced, they walked right on by.

"I feel like a spectacle."

Mother and Mrs. Gladstone exchanged glances. Their sighs were overly loud in Lottie's opinion. And there was a definite lack of excited chatter, now that Lottie had reminded them of her failure in social conversation. But perhaps that was for the best.

A songbird began its notes in the trees up ahead. And that reminded her. There was something to discover in that particular copse of trees. She'd seen it moments ago.

Minutes passed, too much time, where the three of them said little. Group after group of people Lottie had never seen before passed. She stared at her slippers, peeking out from the hems of her skirts.

"Oh, don't slouch, dear."

She lifted her chin and then a laugh carried over to her. The best noise of her whole day. Denny's laugh. She spun around, searching for him. He was taller than most. Surely, he would make an appearance soon. A huge group of women passed them, then Denny, at last.

"Bless that man! And he's brought men!" Her mother nearly swooned herself. She clutched Lottie's arm. "Three men!" But Lottie hardly heard her mother's swooning. Denny was coming. Her heart beat in erratic thumps of great relief. Denny would save her. He laughed again at something the man on his left had said. And when he glanced forward again, she knew the moment he saw her. His mouth stretched even further in the most natural grin of all. He lifted a hand, said something to the man on his other side, and soon all four were looking in her direction.

Her breath sped up, but before she could panic, she focused in on Denny. Her best friend. The man who'd known her forever. She could converse with Denny.

By the time they were close enough for introductions, she thought her gloves would be wet through from the clammy palms they housed, so she offered a hand to Denny first. "Lord Ragsdale. It's good to see you."

His smart bow and happy, teasing eyes made her laugh. "And you as well, Miss Hughes." His voice had a deep singing quality to it. She knew him to have a fabulous voice, as they'd sung hours of duets together while she played the piano. "Might I introduce you to some old chaps from Oxford?"

"Old." The man at his right, full of humor and hints of mischief, shook his head. "He speaks as though we're the grizzly-professor types.

"Right. Young, then. This grizzly here is Lord Hampton. And we have Mr. Wallace, and Mr. Tanner."

She curtseyed to them all and then froze, not knowing what to say. Denny jumped in. "Miss Hughes and I are too familiar. I could tell you her finer qualities, which involve the trees at the backs of our abutting properties, a quick, winding creek, and her ability with cricket, but I think perhaps you are looking for other things to discuss." He laughed when Lottie placed a hand at her forehead, but when she saw him wink, she nodded.

"I too could share all our childhood secrets so be forewarned, Lord Ragsdale."

"Ho ho! Too true. Then I must behave. Miss Hughes is truly a gift this Season, for she dances like none other and paints beautiful, er, chairs?"

"Tables."

"Ah, yes, tables, and is quite proficient on the piano."

Lottie felt much like she was being offered for sale, but instead of allowing the discomfort to rise, she added, "And Lord Ragsdale is precise with a shuttlecock, does undisclosed things at Jackson's, at which I have heard he is quite proficient, and sings rather well." She rocked back and forth from toe to heel, until her mother placed a hand on her arm, stilling her motion.

The others took their cue and shared random facts about each other, until the group as a whole was laughing so hard that Lottie had tears in her eyes. At one point she shared a grateful look with Denny. And he winked again.

Perhaps this Season wouldn't be as painful as she feared.

Or perhaps it would.

Two

LORD DENNISON RAGSDALE BOWED to his sister as her dance instructor called out the next country dance.

Grace's pout was prominent. "I never remember these steps. If I'm ever first in line, I'll be a great mockery."

"You won't. The others will know the steps. Just follow along with your four."

Her curls bounced around her face as she shook her head with great energy. "Unless there aren't four. You know sometimes we start with two."

They stepped together and then walked around two chairs, set up as imaginary couples in their group of four. "See, you know them now. You're not hesitating at all."

"I hope it sticks. I hope I don't freeze up when it's important and bumble through."

"Grace, you worry too much."

"Says you, who isn't about to face your second Season."

"This is my fourth, at least. I've lost count."

He lifted her hand up above his head as she circled. "You're a fantastic dancer. And besides, if you need help, you know Lottie will be there."

"True. I don't know how she's such a proficient, either."

Her instructor clapped out the rhythm. "You're lagging."

They lightened their steps.

Grace relaxed her shoulders, as she had yet to make one misstep. "Thank you for helping me."

"I'm happy to do it for a few minutes more. Then I'll be making a stop at the club. And the stables."

She returned to her original spot, ready to repeat the sequence. "All your stops in town. They're fine, I suppose. The country is just so much more pleasant, don't you think?"

"My horse is closer, if that's what you mean."

"Our horses are closer and there is an actual view out the window. We know all the neighbors already. It's . . . simple."

"I won't argue with you there." They stepped to the left to begin the whole sequence again. "I saw Lottie today at the park."

"How was she?" Grace laughed.

"She looked like she was ready for smelling salts. Too many people she didn't know. She cannot function."

"How will that woman ever marry?" Grace shook her head. "She has to be able to converse, to charm a man. Her dowry being what it is, something must compensate. She's pretty enough, of course."

Denny ran a hand through his hair. "I introduced her, and she was right clever. She floundered for a moment, but we made light of things. I am convinced Lord Hampton will seek her out at a ball."

She took his hands in hers as they walked in a sedate circle. "You can't dance with the two of them to ease the way. When she's left to herself, what will she do?"

He dipped his head. "Unless we were in a foursome. And, you know, she's *able* to converse. She knows how. We've seen her talk to any number of people."

"Well, of course, I'm just saying she won't always have you by her side. And I do think it's sweet you've kept this friendship for so long. But it's also not practical for you to have a friend like her. Someday, you'll marry. You need to be seeking your own wife and making your own way this Season."

He shrugged. "I'm in no hurry. I'd actually prefer not to marry quite yet."

"Don't tell Mother."

They finished up again and he checked his pocket watch. "That's my signal to make my bows. Keep working, sister." He winked.

She groaned.

As Denny left, the dance instructor began working with her on the angle of her wrists. Denny rotated his shoulders, so happy not to require further instruction in dance. It was fine enough, even diverting when Lottie was his partner.

He hurried out onto the street. He could send a servant for his horse, but he wanted to visit the stables. He wanted to brush Cyclone down. Grace was right. There was something about the country that appealed to him as well, and it involved being with his horse.

He hurried in the direction of the mews, skirting in between homes and down back alleyways in order to avoid anyone who might stop him in his progress.

The duke had purportedly returned. And Mr. Wallace had let slip that he was housing his stallion at the same stables with Denny's horses. The very stallion Denny wanted, the one Denny would have purchased, had the duke not beat him to it. But perhaps the man could be reasoned with and Denny could have a breeding opportunity. He had the perfect mare. If he could mate the two, his initial stock would be set.

He'd been studying and preparing to grow his stables to be a premier breeding and racehorse stable. He was on the brink. This stallion had been a key to that success. Curse the duke. How could he have purchased the horse first? The man was a menace. He had his fingers everywhere, sat at every gambling table, negotiated like the devil at Tattersall's, and beat out Denny in almost every situation.

But Denny had something the duke wanted.

He grinned to himself. That one thing was going to win him a chance at breeding with the stallion.

Denny slipped into the mews and breathed deeply the sometimes-pungent smells of a place full of many horses. Their owners were made up of the families who lived in the homes nearest their location, including the Hughes. He wondered if Lottie would be there. They both had an uncanny habit of slipping out to the mews at around the same time.

But as his eyes scanned the stalls, he was disappointed on two counts. No Lottie, and no duke.

He'd have to pay a call to the duke and talk business with him more formally.

Horses were being fed. Great piles of hay and buckets of grain were added to the stalls. Denny leaned his forearms on the door of Cyclone's stall. "How are you doing, big man?"

Denny planned to use Cyclone to breed as well. This stallion had a near perfect lineage. But he was getting older. He would create decent stock, but no one beat the lineage of Smoky, the duke's new horse. That one came from Forrester himself. With these two stallions, he could begin breeding, then raise up his own studs from their colts. A match between his mare and Smoky would be a winner. He was certain of it.

He brushed down Cyclone, more for his own benefit than anything. Their stable hands took good care of the horses. But Denny needed to think.

Then he moved to Smoky's stall. True to his name, the horse was a deep gray. So rare in color and worth his price in lineage, Denny stared with great covetous longing at the beautiful horse.

"Wishing you could rob me of my horse?" The duke's voice grated across Denny's skin, for no other reason than that he'd bought the horse before Denny did.

Denny turned and smiled. "Honestly, yes." He held out his hand. "Good morning, Your Grace."

"Good morning. You're looking for some good breeders, I hear?"

"I am. I'd like to talk to you about getting a cover from Smoky here." He skipped all other pleasantries and went straight to what he most desired.

The duke nodded but didn't answer for many minutes.

Denny was about to repeat the question, when the duke at last turned, his face unreadable. "I think I shall decline your petition."

"Why would you do that?"

"Because I am starting my own breeding program, and I purchased Smoky to be at the center of it all."

"Only because you heard me talking about it."

"I do my research."

What little research the duke did was fully and completely supplemented by his eavesdropping on Denny's conversations. What he couldn't figure out was how the man was able to grab the horse *before* Denny, who had a verbal agreement with Mr. Winson, the previous owner.

"I'm willing to pay extra."

The duke paused. His body went still. It was a subtle reaction, but Denny knew the signs. He also knew the duke had lost big the other evening and that he hadn't had the blunt to pay up.

"What makes you think I'm in such dire need of money? Really, Lord Ragsdale."

Denny knew His Grace was bluffing, but he'd bide his time. He needed one more mare as well.

"Everyone can use a bit of blunt. And I'll pay well." He turned back to admire the horse, leaving his offer to dangle in the air between them.

The duke left long before Denny, who took his time, going down his line of horses, watching them, thinking of all the possibilities, and further solidifying his plan.

By the time he was ready to leave, Lottie showed up. And the sun she brought into the dank and dark place was enough to keep him hovering about.

Three

LOTTIE WAITED WHILE THE groomsman saddled up her horse. She turned expectant eyes to Denny. "Are you coming?"

"Lott, I've been here for hours already."

She shrugged. "Suit yourself. I'll try to remember all the details of the new racetrack I heard they're building..."

His mouth opened and then closed, his eyes narrowing. "They've started?"

"Yes, they have." She knew her smile was self-satisfied, but it couldn't be helped. She also knew she'd soon have an escort to accompany her and ride out to the new track; perhaps they could even circle it a few times. Denny was a gem of a friend.

"You are a regular vixen of the first water, do you know that?" He frowned.

"Is that better or worse than being a diamond of the same?"

"In your case, worse. Far worse."

She laughed. "But you're coming?"

He sighed. "I'm coming." He waved for a man to saddle Cyclone.

"Have you found a good mare yet?"

"Well, we have Clarice."

"True. But you know you'll need another. You'll need

someone from the distance-endurance lineage. Someone like Browning or Merlin."

He ran a hand absentmindedly down her horse. "I know. I've narrowed it down to two. But I don't know how I can find anyone sired by either."

"We'll just have to pay attention. Been to Tattersall's?"

"Not today, no."

She reached for her reins, stepping up on a block to mount. "Do I sense a little irritation coming from you?"

He ran a hand through his hair. "It's the duke. The man won't let Smoky cover."

"That's stubbornness talking." She swung herself up onto her horse. "We can convince him. What sort of man is he?"

"The horse-stealing, competitive, cutthroat kind."

"Ah, I see, so a friend of yours, then?"

"Malcreat."

"Slug."

"Blunderbuss."

"Blunderbuss of the worst kind."

He rose one eyebrow. "If the men of the *ton* could hear you now."

"If they can't appreciate a little real talk from their women, then I can have nothing to do with them."

"You impressed Lord Hampton."

Her face flushed, *curse her ill-timed blush.* He studied her with an odd tilt to his head. "How can you tell such a thing?"

"I'm a man. Trust me. I expect he will come seeking a dance."

She snorted. "Well, that would be a first."

"Not so." He frowned. "We always dance a set."

"Ah, yes, my best friend." She sighed and looked away.

"And what is wrong with that? I could always *not* ask you..."

"You know I wouldn't want you to do that. But you also know that no one else asks me, well, except maybe some of the old, I mean, really old widowers."

He reached out and patted her mount. "I'm certain it will pick up. This is the Season. People come here to dance."

"And I do love to dance." She shifted on her mount.

"You're the best I've seen." He mounted Cyclone. "Grace could use your help."

"Dancing? Is she still concerned?"

Their horses nickered together. "Very. But she's excellent when she's not thinking about it."

"Like me. I can converse when I'm not thinking about it." She sighed, still stinging from the awkward moments in the park.

"Not just converse. You're charming, witty, and can bring me to tears with laughter. You're a regular entertainer."

"Unless someone is listening."

They urged the horses out into the back alleyway behind the townhomes. "You can talk when I'm listening."

"I know. I never thanked you for showing up when you did at the park."

He dipped his head. "What a hilarious conversation. Honestly. The best I will likely have this whole week, or longer."

"My cheeks hurt from smiling."

"You made it even better. I got you started, but you had everyone almost falling over with laughter. That was you." His face beamed with his typical Denny sincerity.

But she just looked away. "It's not the same when I'm by myself. I cannot think of a thing to say. Nothing. My mind goes totally blank and then I panic and then I say the first thing that enters my brain out of desperation. It's not pretty."

He laughed. He didn't even try to hide it.

"You're laughing because it's true."

"Well, now, there was that time—" He snorted.

"Oh, stop."

"With the baron."

Her cheeks flamed. "You would have done the same."

"If the baron wanted to ask me to dance?" He lifted his eyebrows, watching her.

She rose higher on her mount in mock pride. "I'm fairly certain the turkeys on our estate are a perfectly acceptable conversation topic . . . somewhere."

He wiped his eyes. "I know. I'm teasing, but in sincerity, you just need a little more practice. Come, let us pretend we have just met."

"We've done this before."

"Obviously not enough."

They moved out onto the wider streets and headed for the park.

"Come. I'll be the duke." His grin was too contagious.

"His Grace?"

"Certainly. You'll meet him, one day. He shares the same mews as us. And besides, doesn't every woman wish to be acquainted with the duke?"

"I suppose."

"Miss Hughes, you look lovely this evening. Bow, kiss your hand, etc."

She watched him.

"Your turn."

"Oh, very well. Hello, Your Grace. Thank you." And then she froze.

"What's the matter?" He watched her.

"What do I say?"

Denny shrugged. "What do you mean?"

"Well, he told me I look lovely. I said thank you. But now it's my turn to start something, and I don't know what."

"Well, what would you say to me?"

"Some personal joke between us."

"Ah, and you have no intimacy with His Grace."

"Correct. And I freeze."

"You could ask how he's liking the Season."

She huffed out a breath that tickled her forehead. "That's such a boring, asked-too-many-times, dull kind of question."

"But it's better than the alternative."

She sighed, then nodded. "You are correct. Perhaps I'm holding out for the most clever thing in the world to pop into my mind, when I can actually just be lifeless and dull."

Denny tipped his head back and laughed into the blue sky. "You are a wonder, Lottie Hughes, a true wonder."

"I'm just not gifted with clever conversation."

"Maybe you can pretend they are all me . . . with memory loss."

It was her turn to laugh, and Denny turned serious. He leaned toward her. "Now see that?"

She turned this way and that. "What am I seeing?"

"Your face. It lights up when you laugh and you aren't worried about people noticing. And your voice. It has this deeper, husky quality to it."

She raised a hand to her face. "Husky? Really?"

He nodded. "The men are going to love this side of you if you ever let them see." He adjusted his cravat a moment then met her eyes.

"So, all I do is pretend I'm talking to you. That will be my method from now on. The *ton* will be full of memory-deprived Dennys."

"You can take your first test right now." He indicated a group of men on horseback.

Her face paled, and she swallowed what felt like something large.

"Are you well?"

"Petrified." She lifted her eyes and pasted on a smile, and even though he'd seen the transformation a hundred times, he studied her, as though he was amazed, yet again. She watched him try not to make a face. For instead of the vibrant, stunning woman at his side, he was now accompanied by a stiff and awkward-looking creature. She knew it, and it made things worse that she knew.

They approached the group. He rotated his shoulders and pasted on another smile. "At any rate, you could use the introductions, could you not?"

She nodded, pressing her lips together.

They were almost within hearing distance. He whispered, "Get it together," then lifted his chin. "Good afternoon to you."

Three perfectly eligible men paused in front of Lottie, all with curious, even interested, expressions.

Four

LOTTIE TRIED TO GAIN some control. She tried not to panic. Swallowing, clenching her hands together, she tried to pretend like speaking with strangers was normal. But to no avail. Denny's introduction sounded far away, almost as if her head was under water. The three men wavered in front of her for a moment while she clutched the reins.

"Miss Hughes?" Denny's concerned eyes bored into hers. She blinked away the dizzy spell and cleared her throat.

"Yes, hello, I, um . . . hello." She nodded too many times, smiled, then wished to hide. She looked away.

But the first of the newcomers, the one closest to her, smiled warmly. "I see you enjoy riding."

"I do, yes." How could he know such a thing?

"Your seat is so natural. I myself feel rather stiff."

That sparked her curiosity, and she forgot her fear for a moment. "Do you not ride often?"

"I do, when I can, but I find I am often in my books." He dipped his head as though this were a thing to require an apology.

"Oh, well, then, you are absolved. For there are two worthy pursuits, riding and reading." She breathed out in relief. She'd done it. A full sentence of rather interesting dialogue. The victorious look she flashed Denny was answered in kind.

"So, you also enjoy reading. Excellent." He nodded.

Denny then jumped in, involving the others. And the conversation continued around her with little required of herself.

As soon as they'd left, she giggled. "Did you hear that?"

"I did indeed. Well done. See, it is not so hard, and now you shall have an admirer."

"Shall I?" Astounded, she replayed their interactions. "I don't know how it could be so."

"Mark my words, Mr. McAllister will also be asking you to dance."

"I quite liked the looks of him."

He looked twice, adjusting his shoulders. "You did?"

"Yes, something about his cravat."

"His . . . cravat?"

"Right, yes, it was different. All cravats are the same, are they not? He found a way to be unique. I liked that."

Denny didn't respond, but a slight frown line appeared just above his eyes.

They continued riding and then approached a rather large group of women, all with their eyes on Denny. He slowed, naturally. And their giggling commenced.

"Lord Ragsdale." The boldest of the group fluttered her eyelashes and curtseyed. "Have you heard there's to be a ball?"

"I have indeed, to which are you referring, Miss Spelting?"

"Oh, why the one this evening, the Worthingtons' ball? I hear His Grace will be there."

"Certainly." Denny nodded. "Of course." His jaw clenched, and Lottie almost laughed at this sudden surge of dislike. What had gotten into her friend?

"Well, we were wondering—I mean, all of us—we hope you will attend?" Her eyes widened and then she dipped them in such a show of false modesty that Lottie snorted. All eyes turned to her.

She cleared her throat and coughed a bit, attempting somehow to cover up the sound. "I do apologize."

Denny leaned back so that Lottie was more in view of the others. "Have you had the pleasure of meeting Miss Lottie Hughes?"

Lottie didn't think she'd yet met a single one. So Denny went through the names. Every woman nodded briefly at her, then returned their eyes to Denny.

As she looked at her friend, she realized she'd never once considered what other women thought of him. Was he a handsome man? Would they wish to dance with him? Be courted by him? A sudden surge of fear and . . . jealousy raged through her, twisting and curling her satisfaction in unhappy knots. Would she lose her best friend to one of these simpering, eyelash-twittering ladies? As her gaze brushed over them all, she dismissed the entire group as being unworthy of her best friend.

And then Denny's words, "I'd like your first set, if you could spare it," stunned Lottie.

She returned her attention to the conversation. A brunette with striking green eyes did not look pleased enough to be so singled out by Denny. The others maintained hopeful expressions. And Lottie wished to move on. How could Denny have asked one of them to dance?

He turned his face to Lottie, his eyes holding an apology before he nodded to the group. "I do believe we are on our way. It was wonderful to see you all." He bowed from a sitting position on the horse. Lottie nodded with a flat smile that surely could not have reached her eyes.

They moved on, their horses clopping gently away on the soft earth at their feet.

Denny puffed out a small bit of air. "I apologize for my blunder."

"You had a blunder?"

"The first set . . ." He paused and searched her face. "We usually share that set."

Her cheeks reddened unnecessarily and she stammered her way through some kind of response. "I, well, that's perfectly fine. I know you are hoping to dance with others."

"But you're my first choice, perhaps tonight you could reserve the second for me?"

She laughed to herself, knowing she'd have plenty available for him, and nodded. "Yes, of course."

They rode in silence. Then she blurted out, "They want me to marry."

"Who? Your mother?"

"Yes. Her sisters, my grandmother, every female member of my family is waiting, holding their breath until I marry." Her shoulders slumped.

"I'm sure you will marry." He cleared his throat and then he turned an unsettled expression toward her. "But I don't know how much I will enjoy such a thing." He stared straight ahead, but his brow was low over his eyes, his shoulders slumping slightly, his hands fidgeting.

"What do you mean?"

"I don't know. Just all of a sudden, I don't know if I will like Lord Hampton, or Mr. McAllister, or Mr. Tanner, who all seem intrigued, to be the number one man in your life. Where does that put your best friend?"

"How do you think I like being your second dance? Have I ever been your second dance?"

"No."

They continued in silence, Lottie becoming lost to unhappy thoughts of Denny's dancing attendance with other ladies.

"You've flirted with other women in front of me before. Never bothered me."

"And I've always tried to help you meet other men, never bothered me."

Their frowns deepened.

She opened her mouth, then closed it again. What was there to say?

"I suppose we could marry." Denny shrugged. "Each other."

Lottie sucked in a quick breath of surprise, which caused a choking fit she did not try hard to end. What kind of question was that? Was he being serious? Joking? Making light of their awkward conversation? When she at last finished, she turned to him and waited until he met her eyes. "What are you saying?"

He shook his head. "I'm being ridiculous. We both have to marry. We have to marry someone of substance and benefit to our estates. We're just going to have to learn to accept the other people in our lives."

"Oh, ugh. What if I hate your wife?" She couldn't help it. The words came tumbling out. "What if you marry Lady Emily?" She placed a hand over her mouth and shook her head. "I'm sorry, but you cannot marry someone abhorrent."

"I don't plan to. And there is nothing wrong with Lady Emily."

Lottie gasped. "Are you planning to marry her?"

Denny laughed. "Of course not. I haven't thought about it at all, but I haven't ruled her out, either." He shook his head. "This is a ridiculous conversation for you and I to have."

"I don't find it that ridiculous. What if I married the duke?"

His face went white, then red. "You wouldn't."

A laugh grew from deep inside her, delighted she'd found her own button to push with him. "Why on earth not?"

"He's a cretin of the lowest order. Do you know he stole *my* stallion out from under me? The very one!"

"So now I'm likened to the stealing of one's horse?"

"Well, yes! That horse was the best thing that could have happened to my stables." He dipped his head. "However, I'm sorry. You know I don't really think of you that way."

She sighed, choosing not to be offended. Denny was a dear. But she knew him too well. "We'll just have to go to the other for approval, then, shan't we?"

"Yes, most certainly if people like the duke are coming forward as options."

"I don't think we shall have to worry one bit about hordes of men vying for my hand."

"But look at today. You had a conversation you didn't botch up."

"I am quite proud of such a thing."

He nodded with his most tender smile. "You are smashing, and as soon as the men realize such a woman exists, I won't have another moment such as this." He lifted his hand to indicate their ride.

"Certainly not unchaperoned. I do believe Mother will have fits and vapors if she finds out even today happened."

"She might, but then your aunt will talk sense into her. Everyone knows we are the best of friends. Nothing more could be expected from us."

Did his statement have a question? His eyes certainly held an inquiry, but he had since looked forward again as though not awaiting a response.

What an odd conversation with her Denny. They were friends. Nothing would happen to change that. Not even marriage.

Five

Denny watched his valet finish his cravat for a long time. "Are we trying something new?"

"We are. You asked that I make inquiries, learn some different methods from that Brummell-following person. McCallister, wasn't it? These are just a few of his techniques that promise to create an improved knot."

Had Denny asked him to do such a thing? He vaguely remembered perhaps being intrigued by the idea of it all. But now all he wanted was to be away from the hands of his man and in his carriage. But Lottie had mentioned cravats, hadn't she? She liked it when men tried something different.

When he fidgeted again, Smithson dipped his head. "Brummell himself works on his presentation for three hours or more, sometimes six."

Denny's mouth dropped. "To tie his cravat?"

"I understand that is a large part of it. He's been known to tear the thing from his neck and demand that the man start over. He oversees the pressing of the cloth as well."

"You can rest assured I will never be so involved in the process. For a ball, the extra touches are fine, but certainly not on an average day, and not when I'm merely seeing gentlemen friends." He considered Lottie. She was certainly not in the same group as his gentlemen friends. Particularly now, as she was trying to be noticed by the others, he realized that he wanted to be equally impressive to her.

A new development in their relationship, perhaps.

"Understood." Smithson pulled and tugged with his thumbs, pinkies out.

Denny could only watch with a small measure of disbelief. But when Smithson at last turned to face the mirror, he had to admit. He looked good.

"My compliments, Smithson. You've outdone yourself."

"I must say that you've never looked better." He did not even brush down Denny's shoulders with his characteristic final farewell. With a nod, he deemed Denny perfect. And with that, Denny hurried down the stairs, into the waiting carriage.

"What took you so long?" Grace was already sitting with her maid and had been waiting, he surmised.

"I can't really say. Smithson had some new techniques to try." He lifted his chin so that she might get a good view of his cravat.

"Besides the fact that we are nearly late, I approve."

"Do you?" He turned this way and that. "I admit, I've given it little thought before now."

"I've heard all the men are suddenly giving it thought. Perhaps you'll be the declared belle of the ball tonight. So to speak. The male version."

"What?"

"If Beau Brummell comes to an event, he often singles out the man most particularly and carefully dressed, and that man becomes the fashion icon to emulate. Come, brother, don't you hear any of these things at White's or something, somewhere you men converse?"

"We certainly don't converse about our cravats." He situated himself on the carriage bench, trying to get comfortable.

"Well, some men do. And being Brummell-approved is one of those things."

Interesting. Would such a thing be impressive to Lottie? "Well, now that I've spent several hours on the thing, I suppose I shall see if it was worth the effort."

"Trying to impress anyone in particular?" Her smile was too knowing.

"If I am, I'm not aware." He shifted in his seat again, suddenly uncomfortable. "But someday, I must marry. Someday, I must impress a woman."

She folded her hands in her lap. "I'm fairly certain you've impressed your fair share, but you never do much about it."

"Up until now, I've not been ready to take such a step."

Her mouth dropped open. "And you're ready now?" She leaned forward. "What aren't you telling me?"

Lottie filled his mind in an uncanny way since their conversation earlier. She was now someone to consider—at least he thought he might be considering her. "I'm not keeping things from you, sister. But I simply have a new desire to explore my options."

Her smile grew. "Most excellent." She adjusted her skirts and then clenched her hands. "I only hope I don't trip and fall on my face."

He laughed and then observed her pale countenance. "You won't. You certainly won't."

She waved her hand around. "Oh, don't mind me. I'm unreasonably nervous." Her lip quivered.

Denny had to act quickly, or he'd have a crying, red-faced sister to care for in a matter of moments.

"Remember my first ball?" He laughed. "I was talked of for weeks."

"Lottie was with you, wasn't she?"

"Yes, of course. She was at my side, and she'll never let

me live it down. I tripped over my own two feet. But instead of toppling over, I created a new step, a sort of flourish at the end."

She snorted, her worries apparently forgotten. "And then Lottie did it as well?" She raised a hand to her lips. "I love it when you two tell this together. I need a repeat performance."

"Yes, well, she did do it next. She was making fun and then others began imitating. And now, I'm responsible for that toe tip and extra hop at the end of one of our country dances."

She shook her head in apparent wonder.

They arrived in front of a tall brick home. "We are here." A footman opened their door and Denny hopped out, turning to help his sister down. "You look beautiful. Every man here will be clamoring for your attention."

"You will assist us, Lottie and me?"

"Of course. And Mother will be here shortly."

"Yes." She stood taller. "I'm ready."

Everyone seemed to be gathered in the street near the entrance. They were chattering in great animation. Denny paused their approach to the house. "Is it just my perception, or is everyone overly exuberant about something right now?"

"No, you're correct. Something has happened." They both craned their necks but could see nothing out of the ordinary. Then the crowd noise increased, and a new carriage pulled forward. Every neck craned in its direction.

"Isn't that . . . Lottie?"

People crowded forward toward her carriage. Three of the men who Denny had introduced her to stood at the very front, ready to hand her down from her carriage.

"What on earth?" Denny held his sister's hand close, both apparently frozen to the ground beneath them.

"I don't know what to make of this." Grace stood closer to him.

The footman created a path to the door and opened it with a great flourish. The crowd noise increased, then Lottie stepped out, looking particularly lovely.

Grace's hand went to her mouth. "She's stunning. Denny, she's absolutely beautiful."

"I see that." He pressed his lips together. "And she doesn't look pleased."

"Oh, you must rescue her." Grace gripped his arm. "She's going to totally freeze up."

Lottie's eyes searched the crowd and found Denny. But he stared helplessly on. "What can I do? There's no way I could make my way through that. Lord Hampton will take care of things."

The siblings watched as she placed a hand on Lord Hampton's arm. He laughed and then dipped his head toward her. She seemed to be responding.

"Perhaps she is making sense?" Grace shook her head.

"I . . . can't tell."

Grace tugged on him. "Come, we must join them inside."

They hurried to beat the crowd that was attempting to accompany Lottie to the front door.

"I've never seen the like." He hurried with his sister just squeezing ahead of a large amount of people heading for the front stairs.

"Nor I, and why Lottie?" Grace gripped his arm as if afraid to be torn from his side.

The chatter around them became louder as they were soon encompassed by the group. Loud exclamations shed some light. Everyone was talking about Lottie.

"She's an heiress. Close on sixty thousand pounds."

"Not a wallflower anymore."

"Every man in the room is going to be after her hand."

Grace and Denny exchanged looks, then Grace

murmured in his ear. "This might be the worst thing to ever happen to our Lottie."

"Or the best." He studied the men hovering. "Or the worst." He straightened his shoulders. "Looks like we have our work cut out for us."

"I don't think I shall worry any more about stumbling in the dance, at any rate. There are more pressing matters."

"Look at it this way, you will get twice as many offers to dance, just by virtue of standing near her."

She swatted him. "I don't even know what to say about that comment."

"I don't even know what I'm saying. This is astounding. Is our Lottie an heiress, truly?"

"People think she is. And that is how the ball will go, at least."

He wanted nothing more than to pull Lottie aside and hear the whole of it. But time alone at a ball did not exist. This was the block of hours to see and be seen and to care for one's reputation. Unless they had a waltz, he'd not have a moment to share with his best friend.

"At least she looks happy." Grace's voice had a wistful quality to it.

He turned. Lord Hampton and Lottie were just a few groups behind them, and she did indeed look very happy. His friend was speaking with great animation and she seemed entertained.

He shared another glance with Grace. "He's a good match for her, given the way he loves to talk. She won't have to think of as many things to say."

"True. And by the time he gives her a second, she might have thought of something."

As soon as they entered, they made their way to the host and hostess and entered the ballroom. They were immediately surrounded.

A deep voice interrupted. "I was wondering, might you give me an introduction to Miss Hughes?" The first of Denny's friends stepped forward, followed by many more such requests. Grace was hounded with similar requests, but from what he could tell, an equal number of men seeking to dance with her as well, for which he was relieved. The more she was entertained and cared for, the more he could assist Lottie. And his best friend was going to need him.

Six

LOTTIE GRIPPED LORD HAMPTON'S arm as if her life depended on it. How had so many heard of her inheritance?

She'd just read the letter, regarding her newfound dowry and large amount of money willed to her, that afternoon. Her aunt had nearly fainted to the floor. Her mother had, at first, not said anything, as though robbed of intellect. Then she spent the next couple hours fanning herself and beaming with the light of victory. But soon after the initial shock died down, her mother switched into action, and letters had been written. Perhaps she had been the cause of the spread of information. And Lottie's maid had been tasked with making her as gorgeous as she could. The modiste was sent for and new gowns ordered.

The modiste.

Surely the woman had shared the news.

Or Lottie's aunt. She'd left rather suddenly, a new spark gleaming in her eye.

Or any number of their servants. It was news indeed. But to have so many of the families in London already know, and to treat her so differently . . . She prevented the frown that wanted to come and instead pasted on a smile.

Denny and Grace had never looked more confused and concerned. And she did not blame them one bit. She herself was confused and concerned. She would have to converse with all these people at some point. She would have to open her mouth. She wasn't certain she would leave with the respect of anyone present, not when they realized her ineptness in conversation.

All this fuss about money?

Lord Hampton leaned closer. "I'm pleased we have the first set. Shall I deliver you to Lord Ragsdale until then?" His eyes were compassionate. He seemed to understand her great discomfort.

"You might stay with me there if you like. But yes, I would like to see Lady Ragsdale as well."

"We will do our best." He stepped closer, his body shielding her from some of the shuffling and crowding.

"I've never seen an event quite like this." Her gaze circled them, trying to take it all in.

"I fear you've created quite a stir."

"It seems so." She stepped closer. "Thank you."

"We will get you inside and then things will proceed in a more orderly and civilized manner."

"Yes, I assume as much."

He shook his head. But they crossed the threshold, and it was considerably more quiet. They moved forward in a short line that presented them in front of their hosts. Lottie curtseyed. "Thank you for the invitation. Everything is lovely."

"We are so pleased to have you. You've added quite a bit of additional interest in our ball." Lady Worthington smiled. "If you find you need a break, besides the ladies' receiving rooms, might I offer you our family sitting area upstairs?"

"Oh, thank you." She nodded gratefully.

"Bring a servant." Lord Worthington wisely suggested.

The implication that she should perhaps avoid being alone with anyone did nothing to ease her concern.

She moved on with Lord Hampton, and they waited while the footman called out her name. The room went quiet, and many eyes turned to her.

"Oh, help."

"Just smile and nod." Lord Hampton did just that, and he looked perfectly natural.

So, she imitated his methods, smiling and nodding twice before entering the room, attempting to pretend like no one was watching. Out of habit, she searched for the perfect places to wait at the side of the ball, unseen and quiet. But as a line immediately formed near them, she wondered if this ball would be much different from all the others she'd attended.

A smaller group surrounded Denny. He glanced twice in her direction, a helpless expression bringing her some sort of odd comfort. They were both at a loss. "I don't know what to say." She swallowed. "When people talk to me, I never know what to say." She turned a portion of her trust to Lord Hampton.

His eyes filled with understanding. "And you'll be dancing with quite a few more than usual, I'd venture a guess."

She nodded.

"I think you could say the same things to them all. One by one."

Her shoulders relaxed a small amount. "They wouldn't know, would they?"

"I don't think so. We all end up discussing the same topics over and over again anyway. No one would think anything of it, even if they were to compare notes."

"Too true." Her mind raced. "What an excellent idea. And you shall be my first."

He winked. "A position I'm more than happy to be. Might I say, Miss Hughes, my interest in asking you to share the first set came before this newfound popularity?" His eyebrows rose. But when she didn't know how to respond to that kind of statement, he placed a hand over hers, resting on his arm. "Just think about that as the evening goes on."

She nodded. Person after person was presented before her. It seemed Lord Hampton knew half the *ton* and her mother the other half. Then those who knew them, knew others. Soon Lottie would not be surprised if she had indeed been introduced to the whole of the ball.

At last, the music started up and she and Lord Hampton made their way to the center of the floor.

Many eyes were on them.

His eyes sparkled in amusement. "I suspect you have just elevated my presence here as well."

"This is all just utterly . . . baffling." She had no way of knowing such a thing would occur. To be in the center of everyone's eyes because of her inheritance? None of these people had cared one ounce to know her before now. Granted, she'd not given them a chance to know her. That pillar on the opposite side with a plant nearby, that would have been her place to wait out the ball. The longing she felt for a bit of hidden dark space was ludicrous. But real.

Grace joined her with Denny.

"Praise the stars." Lottie shook her head. "What is to become of me?"

Grace squeezed her arm. "We shall have a time of it tonight, shan't we? Then we must compare our experiences. Come for tea tomorrow."

"Thank you, I will. Before calling hours. I predict Mama would like me home for those." She glanced around the room. All eyes were still on her. "Must I smile all the while, lest these people see my frown?"

Lord Hampton tilted his head. "That depends. Let's have a look at your frown."

She gifted him with a gentle lowering of her eyebrows. Several of the women behind him gasped.

"Goodness." She knew her cheeks warmed. "I don't wish people to think ill of you." She shook her head. "What a conundrum. I think I might be utterly exhausted by the end of this."

"Might I have the supper set?" Denny's gaze comforted and excited her at the same time. He had a new intensity, a protective air, that seemed to encircle her.

"Certainly."

"And I the last?" Lord Hampton glanced at Denny and back at her.

"Yes."

The warm-up completed, and the introductory measures began.

"Oh, help." Grace grabbed at her stomach.

"You shall be brilliant." Lottie smiled at her friend, grateful to be focused on someone besides herself for a moment. "Review the order in your mind. You've done this countless times."

Grace nodded. And they began.

Lottie became lost in the steps, distracted by helping Grace remember, aware of Denny beside her, and at last free, for a moment, from the strange feeling of every eye on her. Her feet made magic for her. She lifted her arms, curtsied, circled, skipped, and bounced. And she loved every second. If dancing didn't require conversation, she would be more excited to attempt to do so more. But what she most dreaded were those moments, standing alone, without a dance partner and with eyes on her, wondering all manner of things about her desirability. It was much easier to hide in the shadows, to not have to worry about conversation. But she had missed out on the dances.

She laughed in enjoyment as Denny threw in an extra flip of his feet just to make light. "You wouldn't. Not another."

"I think we should. Why not?"

She gripped his hands and as he moved closer in the steps, he lingered just a breath longer than necessary, his eyes catching hers. Then, with a gentle squeeze, sent her to the next man.

But that moment lingered as she approached every man in the line, her hands tingling from Denny's touch, her heart clenched from the expression in Denny's eyes. She'd always been grateful for her best friend, but this was something completely different.

And she didn't know what to do with it. But she knew she was greatly looking forward to their dance.

When she was back with Lord Hampton, he felt more familiar than the long line of others around them so she felt more at ease.

He appraised her. "You are a beautiful dancer."

"Thank you. I do love a good country dance." She felt not at all nervous saying so.

When the dance finished, she longed for a drink. Grace stepped up to her side. "I could use a lemonade."

"Me too."

The path to the drink table was crowded. And the music for the second set was about to begin. Lord Hampton bowed. "Thank you for our set. I look forward to the next." He turned to leave.

Denny moved closer to her side. "I am astounded. What has happened? Is it true? You are now an heiress?" His words, spoken close to her ear, sent a wave of comfort and a hint of anticipation through her.

"We are parched," Grace said, waving a hand in front of her face, "but trapped here."

Denny glanced around them. "I dare not leave you two alone. Who is coming to dance the next set with you, Grace?"

A tall man arrived directly behind her. Broad, handsome. "I believe I would like to claim that honor."

"Your Grace." Denny's mouth barely formed the words through his teeth.

The Duke of Chester was certainly much more handsome than Lottie imagined, as he was dressed up for the ball. She curtseyed low. "Your Grace."

Denny stiffened. "You know Miss Hughes, I presume?"

"I have not had the honor of a formal introduction, no."

"Then, might I do the honors? This is my dear friend Miss Hughes, and this is His Grace, the Duke of Chester."

"It's a pleasure meeting you." Lottie was astounded. Her words flowed. She knew what to say. "I understand you are not often in town?" Again, a perfectly phrased sentence. Grace nodded in encouragement. Denny narrowed his eyes.

"I have not been, no, but I find there are things enticing me to stay for a while. I wonder, might I have the third set?"

"Certainly, thank you." She nodded.

He turned and offered Grace his arm.

The music for a waltz began and Denny closed his eyes in relief. As he approached and placed his arm at her back, she laughed. "What has gotten into you?"

"I could ask the same of you. I cannot believe all of this. Are you . . . well? Besides being still completely parched, I'd imagine."

"I think so. I have truly inherited. A long-lost relative saw fit to leave the whole of it to me. The steward says I am of age, and therefore the money is all mine, no matter how Mother wishes to govern its use. He said he works for me and will do only as I say." Her voice shook. "I don't know what to tell him."

Denny nodded. "I can only imagine. What a predicament."

"It is good, though, right?"

"Of course. Wonderful. But all these people." He shook his head. "How are we to know who is sincerely seeking your hand and not your money?" His mouth pressed together. "We must come up with an interview or a system of tests. Something. We must have a plan. We cannot just show up at a ball like this again, totally unprepared. Who knows what will happen in the very next set when I leave you with His Grace." He winced. "He must not be allowed to take you outside for a bit of air." He stretched against his cravat. "Though such a thing sounds like just the perfect solution at the moment, for you and I."

"Yes, and a drink if we could." She swallowed the dryness in her throat.

"You are so correct. But a waltz." He stepped closer. "Perhaps we should enjoy a waltz. We've practiced for this moment, you know." His eyebrows wiggled just enough to make her smile.

"We have indeed." Then she lifted her chin in challenge.

"Someone needs to show the ballroom how to dance."

So they did. They twirled and spun and flew across the ground. They added steps, took away steps, leaned, balanced, and moved all within the parameters of their three meters. They'd played dancing often before their coming out, embellishing the steps, as both were easily bored with the repetitive dance moves of their instructors.

By the middle, Lottie was laughing through happy tears and Denny had become even more bold. He paused and pulled her close. "This is what every dance should be." His eyes searched her face, looking deeply into the depths of her thoughts. "I wish we could dance another right after this."

"As do I, Denny. I don't know how to do this." She indicated to all the room with her eyes.

"I will help."

"Will they all come calling? Proposing? What if Mother forces my hand?"

"We will talk it through. I will not leave you. I . . . Lottie, I care for you. More than ever, I want to see you happy."

His eyes shown with sincerity, with hope. And she could only be filled with warmth. "Thank you. I don't know what I would do." She sighed. "Lord Hampton was nice. The duke—"

"He's a cretin of the lowest order. I told you."

"Him stealing your stallion does not mean he wouldn't be a good match."

"But we still have to agree, right?"

"Agree?"

"On each other's choice. We have to agree?"

She hesitated.

He stopped. "Lottie. You cannot go marrying some evil man who I cannot stand to be around."

She nodded. "Right. Agreed."

He let out a great sigh of relief.

They continued.

"What is wrong, Denny? You are unhappy."

His arm circled her back, bringing her closer—as close as she dared. And she wondered at the great feeling of protective care he exuded, at the tingles that rushed up and down her arms. He strained against his cravat again and then looked down into her eyes, giving all his attention to her in that moment. "I realized today that I don't want to lose you."

His face grew closer, and she was astounded that more than anything, she did not want to lose him, either.

"You won't. We'll just have to explain things to our

matches. We are family." She nodded. "That's how it's going to be."

A flicker of relief flashed across his face. Then his mouth flattened in a line. "That cretin."

The duke held Grace close, as close as she was to Denny.

"Is he not a good man, the duke?" She looked from him to Denny and back.

"He's fine. His dealings with me have been aggravating, but beyond that, I've seen nothing in him to be overly alarmed about."

She considered those words for several more measures. Then she smiled. "Your cravat is a masterpiece. I've never seen you wear it like that."

"Do you like it?" His face glowed with pleasure. "We are trying something new."

"It suits you. Women are noticing." Everywhere, women were watching him with interested eyes. Something about that realization made her want to stand in the way of their gazes.

"And you noticed." He smiled. "I wondered if you would."

"You look . . . nice." She felt her face heat, and for the first time in her life, she had no idea what to say to her best friend. He was handsome, and she felt tingly inside, wanting to run fingers up into his hair, which was something that had never happened to her before. But she couldn't say any of those things. What *could* she say? "It makes you look . . . smart." She wanted to bury her head in her hands.

"Thank you? I think that's a compliment." He eyed her. "Are you freezing up in front of me?"

"What?" She shook her head. "N-No. I'm not." She clamped her mouth shut before she said anything else.

"But you are. You don't know what to say about this cravat."

She opened her mouth to say something, unsure what, then closed it. She hoped to impress him. She wanted all his time. She was almost desperate for him. But she daren't say more. She didn't know more. None of it made any sense.

The music sounded as though it was wrapping up.

Her heart hammered. "Now what do I do?"

"You try not to give the duke any reason to believe he has a chance."

Denny bowed just as the duke arrived.

His Grace took her hand. "Before we line up, I believe our partners need some refreshment." He tucked Lottie's hand on one arm and Grace's on the other and directed them to the lemonade. People seemed to part to make way for them.

"That's incredible." Lottie let the words slip before she could stop them.

"That's influence." His Grace nodded here and there. When they got to the table, he lifted a cup for Lottie and then for Grace.

"Thank you." She sipped politely at her lemonade, though she wished to down the whole of it.

Soon she was back out on the dance floor, standing next to the Duke of Chester. And he was charming and handsome.

She had no trouble at all conversing with him.

Seven

THE LONGER DENNY WATCHED Lottie with the duke, the more he wished to stand in between the two of them and take her away.

Her laugh carried over to him, three couples down. Then she said something and the duke barreled out a laugh, equally loud. Her face was animated. Her words flowing freely. What had happened to his Lottie that untied her tongue? And why had she seemed frozen when talking to him?

Denny's partner, a pretty blonde he was sure Lottie would not like, circled around him with a hopeful smile. He turned his attention to her. They could have just as hilarious a time of it. He laughed about nothing, just to get them started, and though she looked a bit taken aback, she joined him. Good-natured woman.

He then proceeded to say all manner of ridiculous things. "And to be sure, we won't be dancing like they did at the country dances this past summer. We were all a bunch of elephant feet. No one knew what they were doing, the lead couple as much as anyone. We were flubbing around as though we'd just learned the steps that morning because we had!" He laughed louder and grinned at his partner with so much teeth, she dimmed her own smile, looking concerned.

But he kept at it.

By the time they were finished with the set, the pretty blonde almost ran from him, barely touching his arm in escort from the floor and turning from him with the briefest of curtseys.

Well, that had not gone well, but at least he'd appeared to be having a glorious time. Did Lottie notice?

He turned to find her, anxious to hear her reaction to that set, but for a moment, he couldn't spot her. His heart began pounding in his chest as his gaze flit around the ballroom. Then he caught sight of the back of her, heading outside on the arm of the duke!

He tore after them, cutting through conversations, pushing through the edge of the next group gathering for a set, almost running over a dowager duchess as he passed, until he stumbled out onto the veranda.

They were not there.

He ran to the edge, looking over the railing. That cretin was leading her out into the gardens. "Oh no, you don't." He pressed his lips together and, ignoring the questioning eyes of all those around him, tore down the stairs and out onto the lawn.

"Miss Hughes!" He called out to her, knowing he might be making a scene for all those behind him on the veranda, but not caring one whit. "Miss Hughes!" He entered a row of hedges that led into an area with a fountain in the center. Miss Hughes and the duke were nowhere to be seen. He exited again and ran along the side garden. Her laugh filled the air around him and he followed the sound.

As he turned into another section of a smaller garden area, he nearly bowled her over. Reaching his hands out to steady her, he forced his feet to stop and regained his own balance. "Miss Hughes." He caught his breath. "And Your Grace." He nodded.

The duke raised an eyebrow. "Lord Ragsdale, what a surprise."

Lottie's eyes were wide, surprised, and not overly pleased. "Are you well?" She studied his face, then looked him over from head to toe.

"Yes, that is, no, I mean, of course I am well. I was merely out for a walk in this night air. I stumbled upon you and thought, surely Miss Hughes would appreciate a chaperone, of sorts." He stared down the duke until he nodded.

"Of course. Naturally, we welcome your company, at any rate."

Lottie just kept staring. He wasn't certain how she felt about any of it. But he wasn't going anywhere, not when they were out, walking alone in the gardens. So, he stepped beside the duke and placed his hands behind his back while he walked along with them.

"Where were we? Oh yes, tell me more about your first musicale. You say you were forced into singing?"

"Oh, certainly. Playing too."

"She has a lovely voice. She is often requested at all the homes, the parties." Denny nodded.

"Then I shall have to hear you myself. I do enjoy music."

"Do you? That's wonderful. Do you sing? I love it when men sing."

His Grace coughed, then swallowed before nodding. "I do. I'm a proficient, certainly."

Denny would have called out his nonsense, were it not for the realization that had just struck him. Lottie was still at ease, speaking with the duke. She didn't look the least bit uncomfortable and didn't appear to be in need of rescuing, either, as everything seemed to be on the up-and-up.

He sauntered along, feeling more and more like an intruder until Lottie tilted her head forward to see him around the duke. "And how has the ball been for you?"

"Oh, excellent. I enjoyed our set, naturally. And the others seem to be moving along as expected. Grace is also enjoying herself, I do believe."

She stared at him a moment more until he realized he'd left his sister in the ballroom to chase after Lottie. Surely his mother could assist there. The thought didn't sit comfortably with him. But he would not leave Lottie and His Grace alone together, no matter what.

Lottie looked away, seeming more confused than ever, and paused at a rose that had broken free from a bush and was hanging in their path. She held it to her face, breathing deeply. "This is the most delicious-smelling rose." She ran her fingers on the tips. "I shall be pleased we took this walk, if only for the chance to see it." She turned to them. "I think we need to return. The supper set will be upon us before we know it."

"Yes, I'll be pleased to claim you for our set." Denny wished to rub that in until it stuck in the duke's mind. Denny and Lottie were close. They had been for a long time. If the duke wanted any headway at all with her, he'd best learn to see that Denny was part of the equation. His frown grew. And to learn to stop stealing his stallions.

"I didn't peg you for the brooding type, Ragsdale."

"I'm not brooding." He softened the frown that had been growing.

The duke snorted and led Lottie further away, moving in the direction of the house. "Tell me, Miss Hughes, what do you enjoy reading?"

"Oh, anything gothic, certainly. But I also enjoy the exploits of Wellington, the stories of his battles with Napoleon's men. And I enjoy poetry very much."

"I'm astounded at your interest in Napoleon and Wellington, but I share your love of poetry and, you may be shocked to hear, a good gothic novel." He pretended to shiver, which made Lottie laugh and Denny frown further.

They arrived at the veranda and took the steps slowly. Lottie laughed at something the duke said. Denny was farther down the stairs and wished they'd just enter the house and be finished with their tête-à-tête. But they paused, so he did as well.

They spoke in murmurs, the duke's face close to Lottie's. She blushed and turned away, then stepped back.

Good show.

At last, the duke offered his arm again and they continued. When they were again in the eye of many others, and Denny could no longer stomach their interactions, he left them at the edge of the ballroom. Cards were just the thing. He would return later for the dinner set.

A space cleared up as he entered the room so he took it gratefully, falling into the chair as though his legs couldn't sustain his weight.

The men smirked, then one started dealing the cards. "Having trouble when your woman is the talk of the entire *ton*?"

"I don't know what you're talking about."

The man to his right, a second son of some earl or other, he couldn't remember, organized his cards. "You're trying to claim you don't have any sort of plans toward Miss Hughes?"

The others stilled and watched him.

He tried to respond with no emotion but his hands shook and his heart pounded through him. He knew he needed to figure something out.

The man at his left pointed at him. "You would be brainless if you didn't."

Denny's own cards were terrible. He didn't even need to organize them. "What are you talking about?"

"Well, you are friends. You know you get on well, and she has enough money to fill the coffers of any estate for a long time."

The others nodded, and one across the table took a long drink. "Of all the men, you have the most chance of any of us, at any rate."

He considered them—he sort of hated himself for it—and their words. He didn't need her money, but he certainly didn't like watching other men chase her for her money. They did get on well enough, excellently to be true, and really, why was he not pursuing his best friend?

"We've talked him into it." The man across the table placed a card down.

But Denny shook his head. "I've not said anything. Miss Hughes will make an excellent decision on who she'd like to be with."

"So, you don't mind if each of us tries his hand at her?"

Denny made some sort of foreign growling noise before he could even stop himself, and they all laughed. He didn't say more, though. He didn't need to prove himself to a bunch of men playing cards.

He lost abominably.

When he at last stood, certain it was now time for the dinner set, the group of men tried to get him to stay. "Come, man. Or, at least, send another sorry sap, wallowing in his indecision, to replace you."

Denny tossed his cards down and left the room. *Sorry sap.* He was not a sorry sap. And he was not wallowing.

The ballroom looked much the same as when he'd left. Dancers were in the middle of a minuet, and he found Lottie immediately. Again, she looked to be having a wonderful time. She was talking rapidly to a man who seemed enthralled with the conversation. Was she now cured of her fear?

Grace stepped up to his side and he almost jumped at the sight of her.

"Did you forget me?" Her accusatory tease struck home.

"I . . . well, yes. I'm sorry." He tried the smallest smile. "Have you been . . . well?"

"Yes, Mother has helped with the introductions, and you were correct, knowing Lottie has made a world of difference. I think between the two of us, we know every man in the room and half the women."

"Oh, well, that's good, is it not? Have they been respectful? To you both?"

"Everyone, and the duke has also been attentive." She eyed him, as if she knew he was particularly bothered. "He's not stealing your stallion, brother. The man seems to really enjoy her attentions."

"Of course he does." Denny huffed. But there was nothing more he could say. The duke would be an excellent catch for any woman . . . he assumed. She would be a duchess, at any rate. Her children would be well respected and cared for. "What do we know about him?"

Grace laughed. "I know less than you. He's the duke. What more do you need to know?"

"I don't know, something. We need to figure out just who Lottie is marrying."

"Marrying? She's not agreed to any marriage with him, but have you noticed that she seems to be able to speak to everyone now?" She searched his face.

"Everyone but me. She froze."

"With you?" Her eyebrows shot up into her hairline. "Well, that's new."

The set ended and Lottie was escorted to the lemonade table.

"The supper set is next. Come, let's go get our best friend."

They pushed through the crowd together until they were, at last, standing in front of Lottie.

Denny bowed in front of her and held out his hand.

Lottie's eyes widened and she gulped down her lemonade, then placed a hand in his. "You're early."

"No, I'm right on time. See, Grace is also being led out to the floor."

The music for a waltz began.

Her face paled and then she blushed. *What had gotten into her?* Her blushing was doing all sorts of odd things to him as well. He stepped close and placed a hand at her back, but all too soon, the closeness of a waltz was not enough. He wished to pull her into his arms, to cradle her, then to taste her full lips.

He nearly choked with the power of his thoughts.

And felt mortified for having such thoughts about his dearest friend. Suddenly he wished to apologize to her innocent and lovely face. His felt heated. He must look a complete fool. *Say something.* But no words came.

She really was beautiful. The dip at the end of her nose, her round and rosy cheeks, her wide smile. She was the most beautiful person in the room. Had he never seen it before?

"Are you going to say anything, or are you just going to stand there, staring at me? What's gotten into you?"

He breathed out in relief. "You can speak to me."

Her mouth opened and closed. "Of course I can."

"No, earlier you froze. I saw it. You've been able to talk to every man on the floor, every man here, except me." He studied her, hoping to see something, hoping she would reveal a hint of what was going on between them.

"I-I didn't freeze." She swallowed and looked away.

"You did. And I . . . I can't stand it that you're dancing with all these men."

Her eyes narrowed. "Why?"

The music started. "I don't know. Do you want to show

these mediocre dancers what a real waltz looks like again?" His grin widened; his eyes challenged her.

She lifted her chin and he laughed, loud and free.

"I do. Just don't step on my feet."

"As if I step on your feet." He shook his head, then swept her in his arms as they twirled around the room once more.

Eight

LOTTIE HAD NEVER ENJOYED a dance more. Her feet skimmed the surface of the floor. She and Denny spun and moved and her skirts swirled. She had no notion of anyone except Denny—her Denny—whose strong hands carried her. Their years of practicing together, all the moments she'd bribed him to join her dancing instructor, all the times they had then practiced on their own, with Grace at the piano—it all came back in a great swirl of music, laughter, and friendship, sweetened by a new sensation, a new consciousness of his hand. His fingers, pressing into her back, the surety of his strength, his arms, the shoulders that rippled beneath her fingers. Denny's eyes sparkled back at her. His lips spread into a large smile, then puckered together. She'd never seen such expressions flash across his eyes before.

He admired her. His eyes searched her face with pleasure.

Denny, the friend she turned to for everything, was also the man she admired? In a decidedly unfriend-like manner. She was astounded.

He slowed their pace, tucking them into a corner, almost in the shadows. His arm circled tighter, he stepped nearer. His mouth, a breath away from her own. "Lottie."

She stared into the blue depths of his eyes, seeing an earnest question, one she didn't know how to answer. His lips appeared soft, but firm-looking. They were almost always smiling, but now, in almost touching hers, they were slightly parted, full. The room went quiet. Soft puffs of breath tickled her mouth.

Denny's breath. Denny's lips.

Someone approached them, waltzing with Grace. "What a cozy corner we have all found." The duke's voice jarred Lottie back into some sense of reality.

"What are you doing?" Denny's voice was almost a growl.

"Just dancing nearby, in case a chaperone is needed." His gaze bore into Denny's.

Lottie sucked in a breath and stepped farther away.

"Your assistance is not required." Denny led her in the other direction. "I apologize." He cleared his throat and wouldn't look at her.

"For what?"

"Hm?" He glanced down.

"What are you apologizing for?"

"For the duke's behavior. I'm sorry you had to experience that nonsense."

"Hmm." She waited until he met her gaze.

"What?"

"Or are you apologizing for your behavior?"

He almost tripped, which would have been uncharacteristic in every way. They'd been dancing together for so many years, they could do it effortlessly, no matter what was going on, or so she'd thought.

"You are acting as though the duke's attentions are unwanted."

He opened his mouth, then closed it.

She dared the next sentence, braved the awkwardness. "And you are behaving as though you . . . you want to kiss me." There, she'd said it.

Denny swallowed, twice, before he stretched his neck against his cravat and tried to respond. "I told you, I don't like it that so many men are showing interest. I particularly don't like that the duke has stepped in as a contender."

"Why not?" This was her best friend, but at the same time, he was a man she'd never seen before, standing in front of her.

He ran a hand through his hair. "And I want to go back to the time when I was your only dance partner. Me, and the widowers. And, Lottie, he stole my stallion."

Her next breath was as painful as any she'd tried to take. Her eyes welled with tears. He'd just ruined everything. Was she nothing more than a horse to him? A prize to win, a competition with the duke?

She went limp in his arms and she looked away. They finished the dance, but it was lifeless, and she refused to speak to or hear him.

During the closing measures, he pleaded, "Please hear me. Talk to me. What have I done?"

But she acted as though the words did not penetrate. And she certainly didn't respond.

The waltz ended and she didn't wait to be escorted from the floor, didn't walk with him into supper, and didn't speak to him the rest of the evening.

She spent the rest of the evening standing in the shadows. The particularly large plants in the back corner she had eyed earlier provided a perfect place to disappear. Her dress looked like any other in the room, her hair didn't stand out in any particular manner, and she could shift her body to move behind the pillar and plants if anyone moved closer.

So much of her life had been spent hiding. As a couple moved closer, no doubt seeking a bit of privacy, she ducked back further against the wall. It was then that she understood herself for the first time.

She had been afraid. She had told herself she didn't need more than a few friends, told herself Denny was enough, but that had been a lie. She'd been afraid, yet longing for a friend, for attention, for love, at the same time. She'd wanted to be that woman, laughing and smiling in the center of the dance floor. She'd craved attention, love and acceptance, but had no idea how to receive it. She'd been uncomfortable with others, yet she wished to feel at ease.

So instead of trying or practicing or being brave, she'd hidden.

Just like she was doing now.

Lottie rested her head in her hands, leaning back against the wall. She didn't have the energy to rescue herself because her previous hero, Denny, was the person she was hiding from.

A voice murmured her name. Relief and fear filled her. Then the duke was at her side, his shoulder touching hers. "Are you well?" He was gentle-sounding, even caring.

She glanced up at him, his soft brown eyes watching her in dim light.

"I don't know."

"Perhaps it is too much? All the news and the attention from so many, even your best friend is caught up in it all."

"What do you mean?" She turned to him. "Denny?" A sliver of dread worked its way into her center.

"It would be hard to resist the kind of wealth you offer now. He's probably as confused as you are."

Her chest tightened and she gripped the duke's arm. "He . . . he doesn't even care about it."

The duke didn't say anything, but her mind raced with all the possibilities.

"Who can know? It can be difficult for those of moderate wealth to understand the truly wealthy. You will see I am less affected by it."

She considered him. He was a duke. He probably had been surrounded by great wealth his whole life. Were his actions sincere? Perhaps he was truly interested in her and not her dowry. Perhaps he was the only person in the room to stand beyond suspicion.

She relaxed her grip and wrapped her hands around his arm. "I'm pleased we met."

"As am I."

They stood together in the quiet for several moments more, and the longer he joined her in the hidden shadows, the more she appreciated him. To not trust Denny was . . . scary. But at least she had the duke.

Nine

DENNY KNOCKED AT LOTTIE'S door, though it was early for calling hours.

The butler seemed relieved to see him—it was always so difficult to understand the man's emotions. "They are in the family sitting room."

Denny took the stairs two at a time and almost went into the room but was stopped by Lottie's voice. "Who can we trust, Mother?"

"I think we need his help. I'm certain he's not become suddenly enamored with you. We could use another person to help us understand these men. And I'm sure he would tell you how His Grace is a highly eligible man."

"I don't think so, Mother."

"Well, I'm going to ask for his assistance, anyway." Her mother sounded determined. Were they speaking of him?

The room went quiet for a moment, and he stepped around the corner, nodding to the servants.

They announced him, which he usually did not even require, but in their house, things felt definitely different for him right now.

Everyone jumped up from their seats. Lottie, her mother, her aunt, and . . . Grace. He'd not even thought about his sister's own calling hours. But her expression was not one of condemnation, only surprise and perhaps discomfort. The others seemed uncomfortable. They had been talking about him.

He bowed. "I thought a little help from the best friend would be useful this morning."

Mrs. Hughes stepped forward, both hands outstretched. "And I am so incredibly grateful to you. We are finding all this just a bit overwhelming and confusing, and we know you will be able to advise Lottie. You will help her see that when a highly eligible man shows interest, she would be wise to accept the attentions, even return them." Mrs. Hughes' eyes widened with meaning Denny did not wish to understand.

"Mother, I don't think this is necessary."

"We've talked enough about it. We need Denny's help. You will help us, won't you?" She squeezed his hands and then led him to the sofa next to Lottie.

His friend sat up as straight as possible in her seat so he sat as far as possible from her. And no one spoke.

Grace cleared her throat. "I believe we might want to move to the front parlor. Guests might be arriving."

He had to hand it to his sister. She was smart to come. Not only did she care for Lottie, which he knew she did, but she would see everyone she'd want to in the Hughes' front room.

Mrs. Hughes stood. "You are so correct. I will have the cook send up the refreshments. Goodness, this is such a to-do. I had no idea we'd be navigating such a new opportunity. But what a blessing." She fanned herself, and she and Lottie's aunt left the room together, leaving Denny, Lottie, Grace, and some servants to stare at each other.

Denny leaned closer to Lottie. "I overheard your mother."

Lottie lowered her head in her hands.

"I'm happy to help."

Her head jerked up and she narrowed her eyes. "Help, or drive away the competition?" She waited, watching him until he sighed.

"I told you, I didn't like seeing all those men hovering around, but I'll do my best to help. We can talk about them, I can do some research myself behind the scenes, and I'll help you, Lottie." He reached for her hand. "We've been friends for a long time."

She studied him and then sighed. "I know. Denny, I can't bear to lose you as a friend. Please just be normal. Can you do that?" She squeezed his hand, and her face was so full of hope, he could only nod.

"Of course. I'll do what I can."

Grace clapped her hands. "Excellent, now that you two are all figured out, can we go downstairs? I'm only going to be able to meet my match if I linger around for your castoffs."

Lottie laughed. "That's just not the way I imagined our Season going. And Grace, you command your own set. I saw the way some of those men were watching you." Lottie linked arms with Grace and the two led the way down the stairs.

Denny was left with his own thoughts, disgruntled and frustrated. But he would do what he could to help her. When he wanted to declare intentions, he would wait. When he wanted to pull her close, he would step away. He could do this.

The butler let the duke in just as the three arrived at the foyer. All of Denny's protective irritation sprung forward. "Naturally you're the first to walk in the door." He almost grunted the words.

Lottie and Grace both turned to him with raised eyebrows, but all he could do was shrug.

"Seems I'm *not* the first to walk in the door. I am taking note." He offered his arm to Lottie. "Might I escort you in?"

"Yes, thank you."

Grace fell back onto her brother's arm. "Well, we certainly know where his loyalties lie."

"Yes, but why?" Denny narrowed his eyes.

Grace stopped him with a tug. "Because Lottie is beautiful and kind and fun and smart."

"Of course, I'm not saying she's not highly desirable, but since when has he seen her?"

"Well, he just got here. Are you trying to suggest that the Duke of Chester is suffering financially?"

"No." He exhaled. "Perhaps he is sincere."

She shook her head.

"What?"

When she wouldn't answer, he rested a hand at her elbow. "Just tell me."

"You really don't see her. You can't see why a man would want to be with her."

He sucked in a breath. Of course he saw her. He was seeing her, even when she wasn't around. She was a part of all his thoughts and constantly beating his heart for him; at least, it seemed that way. "I see her."

"But you didn't. You see her *now* when everyone else is clamoring for her attention. And even then, you assume it is for her money only." She turned away. "You don't deserve her."

"Grace."

"No, you really don't. Is this the way men look at me? Am I valued only according to what financial gain I will bring to a marriage?"

"No." He hesitated. "To the wrong sorts of men, that is how you are viewed. But consider as well that successful marriages have been built on nothing but financial agreements. It is not the worst thing in the world."

Her eyes widened and then she turned away again. "It would be to me. Since you are navigating this part of the agreement, please take note that if a man wants only my money, I don't want anything to do with him."

He nodded. "Of course, Grace. I want you to be happy, both of you. I hope you know that."

"I do. For me, at least. But what do you want with Lottie, really? Because she has the most eligible man of the *ton* actively pursuing her, and your emotions and misplaced jealousy might interfere. Are you prepared to love and cherish her? Are you here for the whole thing?"

"I don't know what you're talking about. Of course I'm here for her. Of course." He stopped talking. He told himself he was ready to court her, to declare himself. Did he know about marriage? Certainly not yet. He assumed he'd be prepared to propose if she too had feelings for him. But everything was so new. "What I know is that I want to explore this. She's the most incredible non-sister woman I know. If I can also love her as a wife, then I will have the happiest of times."

"And you don't need her money."

"No, I don't, and that's the beauty of it. You and I are both sincere."

Grace nodded. "I love her too, you know."

"I know."

They had lingered too long in the hall. As they stepped into the front parlor, they saw the results of their delay.

The duke sat close, whispering to Lottie. Her cheeks were flushed, her eyes alight. The duke reached for her hand.

Denny took larger steps, with Grace hurrying at his side. "Sorry, we were detained in the hall."

Lottie turned and the duke's triumphant grin could not be misunderstood. "Thank you for that delay. Sometimes a few moments alone are cherished indeed." He placed her hand in the crook of his arm.

Lottie wouldn't look at Denny. He was not going to rest easy until he knew the details of their conversation.

Grace sent him a look of sympathy, much like she thought him a sick or mangled cat, then sat on a nearby sofa.

The guests began arriving. Man after man was announced. Each entered with hopeful eyes and then glanced around at all the others before finding a seat.

Soon, Lottie's mother arrived, and she had her daughter stand at her side, greeting the guests, one by one.

Denny fell into the seat beside his sister.

"No, don't sit here." She hissed.

So he stood and offered his arm. "Perhaps we too should attend to the guests?"

Her eyes lit. "Oh, certainly. We can be of assistance there."

In truth, most of the eligible men actually seeking a wife were in the Hughes' front room. And if he was of no use to Lottie at the moment, he could do his duty by his sister.

But every laugh, every word exiting Lottie's lips shook his insides. She was charming, easy to converse with, as if she'd been cured of her previous worries. Somehow, she was comfortable with all these strangers, no matter that he had attempted to cure her himself all these years.

At one point, he left Grace with a group of very entertaining men and went to stand by the window. From there, he could hear snippets of everyone's conversations.

The servants made room on the tables for flowers. Some of them had brought baskets from their kitchens. What would Lottie say if Denny started behaving as a lovesick pup?

He half turned to watch the men, doting on her, urging a laugh from her lips, offering praise and compliments, and living off her every word. At once, he knew he'd not done everything he could for his friend. But there she was, being built up and admired by strangers, things he should have done better all these years.

Or so he assumed.

Why had she been so hesitant and nervous around him earlier?

He had suspected that, perhaps, this new wave of emotion, this new attraction, had taken over her thoughts and feelings as well, but she was so receptive of the duke's attentions. Plus, she hadn't looked in his direction once since he arrived in the room. She must not be feeling any of the same things Denny was.

He could at least be grateful for it. Pining for a woman who did not seem to notice was a torture of the purest kind.

Her husky laugh carried over to him and brought a similar laugh from his own mouth, even though he had no notion what spurred it.

He stayed. Hours and hours he stayed, trying to outlast every guest, until it was, once again, him, the duke, Grace, and Lottie. Mrs. Hughes had escaped upstairs with a headache.

Lottie was sitting in a most unladylike fashion on the couch, slumped in exhaustion.

The duke raised his hand to a servant. "Might we have some refreshment, something to revive the spirits?"

The servant turned immediately.

He was ordering about the servants now too, was he?

Denny reached for Lottie's hand this time and cradled it in his. "You did amazingly well."

"You really did, Lott. That was incredible." Grace grinned at her.

She lifted her eyes to them both. "I had no idea what true participation in the Season involved. This is incredible." Her eyes took on a dreamy look and then she closed them. "And exhausting."

"Anyone would be tired after what you did today." Grace shook her head.

"Thank you. For being here." Her lips said the words, but her eyes remained closed. Denny had no way of knowing who she thanked, though he hoped a portion of her gratitude, even her notice, spread to him.

Ten

LOTTIE WAS AS CONFUSED as she had ever been.

How on earth would she know who to encourage—who to spend more time with—when there were so many offering their attention?

"Mother, I don't wish to play with their hearts." She set her book aside. "But whose hearts are really involved here? None of them know me. None of them have ever seen me before, besides a precious few."

"We do need assistance here." Mother nodded, then smiled encouragingly. "However, you can be governed somewhat by your own preferences. You have the blessed opportunity to simply choose. Among those worthy, of course. Does anyone stand out?"

Lottie had been asking herself the same question over and over. Denny was acting as strange as he ever had, so everything the duke had suggested about Denny being influenced by her inheritance made sense. Was Denny in need of money? His timing of suddenly acting enamored was suspect, at least. Though she couldn't be certain he was acting enamored. He was different. That was certain. The only person who was apart from that suspicion was the duke. He hadn't known her before and had expressed interest before the announcement of her inheritance had been made. Or Lord

Hampton. But he'd faded somewhat after the duke had shown so much attention.

His Grace was a good enough man. Handsome. Attentive. She smiled. "The duke, of course, is someone to consider."

"Oh, certainly. He is the best man we could have chosen for you. The highest of titles, the most respected, and an impeccable reputation. He has no vices that we have been able to detect. Though, I've asked Denny to investigate."

Lottie shook her head and her eyes narrowed. "You asked Denny to help in discovering his vices?"

"No, not specifically that, but it is a man's job to ferret out the gossip, to discover the hidden things that are not spoken of to women or in their company."

Lottie nodded.

"And Denny cares for you. He is such a dear to be of assistance." Her mother eyed her. "Have you considered him?"

Lottie's heart shuddered within her. She'd thought of nothing but him these past few days. "I can't think of him. He has had opportunities all these years and now . . . why would he have any interest, if not for the money?"

Her mother looked as if she was about to say something but must have decided against it. The silence in the room was thick.

"Mother, say what you wish to say."

Her mother adjusted her skirts and fidgeted a moment before speaking. "Sometimes a man sees you more clearly when other men also find something to desire in you."

"Hmm." That sounded as unimpressive as anything she'd heard.

"I think the first thing to discover is how *you* feel about him. You have been friends for the whole of your lives. You already know you get along well together. He is the best of men. He is titled. Before now, I didn't think the two of you would make something of it, but now—"

"Now he's finally showing me that kind of attention?" Lottie frowned. "I haven't thought of him in that way, either, you know. It's not like I've been pining away for Denny all these years."

"Of course not, Lottie, no one thinks that. Sometimes it's timing. Sometimes it's the realization that the two of you will be separated if you marry elsewhere. Who knows what starts the attraction? Sometimes it's even one particular ball gown." Her eyes turned dreamy, and Lottie knew that whether or not she desired it, a long, sappy story of Mother's love would be coming.

"Your father's eyes when he first saw me in my velvet green gown," she said, her eyes welling with tears. "I'll never forget that moment."

Lottie moved to embrace her mother.

Had the duke ever looked at Lottie in a way that would make her cry years later? She didn't think so, but neither had Denny.

Mother wiped her eyes and stepped aside, busying herself. "So, we are considering the duke, possibly Denny." Then she named two other lords that had made Lottie laugh.

"Excellent. We shall put together a dinner."

"With all of them?"

"Women too, of course. We'll make sure the numbers are even."

Lottie nodded, then her mother reached for her hand. "What has changed? How are you so able to be yourself with all of these strangers?"

Her smile grew. "I don't know, but it all seems easier now, fun even. After all this time hiding, I don't worry so much now. Denny helped, I think. The duke as well, and Lord

Hampton. But it's more than that. These men, they smile and nod and respond, as if they are enchanted, no matter what I say. I guess you could say I don't have a care if I sound particularly witty." She laughed. "Though, who's to say if they return home with headaches of their own for having to dance attendance upon my ridiculous turns of phrases."

"It is their job to do so. If they are courting a woman, they must truly court her—convince her that she is going to be happy in their home."

Lottie considered Mother's words. She'd never had the luxury of thinking along those lines before. The idea that she could *choose* her husband, that she didn't have to pine and hope and worry for a single proposal, was as glorious as it was tiresome. "I am blessed indeed."

"I would say so." Her mother patted her hand and then picked up her needlepoint.

Lottie reached for her book but couldn't read. The greatest worry still needled her, but she daren't speak it out loud, for fear she would make it true. Denny. Had he changed his opinion of her simply to win her inheritance as the duke had suggested? The thought was such a betrayal, such a heartbreaking idea, she daren't believe it, not completely, but she daren't trust him, either.

It was a conundrum indeed.

The footman appeared in the doorway. "Lord Ragsdale here to see you, ma'am." He nodded to Lottie's mother.

She and her mother stood, and her mother hurried to the doorway to grab both of Denny's hands and kiss his cheek. His gaze immediately found Lottie, but she could not read him.

Denny entered, being tugged along by her mother, and sat squarely in between mother and daughter.

"Denny."

"Hi, Lott."

And with that, things should have been normal. Except that her *mother* had summoned him.

She didn't have long to wait.

"Denny, as I expressed, we need your assistance."

"I'll do whatever I can. You are my oldest and dearest friends." His gaze found Lottie again. "My affections will be constant."

She sucked in a breath and almost reached for the pounding in her chest, though she knew it would be to no avail. Her heart was unreachable, except to him. Or so she feared. Now that the flood of interest had opened, could she care for anyone else?

What are you saying? She practically shouted the words in her thoughts, though she said nothing. Denny broke their gaze and turned back to her mother. "What is it you require?"

"We must discover the unsavory portions of their lives."

He turned to one and then the other, eventually focusing mostly on her mother. "All men have sides to themselves that women don't wish to see. You'd be hard-pressed to find someone without a secret or two. With any luck, these dark spots remain a secret for the whole of your marriage."

Lottie shook her head. "Surely that is not true."

"As true as I'm sitting here."

She crossed her arms. "What are *your* unsavory dark spots?"

He laughed. "Well, perhaps not all men. I play a bit of cards, but I'm not addicted to the game." He shrugged, and the look of chagrin and innocence that filled his face made her laugh. Was it true, he had no vice?

Lottie's mother leaned toward him, her face full of hope. "Oh, Denny, surely there are men as good as you are out there. You must help us find them. This duke, for example. What is his story? Can you engage a runner, even, some person to learn more about him?"

"Mother, do you really think that would be necessary?"

"I don't know." She turned to Denny. "We don't have Lottie's father around to guide us in these matters."

Denny looked from Lottie to her mother and back, then with a slight expression of sympathy, he nodded. "I think we need to discover his true intentions. If there is something in his life that would make him desperate for the engagement, we must discover it."

Lottie stiffened. "Because you cannot believe him capable of simply liking me? You think I am that undesirable?" She stood.

Denny stood with her. "Not at all." His eyes bore into hers. "Please, Lottie. You are worthy of the highest form of love."

She stepped back, stunned by his words, but he stood his ground and cradled her hand, looking into her eyes until she sat again. "This is all so new."

He squeezed her fingers, then turned back to her mother. "Is there anyone else you would have me investigate? Any man of interest?"

Her mother listed the other men who had been particularly attentive.

"Good men, all. But I will take measures to be certain."

"Thank you, Denny. What would we do without you?" Her mother patted his cheek, and Lottie was suddenly anxious to get outside. When she was about to stand and wander to the window, Denny turned to her. "Would you like to go for a walk?"

"I would love nothing more. But can we avoid the central pathways in the park?"

"Certainly. And the tearoom?"

She shuddered. "I'd really like to go someplace where only a few people meander about and none of them are interested in me or my life."

"That might be quite impossible, but perhaps if I fetched my phaeton?"

A wave of relief flooded Lottie. "Yes, that would be just the thing."

The servants were called to bring around his phaeton, and Lottie rushed upstairs to grab a warmer pelisse, a bonnet, and to splash some water on her face. For the first time in a long time, she was hoping to look beautiful, and this time for Denny.

She laughed at the thought. How ridiculous her young tree-climbing-self would have thought her. Denny. But she couldn't stop her smile.

Her mother joined her in her doorway. "Give him a chance. I don't think he has ulterior motives, other than your best interest."

Lottie nodded. "I hope you are correct, but I have to, at least, be aware. The duke made it sound like he knew things about Denny. Perhaps we should be sending around investigators to discover Denny's situation as well?" She cringed as soon as she said it. "No, forget I said that. I trust his honesty. But Mother, I don't want Denny if he doesn't love me, not when I . . ." Her face grew warm. Did she love him? "Not when I care for him."

Her mother reached out a hand. "To think the men we are choosing from are all titled and well respected." Her eyes welled again. "I couldn't be happier for you."

"Thank you, Mother." She pulled her into a hug as she passed by in the doorway. "I'll see what I can determine as to his sincerity on our ride. One thing he may or may not remember: Denny cannot hide anything from me."

Her mother's laugh followed Lottie down the stairs. At least she had made her mother happy. The reality of her great wealth had not sunk in quite yet. The instant influx of new gowns—certainly the large amount of attention—was all the result of such a blessing, but she didn't know what to do with the knowledge of her new identity. Was she any different, really? Not at all, yet people all around her seemed to think her fundamental value had changed. And, of course, that was doing things to her insides.

She met Denny in the hallway with a deep burgundy-rimmed bonnet. His welcoming, warm smile was everything she needed in that moment.

With a bounce in her step, she walked with him to the phaeton. He helped her up into the high seat and then joined her at her side. "Now we can get into all sorts of mischief."

She laughed. "And what sort of mischief are you planning today?"

"You are the one to plan all our mischief, if you recall."

"Certainly not." Though, as she thought on it, she suspected he was right.

"The time we interrupted the schoolroom in town?"

"Oh yes, that was me."

"And the time we took from Cook's kitchen for our impromptu picnic?"

"You cannot blame me for being hungry."

"I'm certain they all blamed us when the main course, the venison itself, was no longer in the kitchen."

She laughed. "It was so good."

"It really was, and I had a stomachache the whole of that night."

She tapped her chin. "Surely you have also caused mischief."

"I was in charge of our caroling escapade."

She clapped. "And for all of my ruined dresses."

"I suppose that is also true, though how can I be blamed if boys' clothes are much more appropriate for child's play?"

"You must not be blamed, of course."

He moved closer to her. "I had no idea that our time in town would center around desperate attempts to get you alone." The eyes he turned to her were at once sincere, all humor gone. "I certainly should have made more use of all our glorious hours doing whatever we wished, with no one but Grace as a witness."

Lottie sighed. "It does sound rather lovely. What I would give right now to sneak away to our reading hideout."

"See, there you have it. We are not the sorts to get into any real trouble. What do we do in a hideout? Read."

"We have failed at being smugglers, spies, and highwaymen."

"We certainly have."

The sound of the horses clopping along the cobblestone made Lottie smile. "This is just what I needed. I was about ready to escape my front parlor at a run."

"I knew it."

She lifted her eyes to him. "You did?"

"I can almost guess what you're thinking at any moment."

"I said the same thing to Mother. About you. You cannot hide things from me."

His eyes flitted away.

"Denny?"

"There are things I don't wish you to know until you are ready to hear them."

"Things?"

"The sorts of things a man tells a woman when he wants to . . . well, when he hopes—"

"What a happy pair!" a voice called up to them.

Lottie jerked her head around toward the newcomer. "The duke."

Denny groaned.

"Hello, Your Grace." She waved with a large smile, half of her joyous reaction in response to Denny's.

"You're looking fine behind that pair. Denny has the second finest horses in town."

She placed a hand on Denny's arm, knowing he might say any manner of things to His Grace, things he might regret later.

Denny just leaned back with a grin. "We are off. Nice to see you this morning, Your Grace." With a click of his tongue, the horses continued on the path.

"You are gloating." Lottie nudged him.

"Of course I'm gloating. He can be boastful of the stallion he stole all he wants, but nothing beats knowing he wishes to be in my spot right now, nothing in the world." He lifted her hand and pressed his lips to it. "You are the greatest prize."

She stiffened but did not remove her hand.

"What is it? What have I said?"

"Am I a prize, though? A prize?"

He sighed. "No. I'm an idiot who doesn't know what to say to you."

"So we've switched roles?"

"It appears so." He pulled the horses over near a copse of trees. "What I most want you to know is all tangled up in my throat."

"Perhaps you're just not ready to say it."

"Hmm." He leaned closer. "Lottie, I'm first in line. I'm in your front parlor not just to be a friendly support. I'm there because I want in. I am throwing my horse in the running, so to speak."

It was Lottie's turn to groan about more horse references, but she drank in his words as the sweet honey they were.

"Please don't overlook your best friend because we are so familiar or because I don't have all the right words to say."

She swallowed twice, full of emotion that she desperately did not want to show. "Thank you for telling me." She lifted a hand to the side of his face. "You will always be very dear to me."

He nodded once. "I shall be content with that for now." He tapped her nose. "But there will come a time when our friendly ways will no longer satisfy this new and glorious need for you in my life."

She sucked in a breath.

"I know I am bold. But I can only be honest with you."

"I'd know if you weren't."

He clicked for his horses to begin again. "Now, should we discuss the merits of all your other suitors?"

"What?" Her mouth fell open.

"I'm still your best friend, aren't I?"

She laughed. "I cannot believe this of you."

"I thought you said you know me."

"You're going to sit here and discuss the merits of the duke?"

"Well, I can point out his flaws—"

"And the others on my list, you wish to talk of them?"

"Let's go for a ride and perhaps approach things this way." He turned toward the more populated areas of the park.

"Must we?"

"You're up high. No one can join us. We will be but distant communicators and observers."

The beauty of their arrangement descended on her, and with a great grin, she nodded. "All right, then. Let's hear what you have to say."

Their next turn down a well-traveled path put them in the midst of small groups of gowns and jackets. Chattering, happy members of the *ton* there to see and be seen.

"I much prefer this lofty position. Remember my first

day?" She pointed. "I stood right there in the middle of it all. How mortifying."

"I don't remember it that way. Those men were truly interested. In fact, there were two you could've trusted to have interests unrelated to your new inheritance."

"That's right. Lord Hampton and Mr. McAllister. You told me they were interested, though I hardly believed it."

"Why wouldn't you?"

"Well, if you remember, though it was only days ago, I could never speak more than a few words at a time to those men. I scared them away all the time."

"Scared is not the word, of course."

"I don't know. They always looked a bit nervous and then wandered off." She sighed. "Why is it so much easier now?"

"What I'd like to know is why was it difficult with me?"

She didn't want to understand the answer to that question. She already knew, really. "I think you know."

He squeezed her hand but said nothing more. "As long as you can recover your speech now, I'm comforted with any reason. I cannot abide a life without your clever conversation."

She glanced over at him through her lashes. "Though my reason has not altered, I seem to have recovered my ability to at least articulate."

He sat taller, tucking her hand closer to his side. "I could have cured you. Surely a game of charades would have done the trick."

"You are so right. Or a play. We have not read from a script in many days."

He glanced out of the corner of his eye and clucked his tongue. "Oh please, spare me your dramatics."

"You are the very best hero in every scene. You must know that."

He clucked his tongue again and turned down another path. "Or perhaps I was the only hero."

"Perhaps, but I cannot imagine anyone besting you."

He turned to face her. "Even the duke?"

She faltered, but held his gaze. "What are you asking?"

He turned away. "That's what I thought. Let's talk about these men, Lott. You know, you're talking about spending the rest of your life with them, giving over all your money to them, allowing them to raise your children. It's a big step."

"I know that, don't you think I've given those very things all of my waking thoughts?"

"Take the duke, for example. What kind of man knows another is off to get the funds for a horse yet swoops in and offers a bigger price to steal it from him?"

"The stallion, again? Is that your only complaint?" She turned from him. "Honestly, Denny. I can't bear to hear it. Not another time."

"I know. I'm sorry. But it's a big one, and in my opinion, it says a lot about a person."

She sighed. "I'll give you that, but one isolated instance does not a villain make."

"I shall find other things to dislike."

"That's the sum of your complaint?"

"Like I said, there will be more." He pointed into the air. "And Lord Hampton from before."

"Oh? Do you have a complaint about him?"

"He is overly nice. The man can't say a single negative thing about anyone, nothing. I could ask him his thoughts on Napoleon, and the man would have some positive things to say about his leadership." Denny snorted. "He cannot be serious. It gets on a man's nerves."

She laughed. "So your concern about me marrying him is that he would only see the good?" She raised her eyebrows. "I might move him closer to the top of my list."

"No, I mean, certainly, if you wish. I'm trying here. Some of these men don't let their weaker-based selves be known. But I have men working on that, or I will."

"I know, I know. Well, if each of these men is perfect, then what is your purpose in assisting me?"

"But they aren't. Mr. McAllister makes noises when he eats."

"What?"

"He does. It isn't just your typical swallow. The man sounds like he's inhaling half a goat."

She snorted.

"And that man over there."

"Mr. Stringfellow?"

"Yes, he only likes blondes."

"He asked me to dance."

"Precisely my point. Up until now, he's limited his interactions to blondes only. What does that tell you?"

"He's trying to branch out?"

"No. He's only in it for the inheritance."

"I know you're trying to help me, but every time you say something like that, I feel suddenly like another person is proving that, before the inheritance, I wasn't worth anyone's attention."

"But you were."

"My experience at the side of the ballroom floor proves otherwise."

Denny looked as though he wanted to refute all her words, but she held up a hand. "Thank you for always being there." She stopped short of saying *thank you for seeing me* because had he, really?

"You're welcome."

"Perhaps now we can talk of something else?"

"Oh, well, certainly."

"You've tried another new style of cravat." She grinned.

"You noticed!"

"Of course. You started wearing new ones when I mentioned I liked that sort of thing." She looked away, her face heating.

"I admit it. But I've always tried to impress you."

"Not in the same way."

He laughed. "I don't know. Do you remember the fish incident?"

"The fish incident." She shook her head. "Your fish was not bigger than mine."

He leaned his head back, filling the air around them with his laugh. "Still you won't admit it. I brought the fish all the way to your window. It was bigger. So much bigger. I wanted to impress you."

She paused, never seeing him quite that way. "And I would never let you do so. I refused to be impressed because I was busy wanting to win . . . to impress you!"

He shrugged. "Letting you win is twice as fun!"

She swatted him. "You have never let me win! Admit it now."

"You're correct." He held up a hand in defense. "I never have." His gaze out the side of his eye was suspicious, but she let his statement stand. Had he been trying to impress her all these years?

They continued on in the same way they always had, except that every word, every touch, every glance was suspect, was evoking emotion, was capturing her attention like he never had before. Was this what it was like to fall in love with her best friend? If so, it was the most delicious of all things to ever happen to her.

Were his intentions pure? He certainly made it difficult for her to consider any other man. But she must, and she would, after their outing. For the rest of their phaeton ride in the park, she just enjoyed Denny.

Eleven

BOW STREET RUNNERS HAD only been searching for a day or two. Denny let the new correspondence fall from his hands onto the desk. He could hardly believe what he'd discovered about the duke. His Grace really *was* a cretin.

He was steeped in debt and involved in the most disreputable activities. How had he kept himself hidden from the general eyes of the *ton*?

Certainly, he'd just arrived back in town publicly, but the man had been in London for many months before that, spending time in gaming halls, with the worst sorts at the horse races, losing all his money. Some sources thought him completely stripped of wealth, desperate, and on the verge of losing his estate.

Denny's stomach clenched tighter the more he read his report from the Bow Street runner he'd hired. He should be exulting in the news; the duke was out of the picture. But the victory felt sour. The more he learned, the more he knew Lottie would presume that everyone was right—the duke was only courting her out of desperation for her inheritance. She would believe, yet again, that she was only desirable with a large price tag attached to her.

That was simply not true.

Tonight was the dinner Mrs. Hughes had planned.

Denny had been invited, along with the duke, the other two gentlemen she'd expressed an interest in knowing better, and women to give them even numbers. Tonight he would tell her.

He took extra care again with his cravat, with his jacket, with his hair and teeth. He dabbed his neck and the back of his hands with sandalwood water. His boots were shined. By the time he walked out the door, he was as handsome as he'd ever been.

He and Grace were let into the Hughes' home before they could lift the knocker on the door. The butler bowed. "The family is expecting you in the drawing room."

"Thank you." Denny nodded to the older servant.

They turned down the two hallways that led them to a seldom-used room. He stopped short as everyone became visible. The duke was lifting a glass and everyone in the room was smiling. Lottie stood close, her hand on his arm, with a bright smile on her face. Mrs. Hughes sipped her drink and said, "We are so thrilled to have you as part of the family."

"No." Denny barreled into the room.

Everyone turned to him with wide eyes.

The duke burst into laughter. "You all right there, Ragsdale?"

Denny ignored him. "You cannot do this."

Lottie shook her head and took a half step toward him. "This is . . . Denny, it's not what you think." She glanced at the duke. "At least, not yet."

Denny went rigid in alarm. "It can never be. You don't know this man."

Lottie stepped closer to him. "Come, tell me about it in another room."

The butler stepped back into the room. "Your other guests are arriving."

Mrs. Hughes breathed out in relief. "Excellent. Let us move to a more public room in the house. I was just telling

His Grace that there are few we allow access to see these rooms. And he is one. You, of course, have always been here and there and everywhere." She rested a hand on his arm. "Thank you for coming, Denny."

"You are welcome." He relaxed his shoulders, knowing that no proposals or true welcomes to families were going on as he entered. In a lower voice, he cleared his throat. "I have news. I apologize for my abrupt arrival."

"It was unfortunate, but understandable. No need to put everyone on the defensive."

"You are a wise woman." He exited the room last, with Mrs. Hughes and Grace on his arms, while the duke was able to exit first with Lottie.

He was certain she was confused, perhaps even angry with him. He longed for a moment alone with her. Someone must warn her about the duke's circumstances. But there was no opportunity. As soon as they were gathered in the front parlor, they were surrounded by the other guests.

Lottie left the duke's arm, and His Grace joined Denny. "What are you up to, Ragsdale?"

"Do you even like her, Your Grace? Or is all this just a wild hope to fill the coffers of your estate?"

"I could say the same of you. Why did you wait all this time to declare yourself? Something particularly appealing about the wealth, I'd say."

"You stay out of my affairs."

"Then stay out of mine."

They stared each other down and were soon interrupted by soft hands on their arms and a look from Mrs. Hughes across the room.

Denny, chagrined, turned to the woman at his right. "I do apologize, Lady Lucas. I have neglected my duty in getting to know you."

She pouted up into his face. "I know I shall forgive you. How could I not with a face such as yours?"

Hmm? Perhaps she was complimenting him. Her smile and eyelashes indicated she meant to.

He led Lady Lucas farther into the room in the direction of where Lottie was standing. Perhaps he'd get a moment to whisper a few things in Lottie's ear. She continued in the assumption that the duke was a noble man—a misconception that would surely bring sadness.

But there was no time, not before they all walked into supper together.

The duke was given the honor of escorting Lottie to dinner. They entered first. She laughed and smiled on his arm. Denny escorted someone, pretty enough, polite enough, but who said very little. Grace was on the arm of Lord Hampton, and Denny could only be pleased about that. At least someone would benefit from the dinner.

He turned to the woman at his side. "I apologize for my woolgathering. Tell me more about yourself."

"Oh, don't you worry about me. I know I'm only here to round out the numbers." She eyed Lottie. "Thankfully, Miss Hughes is completely charming and easy getting to know. I hope she marries quickly. Then there might be room for the rest of us to consider doing so as well." She laughed a little.

"You don't seem too displeased with the situation."

"I'm not. There's plenty of time, and though I'd like to marry this Season, I'd like to do so with someone not so concerned with a dowry."

"So, perhaps, this rise in wealth of Miss Hughes is helping you see who those focused on wealth might be?"

"Or at least those who find it vastly appealing."

"Who wouldn't find it appealing?"

She studied him. "Have you too changed your opinion of the lovely Miss Hughes because of her inheritance?"

"Not at all. That is, my opinions have been changing, yes, but it has nothing to do with her wealth." He adjusted his sleeve. "It isn't as though my opinions have changed all that much. She's always been an intelligent woman, awkward in social situations, smart, talented. Nothing has changed."

"Except?" Her eyes were too knowing, her manner too prying. He'd said too much already.

"That is all I have to say on the matter."

Lottie's laugh carried over to them.

She sniffed. "It might not matter one whit with someone like the duke, capturing her attention and earning her smiles." Her pointed looks and irritating comments were grating, to say the least.

The pair arrived at their places at the table. He pulled out her chair and then went to find his seat, pleased to leave her overly observant observations to herself.

Victorious, he saw that he was seated next to Lottie and that the duke sat across from her.

His was just the place for him to give her the necessary details of the duke's dealings. But as soon as they sat, Mrs. Hughes, who sat on Lottie's left and at the head of the table, asked him to talk of his estate.

"Our estates share a property line, right along the ridge of a rocky rise." He smiled. "Right now, the buds will be emerging, the flowers breaking through the earth. And our horses are in their stalls, kicking the doors for a ride across the meadows."

The duke smirked. "A rocky rise, meadows. You speak as though every estate in England doesn't have more of the same. The home of my ancestors sits atop a rocky cliff. Everything you can see from horizon to horizon belongs to them—has for generations. Rocky rises, flowers, meadows a plenty." He sipped his drink.

"Are you saying that we cannot appreciate our homes simply because others, *you*, have similar landmarks?" Lottie's eyebrow rose and twitched. Something she did only when highly irritated.

Denny covered his mouth to hide a smile.

The duke lifted a shoulder. "Certainly not. I think I felt intimidated by the love you obviously have for your land. I was hoping to show you that you might find things to love on mine." He dipped his head but then smiled at her in a manner most disarming. Even Denny was almost charmed by the man.

He shifted his foot to touch hers under the table.

"Home will always be home, no matter how far we travel from it." Denny nodded.

"It's remarkable how quickly we can adapt to new places and find new homes." The duke eyed him and then turned to Lottie. "I would be pleased to show you my home. Perhaps a house party is in order?"

Denny stiffened. As if the duke could afford one. His Grace continued on in his charade, making Denny almost too ill to finish his meal. "In times such as these, it is perhaps best to consider which of your holdings to sell, instead of how to recklessly spend more of your estate's resources."

The table went quiet. The duke looked away and took a long drink.

Denny twisted in his seat so that his words would be heard by Lottie alone. "The man is insufferable."

She shook her head.

"He is lying to you."

Then she turned to him. "Stop." Her eyes narrowed.

"But he is. I have news—"

"Denny, please, just leave it be." She glanced around. "He already told me of his financial situation. Don't embarrass him." Her last words came out as a soft hiss.

She knew? He glanced from the duke and back to her and then to the duke. They'd discussed his finances. He was escorting her into rooms. They were together. And Denny was not with them, not really. He felt shut out. For a brief moment, a victorious glint lit the duke's expression, but then he masked it again with the sorrowing, embarrassed, pitiful expression he'd been wearing before.

"He makes me ill," Denny murmured, then turned to the woman on his right. "I do apologize. Please, someone tell me about Almack's. I haven't been in an age. Shall we all make an appearance Wednesday next?"

Lottie shifted so that her slipper no longer rested beside his boot. She turned away from him, and the conversations shifted. Denny spent the rest of the dinner entertaining the woman at his right.

Cards followed, along with a song from Lottie herself. She chose *their* duet, the one she and Denny had sung together for many years—and asked the duke to sing it with her.

Denny shook his head and wanted more than anything to leave the room. But instead, he suffered through some rather terrible singing. He would have laughed if things weren't so dire. Lottie even thanked His Grace with shining eyes.

As the evening came to a close, he almost led the group as being one of the first to leave, but he forced his feet to still. He would say what he'd come to say, report his findings, at least to Mrs. Hughes if Lottie would not hear him.

No matter what lies the duke had told, Denny knew he was not sincere. How could he be? It was too much a coincidence that the duke was in such desperate financial need, then showed interest in Lottie right as her inheritance was announced. But as he watched His Grace stand close to

Lottie, study her face, laugh at her every word, he had to ask himself: did he really believe that Lottie was not lovable? Was it so difficult to accept that the duke was enamored with her?

Considering his many indiscretions, Denny did find it difficult to trust the man, but being a low-level cretin did not make it impossible to fall in love. As he watched them together, he had to give place for the possibility that His Grace really was becoming attached to Lottie, in which case, Denny might need to give them space to explore their new relationship.

As the man rested a hand on the small of Lottie's back and turned to talk to her in a most possessive manner, Denny went stiff. His hands clenched in an effort to stave off the yearning to stand in the duke's place. He knew he could not step aside. He could not stand by while Lottie was wooed by a gambling and irresponsible reprobate.

He made his way closer to where they stood just as His Grace said, "I'll let you pick the mare. We will start our breeding program in earnest this spring, and you will choose the first couple."

"Considerate, especially since you are hoping she will finance the whole of it." Denny stepped closer. He stood taller than the duke and used his height to its full advantage. "Does she know she would be the one funding your lifestyle? Does she know what that lifestyle entails?"

The duke's face colored, and Denny hoped he'd pushed the man to show some of his true colors. "I find your comments highly inappropriate. I'm certain I will be discussing the financial particulars at a later time, were that conversation merited due to a certain closeness we might obtain."

"Oh, don't try to pretend you are the more proper and polite person between us. Shall we detail the events of last weekend? Share with the others how you waste away your own wealth?" He daren't express what he'd very much like to, such as the existence of an actress in a set of rooms, sponsored by His Grace. Lottie might find it heartwarming to rescue a ducal estate, but Denny knew she would not want her money spent on a kept woman. He could hardly believe the direction of his thoughts. The man was disgusting.

"We can discuss them all you like. The children at the orphanage were more than grateful for their meal and the books for their classroom."

Denny opened his mouth to counter the most ridiculous turn of conversation, but Lottie rested a hand on his arm. "Denny, please." Her eyes begged for his silence, and though it pained him—though he opened his mouth to make her hear—he closed it again, dipped his head, and said no more in that moment.

Twelve

THAT NIGHT, LOTTIE LAY in bed, knowing sleep would not come. The moon shone in through her blinds, the night air shifted around in her room. The opened window did nothing to calm her racing heart.

The duke had not known of her inheritance when he'd come to town. And yet he had such desperate need. Certainly, she'd suspected him. She still might. But he was so terribly sincere, so good, so caring. He *saw* her. He'd even found her in her hiding place at the ball, and she very much liked the idea of being involved in his breeding program, liked to think that her money would make a difference.

Those same things were appealing about Denny.

The tightness in her chest grew. She was going to lose her best friend. If she chose anyone but him, Denny would be lost forever. He refused to amicably accept even her consideration of another.

So, did he love her?

She had seen a change in him. But who was to know if it was love? Who was to know if any of the men would love her? She stood and moved to the window. The world was lit by the moon, and everything was quiet. She missed her and Denny's country estates. If she were home, her window could see the rooftops of Denny's estate, and she would guess at what he was doing. Sometimes he would come find her in the middle of the night.

She opened the window wider and rested her head down on her hands on the windowsill. She couldn't lose Denny. But she couldn't marry him, either. Not unless he loved her.

She stayed thus, resting her head, until her legs ached beneath her and her hands shifted. The moon had not traveled too far in the sky, but she felt as though hours had passed, hours with no solution in sight.

Then a whistle below carried up to her. A whistle with a tune she knew well. The melody entered her ears but settled in the happiest places of her memory. She lifted her face and laughed. "Denny."

He stood directly below. "Will you wake the house? Hush now."

"I don't even care. You came."

"How could I not? Things—"

"I know." She leaned out. "Come in. Meet me in the kitchen."

He nodded but stood in place.

"What are you doing?"

"Just enjoying the sight of you in the moonlight, with your hair down. It's magical."

Her skin flamed all the way to her toes. She could say nothing in response, so she turned and threw on the easiest house dress, slipped on some slippers, and tiptoed down the stairs, through the hallways and into the kitchen.

Denny stood in the dark, his face unreadable, but she hurried into his arms anyway. "Oh, Denny. I'm sorry."

His hands ran up and down her back, his caress spreading tingles throughout her. "Lottie."

She listened, but he said nothing more. "Should we warm some milk?"

He nodded, his chin on the top of her head. Then shook his head. "Let's just sit." He left her embrace to find a candle.

The air felt cold, lonely, the way her life would be without him in it.

When the air around them finally held the flickering light of a candle, the darker circles under his eyes and his harrowing expression made her suck in a breath. "Oh, Denny." She reached out a hand to cradle his face.

They sat on the closest bench. He shook his head and took her hand in his. "No, do not look at me like that." He raised her hand to his lips. "Hear me." His pained expression tore at her.

"Is something amiss? How is Grace?"

"We are well, it is not that. I have come to beg your forgiveness."

His eyes welled up, and she was without words, again, staring at him in wonder. She hadn't seen him cry since his father had passed away.

"I should have seen you all these years. I should have done something to win your heart. I was daft. So very daft, and I'm sorry." His eyes begged her to understand.

She could only nod. "Of course I forgive you. What was there to see but a hiding, fearful woman who could only speak to three people?"

"No, that is untrue. You have always been the most incredible woman of my acquaintance. You have been everything to me, the person I most wish to impress, the one I'm most excited to see, the person I trust with my largest dreams. It has always been you. I just assumed you would always be there. You know that I've had no interest in marrying. I've always had you." He shook his head. "I've been an idiot."

"No." She tried to stop his words, but he held up a hand, resting a finger on her lips. "Please, there is more. If I truly cared, I would step away. I would let you move on. If you wish to marry, to have love in your life, someone you can truly love, then I won't hinder you anymore. I won't make ridiculous accusations in public. I won't try to embarrass you or proprietarily stake my claims. I've been the worst best friend I can imagine."

A tear dropped from her own face before she knew it was there. "Denny, no."

"I mean it. I'm done. I'm here for you forever. If you need me, I will do whatever I can. I learned the duke . . . he's the worst sort of person in private and to other men, but men, they tend to be different with women. Maybe he will keep being so good to you. Maybe you can be happy."

She raised his hand and kissed his knuckles, kissing the tears that fell, kissing her love into him. "I need to have a conversation with the duke."

He nodded.

"Thank you."

He stood and pulled her back into his arms.

They stood thus, Lottie in half agony, half ecstasy as she was enveloped in the best, most selfless love she'd ever felt. How could she not just simply welcome Denny into her life?

She would. She could. But first, a moment with the duke was in order. What if Denny was in a frenzy, a rush to never lose her, and would soon go back to feeling only friendship?

They spent a good part of the night together, cherishing the sweet pain of perhaps never spending another night the same way. And just before dawn, he snuck out of the kitchen and she made her way to her bed.

When light and warmth filled the air and morning officially arrived, she wiped the barest of sleep from her eyes and took off for the park with only a maid in tow. She marveled at her bravery. She never would have done such a thing weeks ago, not since the Season had begun. Or if she had, she'd have hidden away. But this morning, she sought information. She set out to listen.

As she made her way, many smiled and nodded, everyone engaged her in conversation. At one point, she was standing where she had on that first dreaded day in the park, at the crossroads of paths, surrounded by people. The shaded woods called to her again. She had never solved the mystery of the shadows inside.

She nodded farewell to the chattering group who she stood with and edged closer to the darkness and the trees.

When she saw movement and heard murmuring voices, she slipped behind a tree, hoping her maid would be sensible enough to stay back. Excellent at hiding, she moved herself well within the shadows and peered around the edge of a tree.

Two men, both of whom were well-dressed, conversed. Then another joined them. The duke! She sucked in a breath and held it, hoping to hear their conversation.

The duke held up a bag of coins. "You were right. You deserve this. Spend it well." He let it slip into the other man's hand with great reluctance.

The man huffed. "Don't act like it's your last coin. You'll soon have more than you know what to deal with."

The duke brushed something from his coat. "Nothing is certain until she's locked away at my estate. She could deny me at any time—that Lord Ragsdale is a thorn. But you deserve the coins. I'd have never known about her potential. Such an unremarkably plain face . . . I'd have never known who she was."

"I make it a business to know." The man glanced around and stopped moving. "I heard something."

Lottie breathed out as quietly as possible, holding perfectly still, trying to ignore the churning in her stomach.

He'd lied. Everything he'd told her was laced in dishonesty. She wanted to be ill, hoping to rid herself of the duke.

"The paths are full of people, even at this hour. Of course you heard something." The duke turned and walked away. "Don't contact me again and stay silent about what you know. I have no further use for you." He moved quickly and was soon out of eyesight.

The two remaining men murmured together. She could no longer hear their words, but she was unsatisfied. She must know the truth.

She stepped out from behind the tree, into their line of sight.

"Blimey, miss." They froze in place. "You're—"

"Miss Hughes."

They swallowed.

"I'd like some more information, if you please." She held up her change purse. The greedy expressions in the men's faces told her she would learn all she wished.

"Tell me what happened."

Lottie left the woods with a new sense of power. Even though she'd just learned of a terrible betrayal, she felt suddenly strong, and she knew what she wanted.

She felt free.

Free to marry who she wanted, and free to turn down any marriage proposal she wished.

The thought made her skip a few steps as she walked out along a well-traveled path. Many walked along it with her, seeking her attention, but she simply smiled and kept moving. She could speak with those she wished.

All these people who never saw her—she had no use for them. She didn't need an introduction; she'd been introduced to them all. And she had no interest in learning about all their reasons for wishing to be her dearest of all friends.

She walked until her feet were sore. She found her way to the head of the fountain she'd so often longed to enjoy and there, she breathed in the smell of roses. She wandered along the hedgerows. Her maid had kept up, just barely. She smiled and turned. "I'm sorry for my meandering. We shall return home soon."

The maid started, then nodded with a quick curtsey. "Yes, miss."

A rush in the crowd sounded behind her, as if a great many were reacting to something. The sound grew nearer and horse's hooves on pavement followed. She turned, hoping for Denny. Had he found her out and followed her there, knowing what she'd want most was a ride on her horse?

Denny always knew. He was always there. If that wasn't love, what was? A bright clarity began to illuminate her mind.

One kiss would tell if he was governed by friendship or something more. She peered her head around a row, waiting for the first sign of him.

Instead of Denny's cheerful face, the duke came into view, wearing his full noble wear. He looked almost royal, with the brocade on his jacket and the bright light reflecting off his buttons. He was leading his own promenade, and the people around him were eating it up.

He stopped in front of her. His smile was large, genuine, but there was a bit of awareness, of self-importance. He was putting on a show and she could tell. But it was a show in part for her.

He swung off his horse, adjusting his cape out behind him. "Miss Hughes." His grin grew and then he went down on one knee.

"What?" She glanced around. A crowd had gathered and

was continuing to grow. Soon she was hemmed in on all sides. "What are you doing?"

"I think that is obvious by now, don't you?" He winked. "Miss Lottie Hughes, I kneel before you, ready to offer myself, my title, my homes, everything to you. I have found myself enchanted."

A few women in the crowd sighed and fanned themselves.

"We are both in need. We both bring strength to a union between us. And we do well together. We laugh. We advise. We could make happy lives. Will you do me the great honor of being my wife?" His eyes were wide and sincere. She knew him to be a good sort of person in addition to all his failings, but she did not wish to be married to such a man.

But her mother? Did her mother know something Lottie did not? Was it that valuable to be a duchess? Valuable for her children? For her future? If her money could restore a ducal estate, was that not a noble endeavor? Did everyone marry for love?

Eyes were on her, many eyes, but she felt one set in particular. She searched the crowd. People smiled at her, some frowned, but she glanced over them all, looking, seeking, hoping. And then a whistle sounded.

She jerked her head and caught his gaze from the branches of a tree. He winked and his eyes held support. Memories. Strength. Love.

Her attention went back to the duke.

"Yes, I'm still here." He shifted.

She went down on her knees across from him. "Your Grace."

He rested a hand at the side of her face. The crowd sighed.

"I cannot."

His expression closed, as if his face was a complete blank. "Pardon?"

"I cannot marry you." The words came out as a soft murmur. Hoping to spare him some social embarrassment, she said as little as possible.

"Speak up, woman. Or has your awkwardness returned?" He stood. His congenial patience, his care, had disappeared, and in its place, a sneering expression. "Tell them all what you said." He held out a hand toward the crowd. "If you snub a duke, will you truly marry any one of us? Let it be known she is cold and uncaring."

She gasped and reached for her chest, hoping to grasp at something. She opened her mouth to respond. To convince everyone of his wretched nature, but she didn't have the words. Her mind raced and grasped at nothing.

"That is not true." Denny swung down from the tree. "And you are the worst sort of gentleman to say so." He pushed his way through the crowd and stood as close as he could to the duke's face. "Apologize." His hands clenched and unclenched. His face was tense, his jaw tight.

"And if I don't?" The duke did not back down. He stared up into Denny's face.

Would they be talking pistols at dawn? Lottie shook her head, stood, and stepped closer. "Denny."

He reached for her hand, which she took as she moved to his side.

"You have insulted my best friend in the worst possible way. Apologize. Now."

The duke stared him down.

"Or do you wish everyone to know what we know?" Denny did not lower his voice.

Lottie cleared her throat, calling out loud enough for those nearby to hear. "Do you wish them to know how you paid off my steward for the information regarding my wealth, that that is why you returned to town? That you came here expressly hoping to win my inheritance?"

The crowd murmured, a few of the ladies gasped. Denny turned to her. "What? Lottie. He knew about your inheritance before he met you?" Denny's eyes searched hers and then his face hardened. Before she could do anything at all to stop him, he swung his hand and punched the duke in the face.

The crowd gasped.

Then, while cradling one hand, he held her other. "Make way," he called, and the crowd moved aside as quickly as possible.

The duke called, "You will answer for this!"

"Talk to a magistrate then. And maybe make a deal with your creditors. You're going to need their mercy."

Lottie ignored the duke and ignored the crowd. She walked as close as possible to Denny. "Please tell me you have horses."

"A horse."

"Perfect."

Cyclone was tied to a tree, and the two hurried to him. Denny lifted Lottie up into the saddle and then swung up behind her.

With his arms around her, his body cradling her, he turned the horse and galloped off, away from the crowds, the people, the noise, away from the park. They raced down the lanes, past London and its buildings, until larger estates lined their sights and great rolling hills of land surrounded them.

Lottie said nothing. She didn't know what to say, and she didn't know what to do, but she trusted Denny and that was all that mattered.

At last, he slowed near a stream. "Let's give water to Cyclone." His voice sounded gruff, full of emotion.

He dismounted and reached up for her. His hands cradled her hips. He steadied her on her feet as she dismounted. With Cyclone at her back and Denny at her front, she could only smile. A great peace filled her. "I'm so happy I don't have to lose you." The relief was so strong, she gulped down a breath and fought to stay standing. The air wavered a bit around her.

"You would never lose me. Ever. Even if you married that despicable person." He tucked a hair behind her ear, his touch doing magnificent things to her skin. "But you know, he did it all wrong."

She snorted. "He certainly did." She searched his face. "Which part are you talking about? Paying off my steward? Lying to me?"

He shook his head. "All despicable things. But I was talking about your proposal." A great tenderness softened his expression.

"Oh?"

He nodded, then he stepped back and took her hand. "No, you need to be proposed to in a place like this." He indicated all the land around them and he led her to a tree. "It would be better under the great oak by our swing. But . . . right about here . . ." He stopped on a bit of soft ground and got down on one knee. ". . . will do until we get back home."

"What? Are you kneeling?" Lottie hardly knew one could feel so much happiness.

"I love you. I have loved you for a long time, in the best sort of way. But I love you even more now. I love you as the woman I cannot wait to hold, to cherish, to . . ." He winked. "To kiss," he whispered.

She clutched at her chest. "Do you think we could?"

He laughed. "I do. Marry me, Lott. Not because I'm your friend who can't share. Marry me because I love you."

Lottie reached her hand down to the side of his face. "Then, yes. Denny, I love you dearly. You are more dear to me than anyone in the world. And I would be honored to be your wife." She tugged him to his feet. "But I must know one thing first."

"What is that?" His eyes held a knowing light. He wrapped his arms around her and pulled her close, dipping his head toward her.

She stood taller, catching his lips with hers, pressing closer to him with an urgency she didn't even know she had. Her hands went up into his hair while she kissed him over and over. His large hands encased her waist, pulling her toward him, responding with equal amounts of love.

"I love you, Lottie. In all ways." He kissed the tip of her nose. "But I think I love you like this best of all." He grinned down into her face, looking just like he had every time they'd stolen some of Cook's cakes.

She laughed. "You would." Then she rose up in his arms and pressed her lips again to his, not wanting to ever let go.

An award winning author, including the GOLD in Foreword INDIES Book of the Year Awards, **Jen Geigle Johnson** discovered her passion for England while kayaking on the Thames near London as a young teenager. She still finds the great old manors and castles in England fascinating and loves to share bits of history that might otherwise be forgotten. Whether set in Regency England, the French Revolution, or Colonial America, her romance novels are much like life is supposed to be: full of brave heroes, strong heroines, and stirring adventures.

Follow her at: www.jengeiglejohnson.com
Twitter: @authorjen
Instagram: @author.jen.geigle.johnson

Letters to a Wallflower

Heather B. Moore

One

London, 1817

MISS ELLEN YOUNG WAS tired of being called beautiful.

As she gazed into the gilt-framed mirror, wrinkling her pert nose, pursing her rosebud lips, and narrowing her lake-blue eyes, she scowled at her reflection. Perhaps if she held this facial expression for an hour, a wrinkle would result. Or perhaps if the rain would stop for an afternoon, she could traipse through gardens and earn a few freckles.

"There you are, dearest," Mother said, coming into the bedroom. "Why, Ellen, you're not even dressed for the ball. Cousin Dinah is downstairs, ready and waiting. What will I tell her?"

Without turning, Ellen said, "Tell her she's ready an hour early, and that I'll be ready on time."

Her mother sighed her usual sigh. In a couple decades, Ellen would probably resemble her tawny-haired mother, with gentle lines about her eyes and lips.

"Now be sure to tell Sally to add plenty of curls to your hair. Curls are most becoming on you."

Ellen hid a grimace. "Of course."

Her mother's gaze was full of affection and admiration, which should make Ellen feel guilty. But it didn't. Stepping forward, Mother smoothed a hand over the sleeve of Ellen's day dress. "The Society papers were right. You *are* the diamond of the Season, dearest. I only wish I had the funds to buy you the latest fashions from Paris—"

"You've spent enough on my gowns," Ellen cut in. "I don't need extra frills or more luxurious fabrics."

Mother tutted. "You're right. You're stunning without them, and you'll have a marquess, or an earl, or even a baron proposing to you in no time."

"Not *all* men of the *ton* are desirable, Mother," Ellen cut in with a firm voice. "In fact, most of them are rakes—is that what you wish for my future? A cold marriage bed after I've delivered the requisite heir and a spare?"

"Ellen Constance Young! I did not raise you to speak of such vulgar matters!"

Ellen felt a little contrite, but only just. "I apologize."

"Now," her mother said, her tremulous voice taking on a new calm. "You must listen carefully to my advice, since I will not be attending tonight." She brought a handkerchief to her mouth and coughed delicately.

Everything about Mother was delicate, even when she was ill.

"There will be many eligible gentlemen there, and Cousin Dinah knows who's who. Don't accept dance invitations from any men beneath your station."

"Of course not," Ellen murmured.

"I will send Sally in," Mother said. "Expect her shortly. Make sure that she takes extra care with your hairdo tonight by adding in the orange blossoms that Aunt Margaret went to all that trouble to send for. They'll set you apart from the other young misses, and you'll earn compliments in the Society pages again."

Ellen nodded, as if she lived and breathed mentions in the Society pages.

This was par for the course—the typical admonitions Mother had been giving her all Season. Thankfully, the Season was half over, and Ellen was happily counting down.

It wasn't that she didn't *want* to marry—unlike Cousin Dinah, who was thirty-one and a declared spinster. Having a wealthy husband certainly would have its perks, but did Ellen have to be on display to secure a husband? Parade in front of the hostess and the eligible bachelors, as if she were at a horse auction?

She couldn't think of one sincere conversation she'd ever been a part of at a social function this Season. It was all gossip, judgement, and speculation: who was dancing with who; who was wearing the most fashionable dress; who had obviously eaten too many sweets the week before.

Would all the henpecking end with marriage?

No.

Married women were criticized even more: who was with child; who drove the nicest carriage; who had the invitation to dine with royalty; who had produced an heir; who was hosting the best event of the Season.

Instead of going to ball after ball, Ellen would prefer to tend to her small garden of flowers and herbs—the one that widowed Aunt Margaret allowed her to fully plant and care for by herself on the back terrace of her London townhome. It had become Ellen's solace, her sanity while she and her mother spent the Season here. Ellen's father had passed away a few years before and left them a widow's cottage, but the estate had gone to the nearest male relative.

So here they were. Spending money they didn't really have on dresses, living on the good charity of relatives.

If Ellen had a choice, she'd return home. She missed the country cottage fiercely—the call of the birds in the morning, the wide, clear blue skies, the scent of flowers, trees, and rich earth. Right now, none of that was to be. She must spend her evenings speaking of music, fashion, and art. She had to refine her skills of conversation and flirtation each evening. She must spend her daylight hours doing needlework or playing the pianoforte. All useless skills, unless one was proficient. Which Ellen was not.

"Hello? May I come in?" her cousin, Dinah Turner's singsong voice was unmistakable.

Ellen couldn't have stopped the smile on her face if she tried. Cousin Dinah was a one-of-a-kind woman, well-versed in literature and politics, and privy to London gossips. Her prominent unibrow and outspoken nature ensured that the young gents steered clear of her. She could talk them under any table, could gamble smarter and laugh louder.

Ellen absolutely loved her.

Now if only she could be as carefree and worry-free as her older cousin.

"Now what do we have here?" Dinah asked, her blue eyes, which were nearly the same color as Ellen's, sparkling. "Orange blossoms? Are these for your décolletage?"

Ellen sputtered a laugh. "Should our mothers hear you, they would be scandalized into a fainting fit. They are for my *hair*, dear cousin."

Dinah's grin was very wicked. "Well, my mother is as deaf as an elderly bachelor, and your mother is already in her bedroom, ready for a quiet night with hot tea." She plucked one of the blossoms from the dressing table and inhaled.

The scent wafted in Ellen's direction. They really did smell wonderful. "Mother thinks I'll be the toast of the ball if I wear them in my hair."

Dinah scoffed and brought a blossom to her own hair. "What do you think? Will my dance card be full tonight, as yours will be?" She frowned so that she looked very formidable indeed. Dinah's dark hair and pale complexion were truthfully a pretty contrast. And gentlemen *did* ask Dinah to dance, but mostly out of politeness, not out of romantic interest.

It didn't bother Dinah one whit. She was content being her mother's companion until the end of their days.

"Better your dance card than mine," Ellen said. "My feet were so sore the other night that I was sure my heels were bruised from all the dancing."

Dinah rolled her eyes. "Next you'll tell me your cheeks hurt from smiling at so many adoring gentlemen."

Ellen nudged her cousin's arm. "Oh, that too. And did I tell you that my head had swollen two sizes from so many compliments?"

The two women burst into laughter.

It felt so good to speak ironies with her cousin and make fun of how much importance others put on social events, when really, no one was ever their true selves anyway.

"I wish I could trade places with you, Dinah," Ellen mused, "if only for one ball. Not to give any offense, but a dance or two per evening sounds quite heavenly."

Dinah's heavy brow creased. "*Trade* places? Well, that would be quite impossible." She tapped a finger against her chin. "You're easily the most beautiful woman in the room, even without all the frippery. Even if you left the orange blossoms at home and stood with the wallflowers, your dance card would be full."

Ellen smirked. "Not likely, cousin. If I remove the polish, the sparkle, the fancy gown, and stand with the wallflowers, no one will deign to look my way."

Dinah folded her arms. "Want to make a wager?"

Ellen gave a surprised laugh. "What?"

"You know, when one person bets on something that the other—"

"I *know* what a wager is," Ellen cut in. "But you can't possibly believe that my dance card will be full if I stand with the wallflowers tonight."

"Maybe not full, but at least *half* full," Dinah said. "What do you say? Leave the orange blossoms at home, wear one of my older, drab-colored gowns, and stand with the wallflowers all night. If you aren't asked to dance at least half of the dances, I will . . ." She tapped her chin again. "I will let you take rose cuttings from my mother's garden."

Ellen stared at her cousin. "Truly?" She'd asked multiple times, but Aunt Margaret was not of a mind to let anything interfere with her superior roses. Ellen was positive that the rose bushes would survive, and the new cuttings would absolutely thrive at her cottage home in the country. She frowned. "What if *you* win the wager, what will you get?"

"I will get a full month's break of escorting you to these ridiculous social events, and you will go with Lady Marble, if your mother doesn't attend."

Ellen scowled at this. Lady Marble was the neighbor next door, and with all three of her daughters married and living outside of London, she had no one else's life to meddle with. She'd offered more than once to accompany Ellen to social events. Lady Marble was also the primary source of Society gossip, where Dinah gleaned all her information.

If nothing else, though, a wager would make tonight more interesting. Different. And Ellen was game.

"It's a deal," she said, grasping Dinah's hand and giving it a firm shake.

Two

LORD AARON BOLTON PACED the entryway of his home in Grosvenor Square as he waited for his mother to come down the stairs. They'd be taking the carriage this evening to yet another social event—a ball hosted by Lady such and such. Apparently, the county where their estate resided didn't have the proper amount of Society misses to choose a bride from.

At least according to Aaron's mother, Lady Bolton.

So here they were, attending the latter half of the London Season, when Aaron needed to be back home, overseeing the flock of merino sheep that the Prince Regent had sent to his estate this past month. Other estates had received several dozen of the imported sheep from Spain, in order to see if raising the merino sheep could be successful in the drier counties of England.

Yet Mother was more concerned about Aaron's marriage situation than helping with the Prince Regent's experiment. The moment Aaron had reached his thirtieth birthday this past spring, Mother had turned into a matchmaker, throwing this woman and that woman his way. Well, not exactly *throwing*, but accepting invitations on his behalf was close enough.

Aaron was a grown man and could find his own wife—once things at the estate were in order and settled. Which would be at least another year. Parts of the manor needed to be renovated and one wing completely rebuilt, after the fire only two months ago. And that didn't even account for the state of the gardens. Atrocious.

What had his older brother, Spencer, been thinking?

Oh, never mind. Spencer had been gambling, drinking, and womanizing so he hadn't been thinking at all. His early demise had brought Aaron from the life he loved in the Navy, back to a run-down, neglected estate and a frazzled mother. Who was coming down the stairs now.

"Oh, Aaron," Mother said in her prim tone. Her copper hair was more russet than red, faded with the years, but her green eyes never missed a thing. "You aren't going to wear that, are you?"

He looked down at his outfit that was perfectly respectful ballroom attire. "What's wrong with what I'm wearing?"

"That jacket looks altered."

"It *has* been altered," Aaron said. "It was Spencer's." Spencer hadn't been quite as trim as Aaron, but he saw no reason to outfit himself in brand new clothing when alterations sufficed. He had an estate to rebuild, after all.

"What about the jacket that arrived yesterday from the tailor's?" Mother asked. "You looked magnificent in it."

"I sent it back since I didn't need it," Aaron said simply as he smoothed a hand over the lapel.

His mother clicked her tongue. "The color brown looked fine on Spencer because his hair was red, but you, my son, are a brunette so now you look positively brown from head to foot."

Well. That was an amusing fault. "Perhaps I'll blend in with the foliage in the corners, then, and can more easily avoid the misses with their fearsome mothers."

Mother slapped his arm with her gloves. "You should not

speak of them in such a manner. You'll be marrying one of them soon enough."

"I don't see why anything has to be done *soon*," Aaron said, opening the front door to reveal their carriage already waiting beyond the stairs. "Spencer was older than me, and—"

"Must you bring him up when we are about to socialize?" his mother asked. "I don't need weepy eyes."

"Forgive me, Mother, I apologize." And he was truly sorry. He didn't want to upset her. He helped her into the carriage, then climbed in behind her. He tapped the roof, and the carriage lurched forward, moving over the cobblestone road.

His mother seemed to recover quite quickly, however. "Remember what I told you about this ball? Miss Castleton and Miss Hertford will be in attendance, and you must meet them. Both are lovely young ladies and . . ."

Aaron gazed out the carriage window at the passing homes as his mind wandered from the ladies his mother was discussing. He could never keep them straight, anyway. Some of the homes were lit up, others were dark, and he wondered about the occupants inside.

"Aaron, are you even listening?"

He snapped his gaze back to his mother. "I was . . ."

Her lips pressed together. "What did I say about Miss Richards?"

"That she is very beautiful?"

"Well, yes, she is, but there is much more to her, of course. She is very accomplished."

"Isn't every young lady of the *ton* accomplished? I almost feel that you don't even care who I marry, as long as it's someone beautiful and accomplished."

"That's not entirely true," his mother said. "Of course, I

want you to be happy, son, but marriage is not a thing to be delayed any longer. And, you know, the sooner you meet someone, the sooner we'll be able to return home. All you have to do is find someone you're interested in, pay her a few visits, bring her flowers, take her on a ride or two through Hyde Park, then propose."

Returning home sooner than later was an appealing thought indeed. But he wasn't sure that wooing a woman was quite so neat and tidy as Mother claimed. "Surely women are more picky and would expect much more than a few bouquets and two carriage rides to decide upon a husband."

Mother leaned forward, her green eyes gleaming in the light of a passing lamppost. "Not when you're a titled gentleman." She shrugged. "Such a gentleman can secure a diamond of the first water."

"Those women are surrounded by hordes of clamoring men, and I'm not interested in worming my way through to offer a bevy of compliments she's heard over a hundred times. Sounds a bit pretentious to me."

His mother bit her lip, her gaze thoughtful. "I hadn't thought of it from a gentleman's angle. But I suppose you're right. If you danced with a wallflower, she'd probably accept a proposal by the end of the evening."

Aaron grimaced. "You think very little of your sex, Mother."

She straightened, then folded her gloved hands. "Try it."

"What?"

"Dance with a wallflower, then propose."

Aaron laughed. "That's ridiculous."

"Well, then, don't propose," his mother said. "But dance with the wallflowers if you don't want all the fuss of the diamonds of the first water. Maybe you'll find your own diamond."

Aaron shook his head, but something inside of him was

warming up to the idea. "All right. In fact, I think that's the best idea I've heard from you about this whole marriage mart thing."

His mother's eyes flashed with approval. "Like I said, son, your happiness is very important to me."

"As long as it includes a bride?"

Her lips quirked. "Yes."

The carriage slowed, then it stopped behind the long line of carriages waiting for their turn to unload passengers. "How about I make you a deal, Mother?"

Her chin lifted as she studied him.

"If I dance every dance tonight and call on at least one woman tomorrow with flowers in hand and take her for a ride in Hyde Park the following day, might I have a week off of attending these functions? I'd like to return to the estate for a few days and check on how the merino sheep are doing."

"They are just *sheep*, Aaron, and what will the young lady in question say about your absence?"

"I'll tell her that I'll be away from London for a week, but I'll look forward to seeing her at . . . ?" He paused and quirked his brow.

"Lady Whitehall's ball," his mother supplied. "It's in ten days' time."

"Perfect."

When their carriage reached the top of the drive and it was Aaron's turn to disembark, he handed his mother down. They walked together up the elegant steps leading to the mansion, ablaze with lights and teeming with music and guests. They were introduced to Lord and Lady such and such, who happened to be Lord and Lady Rueland.

As Aaron and his mother weaved through the crush, pausing every so often to greet an acquaintance, Aaron searched for the wallflowers. It probably didn't speak too well of him that he'd never sought them out before—or noticed them, for that matter. To be fair, he'd only been to a handful of balls in his life, and most of them recently. There wasn't much dancing in the Navy.

His mother tapped her fan on his arm. "There," she said in a low tone, "to the right of the potted tree, and past the three matrons on the settee."

Ah. There they were.

"Thank you, Mother," Aaron said. "I think I can manage on my own from here."

His mother smiled, and although she hurried off to join her gaggle of friends, he knew she'd be watching every woman he danced with. So be it. He touched the knot of his cravat, finding it exact. There was nothing amiss in his appearance, save for the perspiration he felt prickling his brow.

There was nothing to fear, though. The three matrons squeezed together on the same settee was, however, quite a sight, and he did fear that the delicately arched settee legs might crack under their combined weight.

But the row of wallflowers beyond? They were simply . . . ordinary.

Not that Aaron thought he was a great enough catch to attract, as Mother called them, a diamond of the first water. But for the first time since entering the Ruelands' ballroom, Aaron hesitated.

There were precisely six women lined up against the wall. Almost with military precision, which Aaron found both fascinating and bothersome. It was as if these women had been assigned a specific spot and told not to move an inch to the left or to the right.

The first two women were bright redheads. Having a bit of auburn in his own brown hair, Aaron didn't dislike women with red hair, but he also knew that sometimes their personality could be a bit, ah, excitable and decisive. Case in point with his own red-haired mother.

The next three women were brunettes, one darker than the others. Their expressions reminded Aaron of his hound dogs back at his country home. None of them appeared to be enjoying the ball, nor each other's company. The woman at the far end was blonde, her hair nearly gold in the light of the chandeliers. She wasn't watching the dance floor but was looking down at a small book in her hands. Was she . . . *reading*? At a ball?

From this angle, Aaron couldn't see her face because one of the brunettes stepped forward and craned her neck to peer at something. But he'd seen enough to know that the blonde woman wore an ill-fitting, puce-colored dress—clearly a hand-me-down. Life wasn't easy for everyone, he had to remind himself. Whether or not this experiment his mother wanted him to try would have any sort of favorable results, perhaps he could at least bring a smile to one of the wallflowers' faces tonight.

He'd promised that he'd dance all the dances tonight, so it was time to get started. Perhaps he'd start with one of the redheads before he made a better assessment of the blonde who was reading a book.

Three

ELLEN WASN'T REALLY READING a book at a ball, she was only pretending to read. Besides, poetry wasn't her cup of tea, so to speak, and if anyone had quizzed her on the poetry book in hand, she'd draw a blank.

Cousin Dinah hadn't forbidden bringing a book to the ball, so Ellen saw no harm in using it as a deterrent toward men who might prefer blonde wallflowers to every other lady in the room. So far, it had worked like a charm.

That, or the too-large dress from Dinah's closet, which they then covered up with a cloak to make it out of the house. On the way to the ball in the carriage, Ellen had removed every piece of dazzling jewelry and discarded every lovely scented orange blossom.

She'd kept the poetry book tucked away until she reached the wallflower wall.

Ellen had spotted Dinah's scowl across the ballroom more than once, and it was really hard not to lose her composure and burst out laughing.

Still, she allowed silent chuckles to emerge from time to time. Thankfully, the other wallflowers seemed to be lost in their own worlds of whatever they were thinking or wishing. At least none of them had attempted conversation with Ellen, and she was trying to decide if she should be offended about that.

Nevertheless, she'd been here nearly an hour and had yet to be asked to dance. It was a glorious thing. Not only did she have a completely blank dance card, but her feet didn't hurt. She'd sleep well tonight and have plenty of energy tomorrow to work in her garden. Plus, those rose cuttings would make the start of a fine rose garden at her cottage.

She was contemplating what her mother might say if she arrived home tonight with a blank dance card, when a pair of shoes entered her line of vision. Men's shoes. *Oh, please, no.* She'd been doing so well.

"I am surprised to see you here, Miss Young."

Ellen released a silent sigh and looked up.

The man standing before her was at least two inches shorter than she, and his brown eyes and mud-colored hair very familiar. So, Lord Jarvis had found her. Well, it had been tradition that they dance at every ball, whether Ellen cared for it or not.

"I have sought and found a bit of solace."

If there was one thing to compliment Lord Jarvis on, it was his laugh, which sounded like a low-toned bell. Quite pleasant.

He laughed now, and she was certain every wallflower was now staring at the pair of them. "You are seeking solace in the wrong place, Miss Young. You're at a ball, and there is dancing and entertainment to be enjoyed."

"You're quite right, Lord Jarvis."

He nodded with satisfaction. "In that case, might you tear yourself away from the bit of poetry in your hands and honor me with a dance?"

Cousin Dinah hadn't specifically said she had to dance with the gentlemen who might ask, but she was counting the invitations regardless. And how rude would it be to turn down Lord Jarvis? Quite rude indeed.

She drew out her dance card from the back of the poetry book where she'd tucked it earlier. Lord Jarvis took it with a flourish and bent over it and began to print each letter of his rather long name. He could have written "Jarvis," but no . . . Her gaze wandered as he wrote, and she sought out Dinah. Was her cousin observing the first notch in Ellen's demise for the evening?

But Dinah wasn't in obvious sight. Not too far from where Ellen stood, one of the wallflowers was dancing. How nice, she decided. It was one of the redheads, and she was positively glowing—or was it blushing? Her dance partner was quite elegant in his steps, and was dressed fashionably, if Ellen was to notice. Which she wasn't really, but she was curious, it seemed.

She hadn't expected the higher elite to ask a wallflower to dance.

The couple moved through the cotillion, and this gave Ellen a view of the gentleman's face. Another surprise. He was handsome. Quite handsome, in fact.

His dark auburn hair waved to his collar, and his jaw made a fine angle just below his sideburns. His eyes were deep-set, which made him seem a bit broody. She wasn't sure of the color, but she was sure of one thing—he was looking right at her.

She hid a small gasp and refocused on Lord Jarvis.

He handed back the dance card, then extended his arm. "If we may?"

The music was ending, and another would begin soon. Ellen gave a quick smile. "Of course."

As she slipped her hand about the crook of Jarvis's arm to be led to the dance floor, she sensed that the auburn-haired gentleman's gaze was upon her. How she knew this, she couldn't explain, unless it was because her neck prickled.

She and Jarvis moved through the crowd, then stood across from each other as the orchestra struck up a quadrille. She knew the steps well enough that she didn't have to pay them any mind, and she certainly wasn't going to make moon eyes at Lord Jarvis. So, she searched once again for Dinah and spotted her at last.

She stood with a few other ladies, and although the conversation seemed quite vigorous, Dinah sent a triumphant smile in Ellen's direction.

It was everything Ellen could do to not roll her eyes.

As she rotated with Jarvis through the dance steps, she caught sight of the auburn-haired gentleman. Who was . . . dancing with *another* wallflower. This time one of the brunettes. After Ellen recovered from her surprise, she decided that she was curious. Or maybe annoyed. Perhaps the man had made a wager with his friends? To dance with the wallflowers? She'd heard of such ridiculous games before.

Yet his attention seemed to be kind and sincere as he made conversation with the decidedly blushing lady. How did Ellen know this? Because they were dancing not four feet from where Ellen was dancing with Lord Jarvis.

Unfortunately, Ellen didn't look away quickly enough because the auburn-haired man's gaze shifted and landed on her. Again.

This time she saw that his eyes were green, dark like leaves after rain, and she knew instinctively that if he were to wear a richer-colored jacket, his eyes would draw in every lady in the room.

So she was not the only one wearing a poor color choice tonight. She almost smiled at that.

It seemed, though, that she'd *actually* smiled at the

thought because Mr. Auburn-Hair smiled at *her*. A brief smile, but there was no mistaking it. His smile was gone before she could truly verify that such a thing had happened because he was now nodding at something the brunette had said.

Ellen really should be focusing on her own dance partner, even though she knew that Mother would prefer a gentleman more titled than a mere son of a baron. But that was of no concern at this moment. Ellen had to figure out how to remain with the wallflowers and not be asked to dance by any other gentlemen.

Her wish was in vain because shortly after the quadrille with Lord Jarvis, she was met by Mr. Thomas and asked to dance. He must have seen her on the floor because it appeared he'd followed her to what should have been a secluded spot with the other wallflowers. Mr. Thomas was a decent enough man, who had quite a fortune in sugar, but wasn't of the gentry. Ellen could practically hear her mother's disappointment—if she had come. Right now, though, Ellen was trying to be polite, even as she was inwardly gritting her teeth.

Mr. Thomas had the habit of staring at her as they danced. Couldn't his penetrating blue eyes find another person or item to look upon? No, his gaze never left hers and so she felt obligated to meet that gaze. It was all exhausting, really, because he also smiled one continual smile. What could he be smiling at, and what was going on inside that head of his?

Was he thinking of his sugar plantations and the money that his mother had made no secret of him earning? He didn't speak much—no, his mother did all that for him. It was quite the running joke among the *ton*, although he was very well respected for all that money, of course.

And there was his mother now. Standing on the fringes

of the dance circles and speaking to . . . Dinah! Who was grinning. Of course she was. Ellen was well on her way to losing out on the best rose cuttings in London. For the more she danced, the more people would see her, and the more likelihood they would follow suit of Mr. Thomas's example and seek her out. This would not do, not do at all.

Every step closer to the end of the quadrille only brought with it more of a sinking heart because she'd just spotted Lord Avery. Another baron in the making, and he was looking right at her.

She had now danced twice, and two more dances would put her at half her dance card for the evening.

And it didn't help matters that the auburn-haired gentleman who apparently had a penchant for dancing with wallflowers was now paired with the second brunette. It seemed he was on a mission to dance with every wallflower this evening. Ellen determined that she would *not* be one of them.

Four

SHE WAS EASILY THE loveliest woman in the room, Aaron decided. So it was no wonder that she'd been dancing set after set, even though she'd regulated herself to the wallflower lineup. What he couldn't figure out was why she looked absolutely miserable.

Every wallflower who he'd invited to dance had blushed, flirted, stammered, and thanked him profusely. He had yet to dance with one he felt the urge to call upon the next day, though, as per his agreement with his mother.

Aaron was running out of wallflowers now, and truthfully running out of dances. There was only one other redhead to ask, but she'd disappeared someplace. Perhaps she'd gone home early.

But that wasn't his utmost concern right now. His thoughts were full of the woman with golden hair, eyes the color of a summer pond, and skin porcelain smooth. Who was she, and why was she upset? Was she ill? Had she been jilted? Was there some recent tragedy in her family?

Yes, she was beautiful, and Aaron supposed that was why she'd caught his attention in the first place, but worry gnawed inside. He knew enough about tragedy in his own life to empathize with a young woman who might be experiencing some of her own. What had possessed her to come tonight, then?

She didn't seem to have a fussing mother. She must have come with someone, though, perhaps a distant relation? And what of her dress? It was clearly not fitted to her, so it must be borrowed or handed down. This told him, unfortunately, that she was not a woman with a dowry, which would lower her in his mother's eyes.

Yet Aaron found himself drawn over and over, with curiosity and sympathy, toward the blonde woman. She had been asked to dance by a shorter man, followed by two other gentlemen. She didn't seem to warm up to any of them, or even seem pleased to receive their attentions. So what was she about?

At this moment, she was back to reading her book, wedged close to the potted tree at the end of the row of wallflowers. Aaron had found her reading amusing earlier, but now his stomach felt hollow at the thought of the woman truly suffering from something.

He was about to approach her when a man, tall and thin as a reed, stepped blatantly in front of him.

"Miss Young," the reedy man said, "you are much too divine to spend any moment of this evening alone. Might I tempt you into a visit to the punch table? I hear the lemonade is deliciously sweet. We could then walk the terrace."

"Miss Young" lifted her gaze.

Since Aaron was only a handful of steps away in his approach, he now received the full effect of Miss Young's bottomless blue eyes. If he were to be honest, his knees felt a little wobbly, which was certainly ridiculous. Young girls swooned, not full-grown men.

"I am *quite* tired, Lord Grasser," Miss Young said.

Grasser . . . what a fitting name . . .

"Therefore," she continued, "walking along the terrace, or dancing, for the matter, would only send me into a faint."

"Oh dear," Lord Grasser said. "I should not want that. I shall procure a chair for you, then bring the lemonade to you."

Miss Young smiled sweetly.

If there had been a handrail nearby, Aaron would have grasped it for support.

"I am perfectly well right here," Miss Young pronounced. "Thank you for asking, Lord Grasser. Have a good evening."

Lord Grasser had been effectively dismissed. He murmured something, then moved off.

Now there was no one between Aaron and the young lady.

She didn't even notice him and returned to her small book.

Poetry, Aaron deduced.

He took two more steps. "Good evening, Miss Young."

Her gaze lifted, and she stared at him with such dismay, that a coil of guilt shot through Aaron. What had he done wrong? "I apologize for not being introduced to you formally, but I overheard your name and wondered if I might—"

She lifted a hand. "Stop right there. Do not ask what you've come to ask."

Aaron blinked. Then blinked again.

Turning slightly from him, more toward the potted tree, she lifted her book and began to read. But her eyes weren't following any of the words. At that moment, he knew this woman wasn't entranced with the words of some verbose poet, but she was using the book as a ruse.

He waited a moment, his heart thumping in time to the music filling the dance floor, but she continued to completely ignore him. Slowly, he exhaled, then took a careful step closer. "What do you think I've come to ask?"

She turned a page, but still her eyes didn't follow any words.

When she didn't answer after a long moment, he said, "I don't know you, and you don't know me, but I feel that you are dealing with something difficult. I wonder, might I be of assistance? That, Miss Young, is what I've come to ask."

Her head snapped up at this, and she looked at him. *Really* looked at him. He, of course, gazed right back—that was an easy thing to do. Miraculously, her previous dejected expression had softened somewhat. She didn't seem to have the heavy scent of perfume about her as most women did, but he could definitely smell something softer, more floral.

"Why would you want to assist me?"

Her question was simple, yet Aaron wasn't prepared for it.

"There are dozens of women in this ballroom," she continued, "and yet you are here, standing before me. Asking if I need help with something. What about me has brought you to this inquiry?"

Pink dusted her cheeks, and her blue eyes filled with fire. She was angry, which only made her more beautiful. Aaron brought his hand to his cravat, wishing he could loosen the knot without compromising the shape.

"If you do need help with anything, then I, Aaron Bolton, am at your service." He swallowed. "But I am intruding." His gaze flicked to the book in her hand. "I shall leave you in peace."

She tilted her head. "I don't think you can help me."

All right, then. That was her answer. He executed a short bow, then turned to leave.

"Wait."

Her voice was soft, but he would have heard it if he'd been on the other side of the ballroom. Pivoting, he faced her, not daring to hope too much. Hope burned through him regardless.

"If you really want to help me, then there *is* something I am in need of."

He waited, his pulse skittering like the wings of a moth. "I am at your service, Miss Young."

"Stay here, at the wall, with me," she said. "Engage me in conversation until the end of the evening. Be a buffer between me and any other gentlemen who might venture to invite me to dance."

Aaron's brows shot up. "You do not wish to dance any longer?"

"I do not wish to dance *or* be invited to dance."

Unusual. What woman came to a ball and didn't want to dance? But he wasn't going to pass judgment. Besides, he'd long been of the opinion that dancing with a woman wasn't conducive in really getting to know her. Joining Miss Young in conversation for the rest of the evening would be quite productive.

He'd find out soon enough if she was amenable to him paying her a visit tomorrow. Then he'd be returning to the estate in a matter of days.

"Where are you from, Mr. Bolton?" Miss Young asked.

Should he correct her so that she was aware of his title? No. At least, not yet. "Ravenshire."

"Ah. It sounds quaint." She cast him a sideways glance from where she leaned against the wall. He was only a foot in distance from her, and they both had an excellent view of the dancing.

"Do you know it?" he asked.

"I do not, but I assume it's outside of London. Your skin is too browned to be a Londoner."

He felt quite pleased that she'd noticed such a detail

about him. "South of London," he said. "Ravenshire Estate is nestled among the hills, and we've got a nice stream. Our climate is drier than London, which suits me fine."

She turned toward him and placed a hand on his arm.

He couldn't be more surprised.

"And your family?" she asked. "Have you got siblings?"

All the questions. Was she really that curious? Then he saw the cause of her sudden intimacy. A gentleman paused before the pair of them, gave a small nod, then continued on.

Miss Young's smile appeared, and she dropped her hand. "So?"

"Right. I did have two older brothers, but they've passed on." He hadn't quite meant to say so much.

Her brow creased. "I am truly sorry. I didn't mean to be so insensitive. What a difficult thing."

"Yes, it was difficult," he said, "and still is, in many ways. For my mother, who had depended upon my eldest brother to take over from my father. For my second brother, who never had a chance to fulfill his new role. And for me, who lost both brothers, yes, but also had to give up a career that brought fulfillment."

He certainly had Miss Young's full attention now. He'd just told her things that he hadn't confessed to any other soul outside his estate.

Her mouth opened, then shut. Then opened again. "What was your career, if I might ask?"

"Navy."

She nodded. "I can see that. You seem very . . . capable. As if you could command a ship despite a storm."

He laughed.

She blushed.

It appeared she was being serious . . . and he decided he felt quite flattered. "I apologize, I did not mean to make light of your compliment," he said. "Thank you."

She waved her book in front of her face as her gaze moved across the ballroom. "It's no matter. I just meant that you have a presence about you. One which tells me you are used to commanding others."

She stopped using her book as a fan, and her gaze slid to his again. He wondered if the thump of his heart could be heard above the music.

"Perhaps I'm skilled at running a ship and commanding dozens of men, but when it comes to my persistent mother, that's an entirely different story. She's right now probably spying upon me and wondering if any of the young women I danced with tonight might possibly be her future daughter-in-law."

Miss Young's perfectly arched brows lifted. "Oh, goodness. Your mother is one of those."

"Those?"

"A mother who interferes until she gets her way," Miss Young said. "Pray tell, has she forced you to come to this ball?"

"Yes. Although I must say, speaking to you, while the others in the room swap dance partners, is quite refreshing. My feet have been saved."

Her smile was slow, brilliant. "I understand completely. Tell me, do you always dance with wallflowers? I couldn't help but notice you were making your way through each one of us."

"No, I must confess that tonight was an exception. After a conversation my mother and I had about the need for me to marry, I told her that I was not concerned about it this Season because I have more pressing matters to attend to."

"Oh, what's more important than finding a wife?"

She was teasing, and it made him laugh. "Sheep."

Her blue eyes widened. "What?"

He explained about the sheep he was raising and needed to check on, although he left out the bit about it being part of the Prince Regent's project.

"So you are here to find a bride out of the wallflowers?" Miss Young said in a coy voice.

"Not exactly," he said. "I've made a deal with my mother. I meet a young woman tonight, pay a call on her in the morning, take a ride in Hyde Park the following day, and then I'll be free to return and tend to my sheep."

Miss Young's eyes twinkled with amusement. "Oh, that's such a lark. My mother is the same type to run interference instead of letting nature take its course. She's eager that I snag the first titled man for a husband so that my appearance doesn't go to waste."

Five

NOW WHY HAD SHE gone and said all that, Ellen wondered. Just because Mr. Bolton had been quite open and forthcoming didn't mean she had to be as well. He'd agreed to stand by the wall with her the rest of the evening, but that didn't mean she had to tell him personal things.

Too late for that.

"Your *appearance*?" he echoed.

Her face went hot, which meant she was blushing. She didn't need a mirror to confirm that. "You see"—she swallowed—"the Society papers deemed me as a diamond of the first water."

He didn't look surprised, or amused, so she continued. "This went to my mother's head, of course."

"Of course," he murmured.

Speaking of appearances, Mr. Bolton's eyes were not only green but had some lovely gold and brown shades intermixed as well. Standing this close to him, which amounted to about a foot of space between them, assured Ellen that he didn't smell like a dandy. No cloying perfume for this man. No, he smelled of fresh air and warm sun. Very manly.

She refocused to explain. "Even though I am the daughter of a simple country gentleman, Mother thinks I should be able to attract a marquess or an earl. A baron, at the very least."

"A marquess?"

"Oh, you know, a titled gentleman," she said with a wave of her hand. "Mother isn't picky."

Mr. Bolton rubbed a gloved hand across his chin. "What about you, Miss Young? Are you picky?"

"Heavens, no," she said, then corrected. "Well, not in *that* way. I mean, I'm not interested in titles because then I'd have to live with so many more expectations. I'd have to host dinners, pay morning social calls, plan balls, and keep up with the fashions. My children would be raised by a nurserymaid, and my sons would be sent to Eton at the age of ten."

She was going to blush again if she didn't mind her tongue.

Mr. Bolton nodded gravely. "Those are all important things to consider. And if you married a, er, *simple* country gentleman?"

"Oh, that would be less complicated," Ellen said. "Hosted dinners would be limited in number because our dining table would only seat six. And, of course, morning social calls wouldn't be bothered with because I'd be busy with the children, and balls would be completely out of the question in the country. Not enough people, and not enough ballrooms."

Mr. Bolton nodded as if he completely agreed.

This only spurred Ellen more. "Fashions would only have to be fussed over on the occasional visit to London, and no one would care if I wore orange blossoms in my hair."

"Orange blossoms?" he queried.

"They are the secret to attracting the most wealthy men of the *ton*, you know."

"Ah. Do they know this secret?"

"I have no idea," Ellen said, "for the orange blossoms are wilting right now in my cousin's carriage. They'll be quite wilted by the time I return home."

"Quite right," Mr. Bolton conceded. "I don't believe I've ever smelled an orange blossom."

"They are lovely, truly, but devastating to the male senses."

"Yet you chose to go without tonight," Mr. Bolton said, his eyes warm and amused, "in order to *not* snag an elite gentleman."

"Correct." Ellen shrugged. "I even changed out of my carefully selected ballgown and borrowed this frock. I had to leave the house concealed by a cloak."

"Ah." His brows quirked. "You've gone to such trouble tonight. Why not stay home and avoid the social scene altogether?"

"Because, Mr. Bolton," Ellen said, "my mother insisted I come."

"That says it all," he said with a laugh. "I see we have much in common."

"Yes. Mothers." She smiled. He smiled. It was a lovely way to pass the rest of the evening. She scanned for Dinah and found her across the room, engaged in a conversation with two elderly gentlemen.

"Are you typically a wallflower, Miss Young?"

She looked over at him again. His cravat was expertly tied, which told her that he at least employed a valet. Perhaps he was a country gentleman too. "Oh no. I'm in a wager, but I cannot tell a soul, or I'll lose."

His green eyes seemed to dance with merriment. "That explains quite a bit."

"Does it?"

"Might I guess the wager? Then can you tell me?"

Ellen bit her lip. That might be pushing it. She stole another glance at Dinah—who was still in what seemed to be quite the engrossing conversation. What were they doing? Debating the Corn Laws?

"I suppose, maybe." Ellen exhaled. "Well, probably not."

Just then, Dinah turned from the gentleman she was conversing with, and their eyes locked.

Dinah's brows lifted, as if in question. Ellen smiled and shook her head, then she held up her dance card and gave it a little wave.

Dinah set a hand on her hip.

Ellen shrugged, then covered her mouth to hide a laugh.

Next to her, Mr. Bolton folded his arms. "I'm assuming you know Miss Turner quite well?"

Ellen looked over at the man. "Dinah Turner? Yes, she's my cousin." She was surprised when Mr. Bolton looked quite . . . out of sorts. "Is something the matter?"

His face had lost some color, and he tugged at his cravat, sending it slightly off-center. "I don't know her. I know *of* her."

"Oh, well, everyone does, I suppose," Ellen said lightly, although now she was intrigued. Mr. Bolton was probably Dinah's age. Perhaps . . . they'd known each other in the past? Ellen had certainly never heard Dinah speak of a Mr. Bolton.

Dinah had disappeared from her spot, and a quick scan told Ellen she was heading toward the wall. "Oh, look, I guess you'll get to officially meet her. She's coming this way."

"It looks like I'll be apologizing, once again."

"Whatever do you mean, Mr. Bolton?" But before he had a chance to explain himself, Dinah swept up.

"Darling," Dinah gushed. "Are you going to introduce me to your friend?" She turned her perceptive gaze upon Mr. Bolton. "Oh wait, I know you. We were introduced at the Belvins' last month."

Mr. Bolton bowed. "A pleasure to see you again, Miss Turner."

"Wait. Don't tell me your name. I'll remember in a

moment." Dinah tapped her chin, considering. "Ah. You are Aaron Bolton, the Marquess of Ravenshire."

Ellen whipped her gaze to Mr. Bolton, er, Lord Ravenshire. She'd spent the past hour with this man, blubbering about her mother's wishes for her to marry a titled gentleman. What had she said? What had she done? What this... marquess... must *think* of her.

Her throat squeezed tight with mortification, and her cheeks were surely flaming.

But Dinah's gaze was once again upon her, and Ellen focused on her cousin, too mortified to see what was behind Lord Ravenshire's green eyes now. *Laughing, that's what.* "You haven't filled your dance card yet? How is that possible?"

"I have no idea."

"Perhaps Lord Ravenshire would do you the honor."

Ellen wanted to kick her cousin, hard, but that wouldn't be ladylike. So she kept her feet rooted in place.

Dinah was now giving Lord Ravenshire the stare-down. No one could resist Dinah Turner's stare.

"This isn't fair," Ellen hissed.

Dinah winked.

What was she up to? That was what Ellen wanted to know.

"Well, Lord Ravenshire, we are at a ball, are we not? And you've been conversing with the lovely Miss Ellen Young, have you not? What is stopping you from asking her to dance?"

To his credit, Lord Ravenshire looked truly confused—and so he should be. But right now, he needed to be Ellen's ally, not Dinah's.

"I was considering it, but..." he began.

Ellen held her breath.

Dinah tilted her head and offered her most winning smile. Poor man.

"We were so engaged in our conversation that we completely lost track of the dance sets." His gaze flickered to Ellen, then to Dinah, and beyond. "Oh, it looks like the supper dance has already started, and I must get my mother home. She has a delicate constitution and cannot eat the rich foods our hostess is known for serving."

"I am sorry to hear about your mother," Dinah said. "Is there no one else who can accompany her? I am sure Miss Young would love for you to stay and—"

This time, Ellen did kick her cousin.

Dinah yelped, but then she was laughing.

Lord Ravenshire's brow tugged together, not understanding what was so amusing. Ellen wasn't about to explain it to him. She merely grasped his hand and squeezed. The move was bold, but she needed him to feel the impact of her gratitude. "Thank you, Lord Ravenshire. Have a good evening and give my best to your mother."

She released his hand then and turned away from the stunned marquess and the almost-recovered Dinah.

Ellen made her way through the crush, keeping to the edges and away from those she recognized.

She headed straight out of the ballroom, making no detours, and continued to the grand front entrance of the London mansion. There, she told the butler that she would wait on the settee in the front drawing room until her cousin was finished for the evening. Could he please notify her when Miss Dinah Turner appeared?

The butler agreed and let her into the drawing room.

The dim coolness was a welcome relief to Ellen's burning cheeks.

She needed time to think. To remember all that she'd said to the marquess. Thankfully, she'd won the wager tonight despite Dinah attempting to thwart it all, and returning to her cottage with the rose cuttings couldn't happen soon enough.

Six

AARON WAS STILL PUZZLING out what had happened the night before at the ball as he prepared to leave the house the following morning. On the carriage ride home, his mother had pressed him for details about the women he'd danced with. Frankly, he'd forgotten all about the other wallflowers during his conversation with Miss Young. He gave his mother a few basics and assured her he'd be making at least one morning call.

He hoped that Miss Young would receive him.

What was going on between her and the cousin? Aaron guessed it was something to do with the wager, and something to do with Miss Young being a wallflower for the evening. Because her confession about being a diamond of the first water, and her mother's insistence that she not let her beauty go to waste, told him that she was not typically a wallflower.

How intriguing.

Not intriguing enough to deter him from his plans of returning to his estate, of course. Right after he visited and secured an excursion to Hyde Park with Miss Young, he would begin preparing for the journey.

"Thank you, Jones," he told his valet. Aaron was more trussed up than usual, and he was certain it would meet with Mother's approval. No hand-me-down jacket today.

He hadn't heard Mother stir yet, and that was a good thing. Let her rest save him from another round of questioning.

It was perhaps too early for a house call to any young woman who'd attended the ball last night, but Aaron was planning on walking anyway. He'd make a stop at the hothouse first and procure some flowers.

Chuckling to himself, he hardly recognized his thought process right now. He told himself that he was just intrigued by the wager Miss Young had made, and visiting her was a way to find out more. Besides, if he could convince her to take a ride in Hyde Park, that would be an added bonus. It wouldn't be anything filled with romantic promises. Miss Young had already made it quite clear that although her mother wanted her to marry a titled gentleman, Miss Young herself wanted the simple country life.

And if anyone knew that being a titled gentleman was far from simple, it was Aaron.

Still, he found himself whistling as he strode along the sidewalk. The day was early enough that there weren't many carriages out and about. This only made his stroll more leisurely and enjoyable. Less people to greet or tip a hat to. When he arrived at the hothouse, he took his time in selecting flowers.

He moved among the jars filled with cut flowers, then browsed the potted plants. What type of flowers did an intriguing young woman such as Miss Young favor? Lilacs? Daisies? Lilies? Roses?

He bent to smell a few collections, then finally settled on white lilies intermixed with violet lilacs. Once the shopkeeper had wrapped them up and tied the bundle with a green ribbon, Aaron was on his way again.

This time, more carriages were about. His errand would

be quite clear now as he strode along the street, a bouquet in hand. When he turned into the residential section, his heart skipped a beat. Not many more townhouses now, and he'd be in front of Miss Young's residence. Was it still too early to pay a call?

"Good morning, Lord Ravenshire," a woman said. She was dressed as if she were about to appear before Queen Charlotte. In one hand, she held the leash of a tiny dog, in the other, a cane. A few feet behind her walked her lady's maid.

The woman was looking at him as if she knew him. She certainly knew *his* name. But the soft wrinkles and sharp blue eyes brought no memory or recollection.

"Good morning, ma'am," he said with a short bow. "Lovely weather."

"Quite." Instead of moving on, she remained standing before him on the sidewalk. "You don't remember my name, do you? It's Lady Marble."

"Of course." Aaron gave his best smile, although inside, his stomach had flipped upside down. Now he knew exactly who she was. Lady Marble was notorious for her gossip. His mother had told him more than once to steer clear of the matron.

"Give my regards to your mother, young man," she continued. "Now, pray tell, who is the lucky lady this morning? I am sure those aren't for me."

Aaron chuckled, although his neck prickled with annoyance. Why, of all people in London, did he have to run into her on this morning?

"Oh, I shouldn't say," Aaron said. "I don't want to spoil the surprise."

Lady Marble put more weight on her cane and leaned forward. "I won't tell a soul." She waved a hand and her lady's maid took a few steps back.

Aaron didn't trust this woman one whit, and who knew if Miss Young would receive him in the first place. Whatever happened, it wasn't Lady Marble's business.

"Now, there are four young ladies on this street, all unmarried," Lady Marble said. "Mark my words, I'll find out soon enough so telling me in advance will only be beneficial. I'll be sure to put in a good word for you since I know your mother."

"That is very kind of you, Lady Marble, but I'm afraid that I must keep the secret a little longer," Aaron said.

"A secret is no fun unless it's shared—at the utmost discretion, of course." Lady Marble's blue eyes narrowed as her voice lowered. "Now, tell me the young lady's name, and I will offer my opinion and advice, which are both very sound, mind you."

Aaron wanted to begin his day all over. Leave much later than he had. Take a different street. He swallowed down the annoyance and spoke in a perfectly congenial voice. "It's been a pleasure to meet you this fine morning, and I'll be sure to give my mother your regards." He bowed, then stepped past the woman, nearly having to detour into the street.

He felt her astonished stare as he continued past her poor lady's maid. Perhaps he'd go to another street entirely until he was sure the matron was gone, or not peering out of a window somewhere.

"*Well*, I never! I've never met a more rude man in my life. I am quite put out. Come, Miss Darby."

Aaron winced. His ears were burning hot, not to mention his neck. What had he done? Would word get back to his mother? Should he hurry after the matron and apologize profusely?

But his feet continued forward until he reached a hedgerow. He slipped around it and stood under a tree heavy with leaves. Through the leaves, he looked in Lady Marble's direction. She was walking, yet moving slowly. At this rate, she'd take an hour to get to the end of the street—or wherever she was going.

Aaron sighed and leaned against the tree trunk. He needed to stay hidden for a while longer. Miss Young's townhouse was the very next one, and all it would take would be for Lady Marble to glance back at the right moment, er, *wrong* moment.

"If I didn't have bad luck, I'd have no luck at all," he murmured.

Someone laughed. It was cut off in a half-second, but the sound was unmistakable. With his heart pounding now for a different reason, Aaron straightened from the tree and slowly turned. Beyond the tree was an iron fence, and beyond that was a side garden that must belong to the adjoining townhouse.

Was there a child out playing in the garden? Or was it a gardener within hearing distance?

The laugh had been a woman's, though.

He scanned the meandering path, the orderly flower beds, the rose bushes beyond, but he didn't see or hear a soul.

"Hello?" he said in a quiet voice, not wanting to bring attention to himself if there was no need to.

No one answered; no one spoke or even laughed.

Despite the shade of the tree and the coolness of the morning, Aaron lifted his hat and wiped at his brow. He might have gotten all trussed up for nothing because with each passing moment, he was doubting his errand. Perhaps he should abandon his errand completely. If he never delivered the flowers, then Lady Marble wouldn't have her gossip substantiated.

Just as he turned to face the street again, a small yelp sounded behind him.

He whirled.

There. He saw a color that didn't belong in the garden, unless tree trunks were now white. "Hello there. I hope I didn't disturb you. Sorry for any intrusion. I have paused for a bit of shade."

"You didn't intrude," someone said, decidedly a woman's voice.

And then she appeared. As if materializing out of thin air. She was wearing a white dress covered in a long apron. Over one arm, she carried a basket of flowers, and her straw hat was tied under her chin with a blue ribbon, which matched her . . .

Aaron stared. "M-Miss Young?"

Her perfectly rosy lips lifted into a smile, and the way her lake-blue eyes danced with amusement made him quite weak in the knees. With his free hand, he wrapped his fingers around the iron bar of the fence and stepped closer so that he was in the sunshine.

Her brows shot up. "Lord Ravenshire?" Then her brows fell, and she took a step back. "I didn't mean to interrupt, sir. Excuse me." She executed a half-curtsey, then turned to leave.

"Wait!" Aaron called. He took a breath. "Wait," he said in a softer tone. "You didn't interrupt anything; in fact, I've come to pay you a visit."

Slowly, Miss Young turned around. The color of her cheeks practically matched her rosy lips. "You have?"

"Yes." He held up the bouquet of flowers as proof. "And to bring you these, although I didn't know which type you like."

Miss Young's gaze fell to the bouquet, and several expressions flitted across her face at once, as if she were indecisive about something. When she lifted her gaze, she looked directly at him. "You did not tell me you were titled, Lord Ravenshire. We spoke at length last night, and you let me chatter on about my dislike for titled gentry. When you, in fact, have a title. What you must think of me, I do not know. But please accept my apology, sir."

"No apology needed," Aaron said. "I found our conversation refreshing, honest, and vastly revealing. I didn't mean to mislead you, and I apologize for that. But the more you spoke, the more I wanted to hear. Which is why I'm here this morning."

"To hear more?" Her expression was doubtful.

"To hear about the wager, which I think you won last night. Am I right?"

Her smile bloomed.

Aaron tightened his grip on the fence.

"You are right, Lord Ravenshire," Miss Young said in a light tone. "I *did* win the wager. But never mind that. Am I to be the young woman you will tell your mother you checked off on your list? Is a ride through Hyde Park next?"

She'd remembered. Of course she had.

"Would that be such a terrible thing?"

Seven

ELLEN WAS ABSOLUTELY BREATHLESS. She had to get her heart rate under control too. She told herself it was because she'd been caught unawares. First, that set-down from Mr. Bolton, er, Lord Ravenshire to Lady Marble had been entertaining. Then his grumbled words as he passed close to where Ellen had been cutting dead leaves from her flower garden had made her laugh aloud.

Which Lord Ravenshire had heard.

And now he was standing on the other side of the fence, flowers in one gloved hand, and a charming smile that lit up those green eyes of his.

Why was he *here* of all places? He was a marquess. He was handsome. He was well-spoken and didn't seem to have any annoying habits that she could discern. Surely, any of the wallflowers he'd danced with the night before would have nearly fainted if he'd graced their doorsteps.

She found that Lord Ravenshire was studying her as closely as she was studying him. Thankfully, her straw hat would conceal the majority of her blushing.

And forget about the wallflowers. With his titled status, surely he could have his pick of many other women.

"Why?" she said at last.

"Why?" he echoed, a faint line appearing between his brows.

"Why *me*? You could have picked any of those wallflowers last night to visit. They'd be eternally grateful to you and would go to sleep in a swoon for the next month."

His half smile broadened. "Only a month? That doesn't seem long."

Ellen shrugged, suddenly wishing she was wearing one of her newer, more fashionable dresses. "A heart is a finicky thing. A month seems quite enough time to swoon over one man because it will soon be distracted by another."

He leaned closer to the fence, and she wondered if he still smelled of sunshine. "What if I don't want to court a swoony female?"

"If that's the case, then why not one of the young ladies of the *ton*, for your status surely would be to your advantage. Less swooning too, I'm sure, since they've been bred to be marchionesses or duchesses."

He chuckled. "What if I simply want to fulfill an agreement with my mother and not have all the expectations following?"

"Ah, I understand." Ellen breathed out. "If you'd chosen one of the ladies of the *ton,* you couldn't ditch her after a single call and ride in Hyde Park." She held up a finger.

He was nodding, his eyes dancing. "You are an intelligent and insightful woman, Miss Young."

"So, you are *here*," she concluded, "because . . . ?" She paused, waiting for him to complete her sentence.

"Because you have no designs upon, or intentions toward, a man who is titled." His eyes held hers, almost challenging her previous statements.

She kept her chin lifted, her gaze direct. "That is correct, Lord Ravenshire. I confessed quite a deal to you last evening, so you know where my heart lies—in the country, with my gardening. Simple is all I desire. But . . . if I am to help you out in this, what will I get out of it, pray tell?"

Lord Ravenshire sputtered a laugh. But when she didn't even crack a smile, he sobered. "Yes, well. Excellent question." He looked down at his bouquet for a moment, then lifted his gaze. "I suppose it will take more than flowers?"

She raised her basket full of cut flowers. "I've flowers aplenty, sir."

His eyes widened. "Of course you have." He tilted his head, his green eyes assessing her. "Delicious ice delivered to your doorstep for a week? Or boxes of candy? Do you have a sweet tooth, Miss Young? Or perhaps you prefer jewelry. Do you like pearls, diamonds? How about rubies?"

Ellen burst out laughing. "Stop, oh stop! I could not accept gifts of jewelry—what would my mother think? And ice would surely melt before it could be delivered. And yes, I do have a sweet tooth, but I have a much better idea."

"Then I'm all ears, Miss Young."

"It might be a bit inconvenient, though."

"Will it delay my departure?"

"Oh, no, nothing like that."

"Then I agree," he said. "Just tell me what I must do."

Ellen drew in a slow breath. "Pretend you are courting me, until the end of the Season. You don't even have to be in London. You can send me long letters of devotion, and I'll moon over them so much that I won't have the desire to attend any social function where you are not present."

Lord Ravenshire didn't say anything for so long, Ellen began to sweat beneath her bodice. "Or . . . perhaps the sweets will suffice. My cousin Dinah can help me enjoy them."

"No," he said suddenly. "I mean, I think your idea is quite brilliant. It will keep my mother's comments about my absence silent for the rest of the Season, and that will be quite heavenly. Are you sure I won't have to return and perform some sort of obligation?"

Ellen's smile was one of relief. "I am sure. It's not like we'd be engaged or anything so serious, just . . . courting. From afar." Her mind turned with more ideas now. "Perhaps in a few weeks, you can send a letter telling me that you won't be returning at all for the rest of the Season, and I can be so devastated that my mother will let me return to our cottage early."

"Ah, so really, this is a master plan to get us both to our country homes."

"Exactly."

Lord Ravenshire extended his hand through the fence. Ellen stepped forward and clasped his hand. They shook slowly, and she completely ignored how perfectly her hand fit in his larger one. Even with his glove, and her bare hand, the warmth and sturdiness of his grip was a tad thrilling.

When he dropped her hand and stepped back, he said, "Now, might I call upon you properly? In your drawing room? These flowers will wilt before too long." He winked.

"Of course, sir," she said, discounting the fact that his wink had shot warmth straight through her chest. He'd come here as a plan to fulfill an agreement for his mother, and he'd be leaving as part of a ruse in courting her.

"Give me a moment." Ellen took another step away from him. "Just don't let Lady Marble see you."

Lord Ravenshire whipped his head around so fast to look toward the street that Ellen laughed.

"I'm sorry, she is quite frightful, isn't she?"

He exhaled. "Quite."

"Your set-down of her will be one of my favorite memories of London."

He groaned. "Don't remind me. I'm sure my mother will hear about it."

"Well, we're about to appease both of our mothers, at least temporarily." She turned toward the garden path. "See you in a moment."

She didn't wait to watch him leave his spot on the other side of the fence. She'd have to clean up before greeting him. Even though he'd seen her in the gardening apron and her straw hat covering her undone hair, she couldn't greet him in a formal drawing room like she'd just stepped out of a garden. Oh, and her shoes. They were her designated garden shoes, and she'd need to change into stockings and slippers.

It was a full twenty minutes after Jenny had informed Ellen about her gentleman caller that she walked into the drawing room. And stopped cold.

All the women in the household were crowded into the drawing room. Mother sat next to Dinah on the settee. Aunt Margaret sat on the wingback by the fireplace. And Lord Ravenshire? He was perched on the edge of the chair across from the settee.

Everyone looked at her, and all three women smiled.

Lord Ravenshire stood and bowed.

Seeing a marquess in the townhome drawing room suddenly made the room feel small and shabby.

"Good morning, Miss Young," he said in a smooth voice, free from the teasing earlier, although humor lit his eyes. "I hope I am not intruding on your morning by paying you a call and delivering what I hope will be flowers enjoyed by all."

Ellen held back a smirk and tried to keep her composure perfectly serious.

"Good morning, Lord Ravenshire," she said. "What a surprise and honor, I assure you. The flowers are lovely." She stepped forward, willing her fingers not to tremble as she took the bouquet from his hands.

"Jenny will fetch a vase and water for those," Aunt Margaret said in her creaky voice. She was only a few years older than Mother, but Aunt's voice had faded over the years.

"Of course," Ellen murmured.

As if summoned by suggestion alone, Jenny entered, curtseyed to their guest, then took the bouquet.

Ellen made the mistake of glancing at Dinah. Her cousin's mouth was set in a firm line—not with disapproval, but with an attempt to keep her features schooled. Could she already be suspicious? How? Or was she just triumphant in thinking that Ellen truly had the attention of a marquess?

Dinah would prove to be the greatest challenge in keeping such a secret. She was not a woman to miss anything.

"I hope my visit isn't too early," the marquess continued in an easy tone. "I found myself quite eager this morning to pay you a visit and hoped I might arrive before any other . . . gentlemen callers."

Ellen gave him a pretty smile. "It is not too early. No matter the lateness of the hour the night before, I cannot sleep much past the sun's rising."

"In that, then, we are similar, Miss Young."

Oh, how he could charm. Oh, how all the women in the room were practically swooning at his feet. Well, except for Dinah. She was trying so very hard not to smirk.

Ellen moved to the only free chair in the room, which was a handful of feet from Lord Ravenshire. He did smell of fresh air and sunshine.

She tried not to remember, tried not to breathe in his scent, or think of all that she'd confessed to him the night before when she thought he was simply a mister.

"Tell us of your family," Mother said immediately.

Ellen hid a wince. She knew that his father and brothers had died. Was this a painful question for him?

"Of course," the marquess said, as if he was used to this sort of question, and perhaps he was. "My mother, Lady Ravenshire, is here in London with me. Alas, I have no sisters, and my two older brothers have passed away. Which left the title of marquess to me, to which I have been trying to do justice over the past several years."

All of Ellen's relations in the room made the appropriate condolences when he mentioned his brothers.

His gaze landed on Ellen, his smile soft, and oh, so very convincing, when he said, "I am not getting any younger, as my mother reminds me often, and I've joined in the Season in the hopes of finding a wife."

No one spoke for a moment, and they probably weren't breathing, either. Ellen herself was only breathing because she knew his words were likely rehearsed between his short walk from the garden fence to the drawing room.

"It was so very nice to make your acquaintance last night," Ellen said, because apparently all the other women were still speechless.

"And yours as well," Lord Ravenshire said, his gaze still upon her, full of meaning.

How did he do this? Draw her in with his gaze, make her nearly convinced that meeting her *was* the highlight of his year?

"If it's not too presumptuous, Miss Young, and the fine weather holds out, might I invite you to ride with me tomorrow through Hyde Park?"

His invitation was sincere, at least from the outside. He was probably thinking of those merino sheep on his vast estate. Despite that, Ellen gave her most brilliant smile. "I would love to, Lord Ravenshire."

Eight

THE NEXT MORNING WAS indeed fair with not a cloud to be seen in the sea blue sky. What a fine day for a ride through Hyde Park, and Aaron had awakened before dawn with a smile on his face. Tomorrow, he'd make the journey back to Ravenshire. Peace and quiet called to him, and he was looking forward to checking on the merino sheep and making sure they were thriving. It would be a triumph to write to the Prince Regent about the success of the species.

Perhaps part of his chipper mood was due to the fact that he'd be escorting the lively and amusing Miss Young on a drive through Hyde Park. It was fortunate, really, that they could strike up such an agreement that was beneficial for both parties.

He couldn't think of any other woman who might enter into this sort of agreement. Perhaps one day, Miss Young might find a wholesome country squire to marry, and Aaron would . . . well, he'd probably be back next Season, starting all over. His mother would be disappointed, but that was a future worry.

It was no surprise that Mother appeared in the foyer as he was preparing to walk out the door.

"You must take flowers, dear," she said, reaching up to adjust his cravat that was already perfectly tied. "Get the freshest selection they have so that it will last a good number of days. Are you sure you should leave for Ravenshire tomorrow? You don't want to dash Miss Young's hopes."

"Miss Young already knows my plans and is amenable."

Mother touched her hairdo that was already perfectly coifed. "Is she? And you've told her about the merino sheep?"

"Briefly," he said. "She prefers the country herself and does not fault me for attending to my obligations."

His words might have stung his mother's sensibilities a little, but Aaron wasn't going to change his course now. He and his mother had made an agreement, and he was holding up his end of it.

Mother still looked doubtful, but she nodded. "Enjoy yourself and be sure to pay her kind compliments. A woman likes to know she's appreciated."

A double meaning, to be sure. Aaron bent and kissed his mother's cheek. "I will, and thank you, Mother, for your patience and wisdom."

Her cheeks pinked. "Oh, you. Now off you go. All the fresh flowers will be bought out if you delay any longer. I expect a full report when you return."

"I will plan on delivering it to you then."

His mother sighed, but she waved him off with a smile as he climbed into the driver's seat of the open phaeton. Once he reached the hothouse, he found his mother had been right. The freshest flowers were well-picked over, and Aaron ended up with a selection that was quite eclectic. Well, it couldn't be helped.

Once he reached the street that Miss Young lived on, heat climbed up his neck as he searched out Lady Marble. Aaron had brought up the encounter to his mother so that she would be forewarned, though he'd softened what had truly happened in the interaction.

As he drew his pair of horses to a stop in front of Miss Young's, a woman stepped onto the sidewalk ahead of him. The leash extending from her hand to a small dog told him that this was indeed Lady Marble.

Of all the moments and all the chances.

He swung down from the phaeton and was fully prepared to deliver a cordial greeting when Lady Marble locked gazes with him, pivoted on her heeled shoes, and walked the other way. Her lady's maid quickly turned direction too and headed after her.

So, that was his answer.

He wasn't sure if he should be relieved or worried. At least he'd be leaving town, but he was clearly paying a call to Miss Young, and what if the gossip became detrimental to her?

Aaron exhaled. He'd have to give the full story to Miss Young, for better or worse. He hoped she wouldn't think less of him, because he'd hate for that to happen. Even if they were only pretending to be courting, he still valued her good opinion.

After rapping on the front door, the butler let him inside.

Miss Young stood in the foyer, tying the ribbons of her bonnet.

Aaron was struck again by her large blue eyes, the soft pink of her lips, and the lift of her smile when she saw him. He told himself that his pulse was jumping because of his near run-in with Lady Marble, not because Miss Young was likely the most beautiful woman he'd ever been acquainted with.

Surely, she was inundated with attention from other gentlemen, and now that he thought of it, he was surprised that she had this afternoon free.

"You're late," she said.

Aaron's eyes widened, and he glanced toward the door. The sun was in the right position. "Did I not say 3:00?"

"You did. And it's 3:30."

"Ah, I apologize," Aaron said. He'd never been late a day in his life. Had he really dallied so long over the flowers in the hothouse? "I hope you will forgive me."

Miss Young reached for the bouquet he proffered, pulled the flowers close, and inhaled. When she lifted her gaze, he saw amusement in those blue eyes of hers. "I forgive you, sir. But only because I came down the stairs a handful of moments ago."

"Ah. So if I'd been here on time, I would have been kept waiting."

One edge of her mouth lifted. "Precisely."

She set the flowers on the hall table. "Donald, can you let Jenny know about the flowers?"

"Of course, Miss Young."

Aaron extended his arm. "Shall we?"

She turned to him, as pretty as a painting. "We shall."

As her hand rested on the crook of his arm, he felt a surge of... something. Satisfaction? Pleasure? Happiness?

He led her outside and handed her into the phaeton. Her scent seemed to linger around him, sweet and floral. He swallowed back a compliment that he didn't want her to read into, then he glanced down the street. Lady Marble, or her dog, were nowhere in sight. When he settled next to Miss Young, he said, "I must confess something to you that might change your mind about riding with me through Hyde Park today."

"Now you tell me, after I'm all settled?"

He glanced down at her to find her blue eyes on him, dancing with interest. "You do not seem worried."

"Should I be?"

"Lady Marble turned away from me the moment I arrived at your doorstep," he said in a lowered tone, in case the woman had superstrength hearing. "Our happenstance conversation yesterday did not go very well."

"I know," Miss Young said. "I heard every word, and I must say, Lord Ravenshire, you did put her in her place. I could barely hold back my laughter. Be warned that she'll find her information one way or another."

Aaron took up the reins. "But it was all for naught, because today it is clear who I am visiting."

"True." Miss Young's gaze was still clear and open.

"You do not have a problem with the woman speaking ill of me, which might extend to you if we are to ride in Hyde Park?"

Miss Young patted his arm. "An old lady's gossip is no match against a marquess, and as for me, I care not what she says or thinks. The sooner I can attend to my gardens, the better."

Aaron's pulse was leaping again. Was he just relieved, or did it have something to do with how Miss Young's hand still rested on his arm?

"Well, then. We are off." He flicked the reins, and the horses moved forward.

Hyde Park was teeming with couples who had the same idea. Aaron kept the horses at a leisurely pace so that they could greet others when necessary, but he didn't slow down to further any conversations. He was here with Miss Young, and he wanted to speak with her, not everyone else in London.

"Tell me about your family," he said, when there was a break in the greetings. "I've met some of them, of course, but what about the others?"

"I have no siblings," Miss Young said. "No brother to inherit my father's property after he died, but fortunately we were left a cozy cottage."

Aaron looked over at her profile. He couldn't tell by the

tone of her voice if she'd been upset at this change in circumstances.

She peeked at him, likely feeling his gaze upon her. "Oh, my father was the second son of a baron, so it wasn't like we lived on a grand estate or anything." She shrugged. "The cottage is a perfect size for two women who don't expect anything fancy."

"And one of whom likes to grow flowers?"

"Precisely."

He chuckled. "Are you ever going to tell me about your wager?"

She tilted her head, blue eyes sparkling, reminding him of a summer's day at a pond. "I suppose I can, since you helped me win it. Thank you, by the way, for not asking me to dance."

Now he was even more intrigued.

"My cousin Dinah thought that I couldn't be a wallflower for one evening," Miss Young said. "She said that my dance card would fill at least halfway, even if I made myself uninteresting and unattractive."

Aaron's brows lifted at this. "You are far from either."

She cut him a quick, surprised glance, then continued. "I was determined to stay out of the way from all potential dancing partners. But one of them found me, and that's when I danced the first time. When you arrived, I was quite desperate to stay below the threshold."

"Hello there!" a young man called out. "Miss Young, how nice to see you."

Miss Young smiled prettily at the man, and Aaron felt a twinge of something—annoyance? Envy?

"You look well, Lord Jarvis," Miss Young said.

After formal introductions were made, the conversation was short, but much too long at the same time. When they were finally on their way again, Aaron asked, "Another suitor?"

"Heavens, no," she said. "Lord Jarvis is much too short. Did you see that his legs barely touched the floor of his phaeton?"

Aaron laughed. "Ah, I didn't notice." He straightened. He definitely towered over Miss Young. "You haven't finished telling me of your wager."

He felt her smile before he saw it.

"It's rather silly, I assure you," she said. "You seem to have built up quite a bit of suspense in your mind."

"Then you'd better tell me before the suspense is taken too far."

She gave a soft laugh. "If my dance card stayed under half full, then Dinah would give me rose cuttings from my aunt's garden to take back to the cottage. If my dance card was filled more than half, then Dinah would be relieved of chaperone duties, and they'd fall to either my mother—who is a fuss pot—or Lady Marble, and I don't need to explain her to you."

Aaron slowed the horses down, and they came to a stop in a shady spot beneath a tree. "Wait a moment. Rose cuttings? What in the world are those?" He decided that he'd never seen Miss Young more beautiful than she looked now with her flushed cheeks and twinkling eyes.

"It means that if I transport the lower part of the rose plant carefully enough to our cottage, I can grow the same type of roses," she said. "These particular species are absolutely beautiful."

You are absolutely beautiful, Aaron wanted to echo, but he stopped himself before the words slipped out. He didn't want to change anything about her easygoing manner with him. He was soaking up every smile and word she spoke. And the longer they spent in Hyde Park, the more memories he'd have of Miss Young.

Nine

"He must be quite serious about you," Aunt Margaret said as Ellen sat with the women of the household in the drawing room on a quiet evening.

Lord Ravenshire had been absent from London for two weeks now. Well, fifteen days, actually. Ellen wasn't meaning to count, but she'd counted anyway. And true to his word, he'd been writing letters to her. The first ones had made her laugh because they were full of flowery language of devotion. No suitor, no matter how in love, would have ever said such things to her or any woman.

"His letters are very sweet," Ellen admitted. She'd read a few parts aloud, trying not to laugh as she did so. Her mother and Aunt Margaret had stopped their stitching to listen closely.

Cousin Dinah had only smiled and resumed reading her thick book that discussed weather patterns across the ocean.

But this last letter, the one currently in her hands, held a more serious tone. Yes, it had started out with the usual dramatic sentences of Lord Ravenshire claiming he missed her as the earth misses the sun on cloudy days. But then, he'd said something curious.

I had hoped to write a favorable report on the merino sheep under my care, but their coats are dull and becoming coarser by the week. We are in the midst of the warmest part of the season, and they should be thriving. I suspect they are adjusting to the cooler climate, compared to their homeland.

His tone was positive for the most part, but Ellen sensed the worry behind his words. That afternoon they'd spent in Hyde Park, he'd confessed to her that raising merino sheep on his estate was a pet project of the Prince Regent's.

Ellen had been surprised that Lord Ravenshire had such an established relationship with the Prince Regent, but then again he *was* peerage. So she shouldn't have been surprised at all. If she'd had a man writing to her a few weeks ago, talking about his connection to royalty, she might have been quite put off. But this was Lord Ravenshire. She knew he wasn't a braggart and he was truly concerned about those sheep.

The thought made her even more impressed with him.

"Oh, pray tell, what does the letter say?" Mother asked in a tone teetering on the edge of sharpness. Pride was also in her voice because she was pleased that her one and only daughter had caught the eye of a marquess.

If only Mother knew the truth . . .

"He writes of how much he misses me, and he's included a few matters of his estate." For some reason, she didn't want to share the entirety of Lord Ravenshire's letters. No matter how farcical they were, they were still written by him to *her.*

"And he still does not say when he will return to London?" Aunt Margaret asked. "Does he not know that we have only a few weeks of the Season left? It would be so nice for him to declare himself, and then the both of you could attend events together, on his arm."

"Mother," Dinah said, finally joining in the conversation. "Ellen's been on *one* outing with the man, then he hightailed it back to his country estate. Just because he writes letters that are charming enough to make any woman swoon doesn't mean you or I have a say in his schedule!"

The room fell completely silent, only broken by the ticking clock, then followed by the sniffle of Aunt Margaret.

"Oh, for heaven's sake," Dinah said. "I apologize, Mother, but I am tired of these simpering letters. They are words, all words, and no actions."

"What are you suggesting, Dinah Claudia Turner? Surely you aren't implying that Lord Ravenshire is stringing along our Ellen?"

Dinah folded her arms and narrowed her eyes. "I haven't said any such thing, but something is not right here. Every bachelor of the *ton* is in London for the Season, except apparently Ellen's marquess. Does he not have a capable estate manager or man of business to handle his affairs back home? He came on very strong and suddenly to Ellen, and now she refuses to attend any other ball or function because she can't 'bear to face them without Lord Ravenshire' in attendance."

Ellen stared. Dinah's face was as red as a Christmas ribbon, but her gaze had hardened.

"You are simply envious, Dinah," Aunt Margaret said in a wavering tone. "You're a spinster and seeing your younger cousin being courted is bringing up—"

"I am not envious," Dinah shot out, her furrowed brow quite fearsome. "Who's to say this man doesn't have a mistress in the country? Why else would he delay when he is supposedly enraptured with our dearest Ellen?"

Aunt Margaret gasped.

Ellen decided she'd had enough of this argument over a man none of her relatives truly knew. "It's his sheep."

Dinah snapped her head to look at Ellen. "His what?"

"He's . . ." Ellen cleared her throat. "He's raising a special breed of sheep called merino sheep, and they take extra care and expertise. He's gone back to his estate to ensure that all is well."

Dinah's frown softened, and she laughed. "His *sheep*,

Ellen? Is that what he told you?" She shook her head, then let her chin fall. "You are more naïve than I thought."

Ellen's face burned, and the heat spread to her chest, filling it with indignation. Perhaps Dinah was envious, or why else would she speak so cruelly? Besides, what *if* sheep had only been an excuse? It didn't matter, because there was no true courting between her and Lord Ravenshire anyway. She wasn't going to let Dinah's sharp words get to her, though. And she wasn't going to disclose that this was a project commissioned by the Prince Regent.

Even if doubt did niggle in the back of her mind, she wasn't going to think ill of Lord Ravenshire. They were helping each other out, that was all, and that was all that it would ever be.

Ellen's emotions were like a tidal wave moving through her body, though, and she needed to be alone. She rose, clutching the letter to her breast. "Good evening, I think I will retire early."

"Ellen, I apologize for my bluntness," Dinah said, "but we cannot be blindsided by such things."

"Dinah." Aunt Margaret's voice was clear. "You have gone too far. Leave your poor cousin alone."

"But Mother, we both know that men can be conniving—"

Her words cut off with the closing of the drawing room door.

Tears burned trails down Ellen's cheeks as she hurried up the stairs to her bedroom. She slipped inside, then shut and locked the door. Without bothering to light any candles, she headed to the tall windows. The night was foggy, which meant tomorrow would bring rain, but the cool panes of glass against her palms and forehead was soothing.

She closed her eyes, pushing out Dinah's words.

Ellen focused on Lord Ravenshire. The real man behind

the flowery and sometimes ridiculous words. She believed him when he told her about his sheep. She did. Yet . . .

"I will write to him," she whispered. "Tell him of Dinah's outburst and see what his response is." She might be talking to herself in a darkened room, but it made her feel more steady, more confident.

A plan of action was surely a thing to hold on to.

Ellen crossed to her writing desk, lit a candle, then dragged out a sheet of paper. In the next several moments, she poured out the events of the evening. She wrote it all humorously, but underneath she was really seeking his response, concluding with:

So, you see, dear admirer, I have kept your commission from the Prince Regent utterly secret. Although it pained me not to defend you properly, I feel that you will forgive me in that small thing. I do ever so hope that the merino sheep will turn a corner and begin to thrive. On that note, I've reached the point where I am nearly mad being inside this townhouse with only a small garden plot to work in. Perhaps in your next letter or two, you can break the news to me that you won't be returning after all. I can fall into a proper melancholy, in which the only cure is to return back home to my beloved cottage.

Yours always,

Miss Ellen Young

She signed it with a flourish. Then, unprecedented, she picked up her bottle of perfume and added a light spritz. The scent of roses filled the small space around her. Would the scent last all the way to Ravenshire? Would he remember her by it?

Her eyes welled with tears again. She hadn't written a love letter, and Lord Ravenshire wasn't a true beau, so why was her heart suddenly aching?

Ten

AARON SIFTED THROUGH THE handful of letters on the silver tray that Leonard had brought into his study. There were some of the usual missives he recognized—one from his solicitor, another from a Navy friend, a third from the Prince Regent. He frowned at the fourth in the pile. Mother had written. Beneath that, the familiar loopy handwriting of Miss Young. He set aside that letter to be read, and savored, for last.

First, though, he rose and crossed to the marble top table that contained a container of port and crystal-cut glasses. He poured a half glass, then settled back in the chair behind his desk. The day had been a long one, and the condition of the merino sheep hadn't improved. Not even when Aaron had ordered his laborers to completely clean out their sheds and replace the damp straw with clean, dry straw.

He'd also sent several letters to the other estates who were housing merino sheep as well to discover the progress and method of care being employed. Their return replies couldn't come fast enough.

If this first run of raising merino sheep was successful, it could be a boon to the British economy. They wouldn't have to import the merino wool from Spain that was so popular, and perhaps as early as this winter, the woolen mills throughout the country would be producing the higher quality wool.

Aaron opened the Prince Regent's missive first. It was signed by him, but written by his private secretary, consisting of an inquiry into the progress of the sheep. Aaron frowned. He'd sent an update the other day. Perhaps the letters had crossed paths *en route*. Regardless, Aaron would write a second letter in case the first had gone missing.

Next, he opened his mother's letter after taking a healthy swallow of port. His eyes nearly bugged out when he read the lines after her opening salutation and general well-wishes.

I've twisted my ankle. Nothing serious, but it will greatly hamper my activity for the remainder of the Season. So I've decided to return to the estate. Perhaps we can put together a house party? We'd invite eligible young ladies, of course, but you'd also have the company of young men who could form hunting and gaming parties. It will be such fun, and just think, your sheep will be well on their way to producing the finest of wool, and everyone will be so impressed.

Aaron didn't even read the final lines, but set the letter aside, and closed his eyes.

Mother's twisted ankle wasn't serious, thank goodness, but the solace at the estate had been truly a balm these past two weeks. Despite the worry over the sheep and the frequent dwelling of thoughts upon Miss Young—which he refused to analyze—he was his own man. He rose early, breakfasted alone, collected his thoughts, made lists, followed through until the day was over, then with satisfaction, drank a glass of port before retiring for the night. Very little social interaction, unless one counted his men of work, or the housekeeper who was the quiet type anyway.

Yes, he'd enjoyed these past two weeks immensely.

And now it would be all coming to a rather abrupt end.

His gaze slid sideways to the last paragraph of his mother's letter: *Next Tuesday, I shall arrive.*

Gads. He had three days.

He read the letter from his Navy friend, who had also retired. Aaron smiled at some of the memories his friend brought up. He missed the days at sea, but he was also enjoying the challenges at home. More and more. The last letter was the one from Ellen, and he cracked the seal. A faint floral scent tickled his senses, and he brought the page to his nose. She'd spritzed her perfume on it. He was smiling before he even started reading her words.

Dear Lord Ravenshire,

I hope this letter finds you well. I've greatly enjoyed your replies, and I hope that everything is going well at your estate. I wish I had enough knowledge about merino sheep, or any sheep for that matter, to offer a solution to your concerns. Perhaps by the time you receive this, you'll have discovered something already, and the news will only be good.

His concerns were still there, but it was nice to have someone sympathizing with him. He continued to read, a smile playing upon his lips, when he read about Miss Dinah Turner's speculations about him. Miss Young's words might be lighthearted, but Aaron didn't care for Miss Turner's near accusations.

She thought he had a mistress tucked away at Ravenshire and was playing Miss Young for a fool?

Even if they didn't have this agreement between them, he was no womanizer. Besides, it was laughable to think he'd be able to keep a mistress hidden from his very astute and over-nosey mother. Did Miss Turner have no idea who his mother was?

Instead of smiling through the rest of the letter from Miss Young, Aaron was frowning. Could her relations truly think so ill of him? Did other members of the *ton*? What about Lady Marble? Had she set tongues wagging?

Aaron downed the last swallow of port, then stood and paced to the windows overlooking the rear gardens. The amber sky was fading to violet, the sun now below the western horizon. He would write back to Miss Young immediately and post first thing in the morning. But would a letter refuting Miss Turner's claims be enough?

Aaron exhaled. Perhaps he needed to show up in person at their townhouse. Take Miss Young on an outing. Escort her to evening events. Keep her on his arm to prove to her family and the Lady Marbles of the city that he was true to . . . Aaron shook his head. He'd be straying too far from their plan. He'd be making too big of a statement by doing so, and if an engagement didn't quickly follow, then Miss Young ran the risk of being looked down upon as a flirt. Or something worse.

Besides, Mother would be arriving in three days, and he really couldn't leave his sheep. If the switching of hay didn't work, he'd need to come up with something else, and he hadn't heard back yet from the other sheep owners. Perhaps they'd have advice that needed to be immediately implemented.

Aaron's shoulders sagged. No. He couldn't leave. Not now.

A letter would have to suffice.

With a heavy sigh, he returned to his desk and wrote a four-page letter to Miss Young, spilling out all the reasons why the claim of her cousin was at severe fault. Then he tore up the pages, crumpled the pieces, and tossed them into the cold hearth.

He began again.

Dear Miss Young,

Thank you for your continued concern about my sheep. I have written to other sheep owners in the same experiment and hope for some answers. In the meantime, my mother is returning home from London and has indicated she'd like to throw a house party at the close of the Season. Even though we have yet to discuss in person, I am sure that my mother's natural persuasiveness will win out over any protest by me. I can't think of anyone I'd rather have in attendance than you— that is if you are available and can abandon your roses for a week or two.

Also, please bring your cousin, Miss Turner. I'd be happy to give her a tour of the estate and prove that there are no locked doors hiding mistresses. I hope that her opinion will be quite changed of me. You are welcome to tell her that our letters were not one of courtship, but simply a way of getting us back to where we will both be the most happy.

Yours always,

Aaron

There. He folded the pages, added his seal, then set it on the far corner of the desk. He'd been perhaps more frank than he'd intended. The four-page discarded letter made him realize he *did* want to see Miss Young again. As a friend, of course. They were comfortable together. No pressure, no expectations, no wedding bells clanging in the distance. Time would come soon enough for him to find a bride, but for now, he only wanted a friend.

Eleven

Dinah leaned forward, peering out the carriage window. "The Ravenshire Estate is impressive, I'll give you that. Many rooms mean many locked doors."

Ellen sighed. She should have never told her cousin that Lord Ravenshire had written about giving them a tour to inspect for mistresses. Dinah had laughed aloud, then declared, "The man has a spine. I am impressed."

As if he *wouldn't* have a spine.

Since the invite had included Dinah, and Lord Ravenshire had given Ellen permission to confide in her cousin, there would be no pretense at the house party. A welcome relief. It was clear that Lady Ravenshire was aiming to bring a bride to his doorstep if he insisted on abandoning the London Season. What a determined woman.

Ellen couldn't help but be a bit impressed.

Regardless, Ellen had confided in Dinah the night before she left London for the cottage. Dinah had found the entire thing vastly amusing, and Ellen was sure her cousin had laughed half of the night.

Dinah had been sworn to secrecy, which she dramatically crossed her heart over. The result of the invitation to the house party was that Ellen's mother was more than happy to let her leave London and abandon the few remaining weeks of the

Season in order to transfer Aunt Margaret's rose cuttings. They were already thriving.

When a formal invitation to the Ravenshire house party had arrived at the cottage, Ellen had tucked it away in her chest of mementos. She didn't want anyone to handle it, bend the edges, or sully it with a speck of dirt. Also tucked in the chest were the letters she'd accumulated from Lord Ravenshire. They still began with flowery language, making Ellen giggle, but now they were filled with real information about the merino sheep, other tasks of the estate, and the flurry of plans for the house party.

In Ellen's last letter before preparing to leave for Ravenshire, she'd asked the marquess to tell her about the gardens.

Now she carried that letter, which was more descriptive than she'd expected, in her reticule. Lord Ravenshire had greatly indulged her, she was sure, because he wrote out details that she was fairly certain he'd never given a second thought to. Such as, *There are purple flowers that have stems as high as my knee, and heads that are as large as my palm. I have no idea what they're called, but the bees are sure in love with them. They're buzzing about all day, it seems, and I'm quite sure the bees are going to drop dead any moment from all their flying.*

Ellen smiled, and Dinah's brows shot up.

"You like the big estate, after all?" Dinah tutted. "You are going to change your mind, I know it. A marquess might be in your future, dear cousin."

Ellen's smile dropped. "I was not smiling at the view or ogling over the size of the estate. I was thinking of something else."

"Mm-hmm."

How was Ellen going to make it through the next two

weeks with Dinah at her side, watching her like a hound dog stalking a fox? She hid a sigh. It was either bring Dinah or Mother. Besides, Ellen wanted Dinah to eat her earlier words. That would be quite satisfying. Not that Ellen would ever judge, or care, that Lord Ravenshire had a mistress, but it was nice that he was an honorable man all the same.

As the carriage slowed while turning into the long drive leading up the estate, Ellen's stomach danced. Maybe Dinah was a tiny bit right. The estate was spectacular, well cared for too. And from what Ellen had seen of the grounds, she'd be spending many happy hours exploring. If only Dinah could be distracted enough by the other house party guests, then Ellen would have plenty of time to see everything. Including those giant purple flowers.

"You're smiling again."

Dinah's observation didn't get under Ellen's skin this time. She only nodded, then reached for the interior handle of the carriage door. Before she could turn it herself, it opened from the outside.

Instead of a footman come to hand her down, it was Lord Ravenshire himself.

Had she truly been inside her own thoughts so much that she hadn't seen him approach the carriage?

"Miss Young," Lord Ravenshire said, his voice low, mellow.

His green eyes were darker than she remembered, and they were crinkled at the corners with his welcoming smile.

Ellen returned the smile as she placed her hand in his. She was wearing gloves, but he was not, and the warm sturdiness of his fingers made her want to keep his hand in hers. If only to steady her knees.

All too quickly, he released her hand, then handed down Dinah.

"I trust your journey was pleasant?" he asked, his gaze moving from Dinah to Ellen.

"Yes, thank you," Ellen said.

"We have no complaints, Lord Ravenshire," Dinah added, "but we'd like to be shown to our rooms and given a chance to refresh ourselves before that tour you promised."

Lord Ravenshire's eyes gleamed. "You remembered."

Dinah's laugh spilled out. "How could I forget?" She lowered her voice, which was really only one notch softer. "When Ellen told me of your agreement to write letters, as if you were courting, so you could get back to your sheep and she could fuss over her roses, I don't think I've ever laughed so hard in my life."

Lord Ravenshire chuckled. "I'm pleased we could be such a high source of amusement for you."

"Except," Dinah continued in her loud whisper, "her mother will be quite let down—she had high hopes for her most beautiful daughter securing a titled man."

"Dinah," Ellen cut in. "Lord Ravenshire doesn't need a review of my mother's obsession."

Dinah waved a hand. "Oh, that's right. You've already told him all about how you refuse to marry a title." She gave a dramatic sigh. "Such a shame, dear. I would have dearly loved to visit you here every Christmas."

"Please ignore everything my cousin says in the next fortnight, Lord Ravenshire."

His smile was broad. "I intend to. Shall we?" He offered his arm to Ellen, then to Dinah. "My mother is inside the drawing room and would love to say hello before you are shown your rooms."

"Lead the way, good sir," Dinah said.

They accompanied Lord Ravenshire into the house. Walking on his arm was only a simple thing, yet Ellen's stomach buzzed about like the garden bees.

And what a house it was. High ceilings, gilt-framed paintings, luxurious rugs and furniture. They continued to the drawing room, where Lady Ravenshire sat on an elegant wingback by a marble fireplace.

Ellen might spend as much time exploring the house as she did the gardens. Even Dinah seemed impressed. For once, she was silent.

"Welcome, welcome." Lady Ravenshire rose from her place, using a cane. A small dog that had been on her lap hopped off and began to bark. "That's enough, Frisky."

The dog quieted down immediately. Impressive.

"Mother, this is Miss Young, and her cousin, Miss Turner."

Lady Ravenshire had the same color of eyes as her son, but her hair was more of a deep red compared to the darker color of her son's. Although the woman's smile was warm and friendly, Ellen couldn't help but think of the woman's losses. Her husband, *and* her two sons. How had she borne it all?

"It's lovely to have you both," Lady Ravenshire said. "I hope you'll be very comfortable here. You are the first to arrive, but everyone should be here in time for the supper hour." Her gaze turned fully on Ellen. "My son has told me a great deal about you, Miss Young, and I understand you are an expert in roses."

Ellen's face heated, but she smiled through it. She didn't dare glance at Lord Ravenshire. "I am an amateur, to be sure, but it is a cherished hobby of mine."

Lady Ravenshire's head tilted. "What are your other interests and accomplishments?"

Well, this was unexpected. "I enjoy playing the piano in the evenings, but mostly I enjoy cultivating flowers."

"She embroiders, paints, reads, and sings as well," Dinah cut in.

Ellen barely refrained from rolling her eyes.

Lady Ravenshire smiled. "How wonderful. An accomplished young lady is always a delight as a guest. Do you enjoy those things as well, Miss Turner?" Her gaze danced with amusement at turning the tables.

Well, Cousin Dinah might have met her match.

Dinah tapped her chin. "I am passable in all those areas, but I much prefer card games and discussing politics."

If Lady Ravenshire was shocked, centuries of genteel breeding in her veins stopped her from showing it. "I am sure there will be plenty of activities to keep the both of you satisfied over the next two weeks."

Ellen had to do something, anything, before Dinah said something more outrageous. "What a sweet dog you have there, Lady Ravenshire. How old is he?"

It worked. Lady Ravenshire tore her gaze from Dinah and looked down at her little dog with an adoring expression. "Two years old now. He's a darling, so very obedient. Do you have a dog, Miss Young?"

"I do, but he's not small, nor sweet. He's a bit of a brute and prefers to be outside most of the time."

"I didn't know you had a dog, Miss Young," Lord Ravenshire said.

She looked at him then. It was interesting, seeing him in this place, this lovely and extravagant home. His mother fit in these surroundings more than he did. This was a good thing to see him here, in his own home, because it only solidified how far off she was from ever being interested in marrying a titled gentleman. Not that she was thinking of him that way, but it was still good to know regardless.

"I do," she murmured.

"What's his name?"

"Brandy."

His brows shot up, and Ellen hurried to clarify. "His fur is a golden brown color, like the color of brandy."

Lord Ravenshire's mouth lifted into a half smile, then he looked over at his mother. "I shall be taking the ladies on a tour about the house and grounds in a half hour. Would you like to accompany us?"

"Oh, you go ahead," his mother said. "I'll slow everyone down."

Ellen dared say she was relieved.

"Ah, here's Sybil," Lady Ravenshire said as a maid with curly, dark hair appeared in the doorway. "She'll show you to your rooms."

"Thank you," Ellen said.

The sound of an arriving carriage came from outside the drawing room windows.

"Someone else is early," Lord Ravenshire said. "If you will excuse me, ladies." He gave a short bow and strode out of the room.

"If I might have a private word with you, Miss Young, before you head up," Lady Ravenshire said.

Ellen paused.

Dinah nodded, her eyes dancing with curiosity, but she left with the maid.

Slowly, Ellen shifted her gaze to Lady Ravenshire. Without Dinah or Lord Ravenshire here, she felt like she was under scrutiny.

"We only have a moment alone," Lady Ravenshire said, "and once everyone arrives, it will be too difficult to speak privately. But I wanted you to know that my son has told me about your exchanged letters, and how it helped you return to your cottage instead of remaining the entirety of the Season."

Ellen nodded dumbly. She knew that Lord Ravenshire hadn't deceived his mother as she had hers, yet it was disconcerting to have it spoken out in the open like this. "I-I didn't want to lead my mother and aunt along, but I couldn't stay in London another week. It was suffocating me."

"I understand, dear," Lady Ravenshire said in a quiet tone. "In that way, you are much like my son. He, too, had his mind elsewhere."

"Yes." Ellen was at a loss for any other words or explanations.

"Now, I want you to hear one thing from me, then I'll be quiet," she continued. "My son also told me about your vow to not marry a titled gentleman."

Ellen blinked. This was quite . . . beyond what she thought Lord Ravenshire would tell his mother.

"I understand your concerns, I truly do," Lady Ravenshire said. "But I also want you to take one thing into consideration. I have never seen my son more happy than these past weeks when he is speaking of you. After so much loss in both of our lives, all I want is for my son to be happy. He is titled, and he does have a lot of responsibilities, but he's also a man who deserves happiness in this life."

Ellen opened her mouth, then closed it. What ever could her response be to something like that?

Voices rose and fell from outside—Lord Ravenshire was greeting the next round of guests.

"Now, do what you will with that information," Lady Ravenshire continued. "I hope you enjoy your stay here."

"Thank you," Ellen choked out. If it weren't for the approaching voices, she might have sunk onto the settee and let her weak knees recover. Instead, she gave a brief curtsey to Lady Ravenshire, then hurried out of the room. She headed up the stairs, not exactly knowing where she was going. But Sybil appeared in the upper hallway and directed her to her bedroom.

"Your rooms adjoin with your cousin's," Sybil said. "Lady Ravenshire thought you might enjoy being close to your cousin."

"Oh, how very thoughtful of her," Ellen murmured as her thoughts continued to spin. She barely saw the room as she entered, and once the door shut behind her, she sank onto the edge of the bed. Lady Ravenshire's words rang in Ellen's head.

She had to put them out of her mind. Lord Ravenshire was happy because he was home with his sheep and amused because of their letter writing. Not because of . . . her.

Ellen closed her eyes. Not until this moment had she felt guilty about misleading her mother and Aunt Margaret.

"I must confess all to Mother," Ellen whispered to herself. After the house party, though, because she had to tell her in person. A letter might shock her too much.

After Ellen removed her bonnet and adjusted her hair, she tapped on the adjoining door.

"Come in," Dinah said immediately.

Ellen stepped into the room and found it much the same as hers. Elegant furniture, consisting of a writing desk and a four-poster bed, with high windows overlooking the back gardens. "Lovely, isn't it?" Dinah asked in a cheerful tone from where she was standing by the window, but her eyes narrowed. "What did Lady Ravenshire tell you?"

Ellen sighed. She wasn't about to tell her cousin exactly what was said. "She knows the truth about our letter writing, which I'd assumed. Perhaps she wanted to clear the air, in case I felt like I had to conceal something. It only makes me feel awful now about deceiving Mother."

Dinah folded her arms. "Ah. Does this mean you're going to write to your mother?"

"I should tell her in person, I think. Which means I need to do it the first day I arrive home."

Dinah nodded, but her gaze was thoughtful. "Perhaps you won't need to tell her."

Ellen frowned. "It's only fair. She'll wonder why Lord Ravenshire is no longer sending letters full of how much he misses me."

Dinah smiled.

"Why are you smiling?"

"No particular reason." She crossed the room and picked up her bonnet. "Shall we join Lord Ravenshire?" she asked in a perfectly innocent voice.

Ellen wasn't fooled. Dinah was up to something.

Twelve

As Aaron led the women on a tour of the house, Miss Turner was oddly quiet. More than once, he found her speculative gaze on him, her unibrow pinched. It was as if she were trying to study him as one might an insect beneath a microscope.

Miss Young was her usual sweet self, but quiet as well.

What was going on between these two cousins?

"This wing is original to the house," he said as they walked, "and rumor has it, there's a hidden room, although I've never found it." He expected Miss Turner to react to that bit of news, but she only nodded and smiled.

"These are lovely paintings," Miss Young murmured as they paused in a studio that had belonged to his grandfather.

His grandmother hadn't ever relocated the paintings, so the following generations had left them as is, sort of a memorial, Aaron supposed. Grandfather had loved landscapes, and now, standing in the room, he noticed how many included roses.

"Grandfather spent his last years highly focused on painting," Aaron said. "I remember Grandmother's complaints at our family dinners, although she always wore an affectionate smile." His eyes stung, and he didn't know why.

He turned to examine another painting so that he might blink back any tears.

"Does anyone else in your family paint?" Miss Young asked.

Miss Turner stood on the other side of the room, near the windows, gazing out as if she didn't care one whit about art.

"My mother does, but not extensively. She has an easel set up on the back terrace from time to time. Although she hasn't used it since the passing of my father and brothers."

Miss Young stepped closer. He caught her scent of something floral. Sweet and familiar. "Perhaps your mother will take up painting again someday."

He nodded, his throat too thick to speak. After several moments, he finally asked, "Care to continue to the gardens next? Breathe in some fresh air?"

"Of course, that sounds lovely," Miss Young said.

They headed down the stairs, then toward the back doors that led to the rear terrace. But as they reached the doors to the terrace, Miss Turner stopped.

"I feel a headache coming on," she said in a perfectly lively voice, not sounding at all ailing. "I should rest until it's time to get ready for supper. I wouldn't want to miss meeting everyone else."

"Of course," Aaron said, while at the same time, Miss Young said, "Perhaps I'll come with you, in case you need anything."

"No," Miss Turner said. "You enjoy the garden. It's what you've been most looking forward to. I'll be fine after I close my eyes for a bit."

Miss Young bit her lip, looking hesitant. "If you're sure..."

"I'm sure," Miss Turner replied in a decisive tone. "Have an enjoyable walk." She glanced at him with a quick smile, then headed toward the staircase.

There'd been something in her eyes, something like expectation. Or was it something else? Oh, he couldn't quite define it.

"Shall we?" Aaron asked, extending his arm for Miss Young, in case the ground was uneven.

She hesitated a moment, looking after her cousin. Then she turned toward him and slipped her hand around his arm. Aaron couldn't explain the relief he felt at her action. Not only would he be able to spend more time with her, but they would be without the company of her cousin, or his mother, or any other nosy person, for that matter.

"I'm sorry," Miss Young said as they moved off the terrace and onto the first walking path that would take them to the rose garden. "I don't know why my cousin has been so quiet on the tour. She was very much looking forward to it earlier."

"Perhaps she has a headache as she said?"

"Perhaps," Miss Young muttered, but she didn't sound entirely convinced. "I think she abandoned us purposely. She seems to think . . . Oh, never mind."

"Seems to think what?"

She stopped, so Aaron stopped with her. Miss Young sighed, her eyelashes fluttering over her blue eyes. "We are friends, are we not?"

"I think we've well established that." Why was his heart suddenly racing?

Miss Young dipped her chin. "Dinah has created a fanciful scenario in her head. Ever since I told her about our ruse, she has found it vastly amusing, yet she thinks that despite our friendship, I am somehow pining for you."

Aaron was pretty sure his heart skipped a couple of beats. He drew in a breath. "Oh. I'm assuming you are not pining for me?" he teased.

"Oh, of course not," she exclaimed, but the color of her

cheeks had bloomed. She took a step, so they began to walk again.

"That is very good news because I wouldn't want you to break your vow."

She looked up at him. "I didn't make any such *vow*, per se. But I know my limitations, that is all."

"I understand," Aaron said. "Although I don't think you have any limitations, Miss Young. If you do, you've kept them well hidden."

Miss Young's laughter was light, but it was music to his ears all the same. He hadn't heard it since before she arrived, and he realized that he'd missed it. Dearly. Laughter didn't come through a letter, as hard as he might try to imagine it.

Aaron paused their walk before they stepped beneath an arbor. On the other side was the rose garden, and he wanted Miss Young to feel the full effect.

"Now, close your eyes," he said. "I'll lead you to the other side of the arbor, then I'll tell you when to open your eyes. Do you trust me?"

"I trust you."

Her words seemed to reach into his heart, but he pushed that aside to analyze later. Miss Young's eyes slid shut as a smile played upon her rosy lips.

Aaron gazed at her for a moment. Did she know how beautiful she was? How sweet? How delightful? And . . . his pulse was skipping ahead.

He gently steered her beneath the arbor, then to the center of the rose garden. She *had* trusted him, he realized, and kept her eyes closed.

"All right," he murmured. "You may open your eyes now."

He watched as her eyelids fluttered open, then he watched her expression transform into sheer delight.

"Lord Ravenshire, it's breathtaking."

Yes, yes, *she* was.

Miss Young spun in a slow circle, her eyes bright with excitement. "I cannot believe you ever leave this place. I might have to bring down my bed and order all my meals to be brought out here."

"That can be arranged."

She shook her head, still smiling, then she walked toward one of the bushes that was currently covered in peach rosebuds.

Miss Young bent to breathe in the fragrance. "Lovely, just lovely."

She spent the next hour inspecting each rose, touching petals, breathing in their scents, and sometimes asking him questions, which he had no idea what the answers would be. So he made up the answers, which made her laugh.

It was perhaps the most pleasant afternoon he'd ever spent.

At one point she turned to him and said, "You have a kind heart, Lord Ravenshire."

"You might change your mind after I take you to visit the sheep and talk your ear off."

Miss Young only smiled. "I'm looking forward to seeing the creatures that have so fully kept your attention."

"Not all of my attention," he said. The words just slipped out. "Now that you're here, I might forget them altogether."

At this, Miss Young smiled. A full smile. Her brilliant, beautiful smile. "There's the charming Lord Ravenshire I've come to know. Now, lead me to your sheep."

Thirteen

THE MERINO SHEEP WERE much larger than Ellen had expected. The males also had large, curling horns. She'd never known anyone with such knowledge of sheep as Lord Ravenshire. Not that she knew any sheep owners personally, but she was impressed with the history Lord Ravenshire divulged.

"It used to be illegal to export merino sheep from Spain, upon penalty of death," he said as they leaned against a stone fence separating them from the flock. The sheep seemed quite content, grazing or napping. "But over time, the king of Spain gifted merinos to other royalty. It wasn't until the Peninsular War that Spain was forced to sell off large flocks. This created a merino craze, you might say."

"And the Prince Regent is part of that?"

"It's all about money and having our own breeding program in Great Britain."

Ellen eyed the grazing sheep. "Why do you say they aren't thriving?"

"Their fleece should be twice as long and thick as it is now," he answered. "Merino sheep thrive in the drier climate of Spain. Their feet and coats need to be dry at all times, which is why they only come to pasture on sunny days like today."

Ellen watched the sheep more intently and tried to

imagine them with thicker and longer fleece. "What about rainy days?"

"Come, I'll show you."

He offered his arm again, and she gladly accepted. It felt quite natural now to walk on his arm and fall into conversation. Lord Ravenshire was easy to speak with, and despite his wealth and status, he was kind and considerate and witty. Not austere or brooding or demanding.

When a large barn came into view, Lord Ravenshire said, "This is the sheep barn, and we are working to improve it by keeping things very dry inside, short of building fireplaces, that is."

"This seems like a lot of work for an experiment," Ellen said.

"Yes, well, it's the best I can come up with for now," he said. "I've received letters from two others who are part of the project, and one had tried keeping the sheep inside at all times, but the sheep don't seem happy."

"Happy?"

He looked down at her with a smile. "Yes. Not that the sheep are pets we coddle and hand-feed, but they thrive when happy."

Ellen smiled back. "I guess I've never thought a sheep's happiness would be connected with its quality of wool."

"It's not scientific, but I believe it has an effect."

Ellen studied him for a moment; he was absolutely in earnest. "May I see inside?"

His brow creased. "Your footwear might not appreciate it."

She shrugged. "I can clean them if necessary."

"Come, then."

They stepped inside the barn, and after Ellen's eyes adjusted to the dim interior, she saw them. Lambs. "Oh, I didn't know you had babies here." She rushed over, lifting her skirts to preserve them, but not caring about her shoes. The lambs had spotted their visitors and were now bleating and jostling toward them, only to be stopped by the pen wall.

Her nose wrinkled involuntarily due to the smell, but she didn't mind it, not really. "They are adorable."

Lord Ravenshire chuckled as he reached her side. "I don't think I've ever seen you move so fast."

She ignored him and reached out a hand toward one particularly curious lamb. It butted against her hand. "Oh, he's so soft, can I hold him?"

"I don't think it's wise with your dress—"

But Ellen had already grasped the small lamb and picked it up. She held it against her, delighting in the soft, warm fleece. "What an angel." It bleated, and she laughed.

The other lambs were now all bleating at once.

"What is it?" she asked them collectively. "Do you want me to hold you too?"

"Miss Young, you can't possibly—"

It was a bit of a feat, but with one arm cradling the lamb, she used her other hand to lift her hem and step over the low wall. She set the first lamb down, then gathered another one in her arms. The lambs surrounded her now, bleating for attention.

She picked them up one by one, cradling one, then trading it for another. The others pressed against her legs, trying to get closer and closer. One of them started to suck on her finger. She laughed at the way it tickled.

Lord Ravenshire shed his jacket and joined her inside the pen. He bent to scratch the heads of a few of the lambs. "They think you're going to feed them, you know. Their mothers are outside in the sun."

"Oh, are they hungry?"

"They're always hungry," he said with a smile.

Ellen grinned back. After only a few moments with the lambs, Lord Ravenshire's hair was tousled, and his pristine clothing not so pristine. She could only imagine how she looked as well.

"Ho there," a voice came from the barn entrance, startling Ellen. She turned to see a burly man walk in wearing work clothing.

"Mr. Smith, this is Miss Young," Lord Ravenshire said. "Mr. Smith runs the barn."

Mr. Smith's expression relaxed. "Oh, it's you, my lord. I heard the bleating and was worried a predator got inside."

"Miss Young wanted to see the barn and then, well, one thing led to another." He looked over at Ellen, and she couldn't help giggling.

His cravat had come loose, and one of the lambs was determinedly tugging at the top of his boot.

"Do you need my assistance?" Mr. Smith asked, looking from Ellen to Lord Ravenshire, as if he couldn't figure out what was so funny.

When Ellen shook her head, Lord Ravenshire said, "No, we were about to leave. I hope we didn't get them too stirred up."

"That's a bit of an understatement," Mr. Smith said with a chuckle. "But it's good for them to be lively, I suppose. Just shut the door tight when you leave. I won't be too much longer, then I'll check on them again."

After Mr. Smith left, Ellen asked, "Do you get predators?"

"Not inside yet, but it's always possible." He gazed at her for a moment, his green eyes darker beneath the barn roof.

She'd always thought Lord Ravenshire a handsome man, but disheveled was his best look, she decided.

Their gazes held for a long moment, and by the time Lord

Ravenshire finally spoke, her heart rate had more than doubled. "I hate to tear you away from all your . . . lambs, but we should probably get back. I'm going to have to completely change my clothing."

"Me too," Ellen said, looking down at the dirt and bits of hay on her dress. The only thing that had probably saved her hair was her bonnet. She set down the lamb she was currently holding, then patted all the heads she could reach. "Goodbye, little ones, see you tomorrow."

"Tomorrow, eh? Planning to make a habit out of this?"

She looked up at Lord Ravenshire. He now stood on the other side of the low fence, his hand outstretched to help her over. "Is that all right with you, sir?"

"It's more than all right," he said. "I will be sure to carve out time for it."

She placed her hand in his and stepped over the wall. He didn't let go of her hand immediately, but instead, his thumb moved over the underside of her wrist.

The barn was definitely too warm now. Fresh air would do her good.

Ellen pulled away first because the look in his green eyes was making her pulse do all kinds of leaps. "Our appearances will give your mother a fright."

He chuckled. "Only if she sees us. We can enter through the kitchen entrance, and Mrs. Goodwin will cover for us."

"Oh, really? And you know that because you've made a habit of mischief in the past?"

He winked as he pushed open the door and stepped aside so she could pass through first. "Perhaps, but never anything too terrible."

"Oh, that's a relief, then," she teased as she stepped outside. "As long as there aren't any mistresses locked away, I guess I can continue to be in your company."

The edges of his fingers touched her elbow. She stopped and looked up at him.

His eyes were lighter in the light of the sun, and the edge of his mouth had lifted. "Hold still."

She did, although her heart thumped quite heartily.

He plucked off a few pieces of hay from her upper sleeve. When he dropped his hand, he said, "I think you're a natural, Miss Young. Those lambs took to you instantly. They will be sorry when you depart."

She took a shallow breath. "I will be sorry to leave them."

"Will you?" His voice dropped, and his gaze searched her face, his eyes intent. He seemed to hover over her, as if he were thinking of something that wasn't sheep.

She took a step away from him, if only to clear her thoughts that were becoming quite muddled. "Like you said, we should hurry back."

"Right."

They headed toward the house, and a comfortable silence fell between them. Just before Lord Ravenshire opened the door that must lead to the kitchens, she said, "Thank you for the tour, both inside and out. It was an honor to see the place you love so much."

He paused at this, his expression thoughtful. "It was a pleasure, and I hope one day to see your beloved cottage and all your pet roses."

Ellen couldn't help but laugh at his teasing—*was* he teasing? Apparently, her heart didn't know the difference. It was off to the races again. She determined that by the time she was ready for supper, she'd be back to a calm coolness. It wouldn't do to have Dinah catch her in this state of . . . wild happiness. No, it wouldn't do at all.

Fourteen

THE NUMBERS WERE EXACTLY even, Aaron noted. Mother had done an excellent job, and now he was seated between Miss Turner and Miss Whiting. The two women were getting along famously and were currently in a lively discussion about whether women should write novels or not, completely leaving Aaron out of the equation.

This gave him more time to observe Miss Young, and he wasn't sure he liked all the attention the men were already paying her. Not that he could blame them. She was beautiful, sweet, intelligent, and vastly amusing.

Still.

She laughed at something Lord Browning said, and it made Aaron's neck feel hot and itchy. He rubbed at it, but there was no relief.

How was he supposed to stand two weeks of this? All the conversation? All the flirting? All the boasting? None of these people were really his friends. He'd left those behind in the Navy and had been too busy upon his return to organize hunting parties or attend card games.

He caught his mother's eye, and she smiled, but her brow had lifted. This meant she had something to say to him, which would happen later, he suspected.

Aaron turned to his food and cut up another bite.

The meal finally concluded, and the men retired to the library for a round of port before joining the ladies. Even there, he felt bothered. Lord Browning shared some quip by Miss Young and the other men laughed, then they all commented on her beauty.

It was irksome, very irksome.

Yes, she was beautiful, and *he'd* surely noticed it. Had been bowled over at times by it, but she was so much more.

By the time they joined the ladies in the drawing room, he was nearly seething. It seemed all the men took their turns chatting with Miss Young and bestowing compliments upon her. She was gracious toward each, but Aaron knew her smiles were far from genuine. Perhaps he could take some pride in the fact that around him, her smiles were sincere. They were friends, good friends. And he valued that above all else.

"Son, you're in a corner not speaking to any lady." His mother paused before him with a staged smile. "You are the host, remember?"

He blinked. "Yes. Apologies. I don't know where my head is."

"I know exactly where it is," she murmured, then moved off before he could ask what she meant.

Aaron exhaled. He had to focus on the task at hand. Speak to the guests, women included. Stop focusing on who or who wasn't engaged in a conversation with Miss Young. He moved among them, one by one, joining chats, adding his own thoughts and opinions. There, of course, was no opportunity for any private conversation with Miss Young.

How was it possible to be in the same room and the same company with a woman and miss her? The realization rocked through Aaron. He could not allow his thoughts to progress. They had to stop here and now.

When the evening finally ended and everyone retired for

the night, Aaron found himself in the library, nursing a port that he couldn't even taste. His gaze stayed riveted on the box where he kept all the letters from Miss Young. Her words to him were inside, nestled into a tidy bundle.

He should resist. He didn't need to read any of her letters again. She was under his roof, for heaven's sake.

"Here you are."

Aaron snapped his head toward the door. His mother stood there in her dressing gown. To the right of the door was the tall clock telling him it was well past midnight.

Aaron shot to his feet. "Is everything all right?"

"Everything is fine, son. Sit down." She came into the room and settled on the chair across from the desk while he retook his seat. "Can't sleep?"

"I have things on my mind, I guess." He eyed his mother. She looked tired, and she had to be worn out from so much entertaining that day. "Don't let me keep you from your rest. I'll be fine."

"I wanted to talk to you with no one around," his mother said. "I think you need to let Miss Young know how you feel."

Aaron opened his mouth, then closed it.

"It's no use denying anything, Aaron. It's plain as day on your face. I've noticed it, and I wouldn't be surprised if Miss Turner has noticed as well. Others will too—especially if you keep glowering at the men speaking to her and ignoring every other female in the room."

Aaron propped his elbows on the desk and let his head drop into his hands. "Was it that bad?" he mumbled.

"Worse, I should think."

"She doesn't want to marry a title."

"I know, son, but what would you do in the Navy when you had a differing opinion about protocol?"

He parted his fingers and peered at his mother. "Explain the reason behind the protocol."

"Can't you do the same now?" his mother asked. "Is this really any different? Explain how you feel, explain why you think she would be an excellent marchioness, then see if there are compromises to make."

"Compromises?"

His mother's face flushed. "I might have read one or two of her letters. I understand her a bit more now, and I think if she feels the same way about you, there can be compromises. For both of you."

Aaron wasn't too happy to hear his mother had read Miss Young's private letters to him. He'd have to transfer them to a locked box. "That's the thing, Mother. Miss Young has this block in her mind to not even consider me as a true suitor. I very much doubt she has allowed any feelings to creep in."

At this, his mother smiled.

"Why are you smiling?"

"She was watching you as much as you were watching her tonight." Mother rose to her feet, and Aaron rose too. "Trust me on this, son. A woman knows when another woman has set her eyes upon a man. Even if her brain is telling her no, her heart is saying something else."

She walked around the desk, kissed him on the cheek, then left the room.

Aaron stared after her, his heart pounding for a new reason. *Hope.* Was it possible? And if it was, how would he go about asking Miss Young to change her mind?

It was another hour, or maybe two, that Aaron sat in the library, thinking. Just as he fell asleep, someone began pounding on his door. Disoriented at first, he sat up. He'd fallen asleep in the library, and someone was knocking on the *front* door. The nearly gutted candle he'd left burning told him it was the wee hours of the morning. If the pounding continued, then the entire household would soon be awake.

Aaron staggered to his feet, then hurried to the door and opened it.

On the other side stood Mr. Smith, his hat in hand.

"Something's wrong with three of the sheep, sir," he said. "I'm sorry to wake you, but I didn't know what else to do."

Aaron scrubbed a hand through his hair and glanced about. He'd shed his jacket some time ago, and he didn't want to go search for it. "No worries. Let's go." He hurried toward the barn with Mr. Smith, the moon lighting their way.

"Tell me everything," Aaron said through gritted teeth, hoping that this was a false alarm.

"I went to check on them like I always do halfway through the night, and three of the ewes were listless, laying down and moaning."

Aaron cursed. If it was the fever, more sheep could get it. He couldn't get to the barn fast enough. They'd also have to separate the lambs out as well. The merino sheep couldn't be lost. Not now. Not in this way.

Inside the barn, Mr. Smith lit a couple more lanterns while Aaron crossed to the three ailing sheep. Their stomachs were starting to bloat. They were as good as gone. The only thing he could do now was get the other sheep separated so that the fever didn't spread.

"Go fetch the groomsmen," Aaron said. "We'll need to bury these sheep as soon as they pass, and they don't have much longer."

After Mr. Smith left, Aaron set to work, herding the adult sheep into another section of the barn. Then he scrubbed his hands, and lifted the lambs over the fence two by two, and put them in yet a third section.

By the time Mr. Smith had returned with two bleary-eyed groomsmen, Aaron was nearly done. The moaning from the sheep had stopped, and the groomsmen set to work in the field outside the barn, digging graves. Aaron didn't want to take any chances of the fever spreading from a dead animal.

"We're finished, Lord Ravenshire."

Aaron looked up from where he sat on a low wall. He hadn't realized he'd nodded off. "Buried?"

"Yes," Mr. Smith said.

Aaron nodded. "Go get some sleep," he said. "I'll keep watch for a few hours, then you can relieve me."

"You don't have to, sir, I have the groomsmen to help."

But Aaron held up his hand. "I want to be here."

The minutes passed agonizingly slowly, and Aaron continued to check on the sheep. It wasn't until the sun was well above the horizon that Mr. Smith arrived, full of apologies for sleeping longer than he'd intended.

Aaron waved him off. "If there are any signs of fever in the others, fetch me immediately," he said. "I won't be going on any excursions today with my guests. And after I get a bit of sleep, I'll return here."

Mr. Smith nodded, and Aaron set off. He'd missed breakfast with the guests, and his stomach was loudly protesting. He was a mess again from moving and handling the sheep, so he'd take the kitchen entrance. But when he saw the mail coach heading toward the front entrance, he detoured.

He greeted the driver, then took the letters he handed over.

Leafing through the post, he found two letters from the other breeders he'd written to and hoped for a reply. Right there, sitting on the front steps, he opened the seals and read the grim news.

No, fever hadn't plagued their flocks. But their sheep weren't thriving.

Aaron released a frustrated breath. The project was over. There was nothing to be done about the climate, and even sheltering the sheep in barns and sheds wasn't working. He dreaded being the one to report to the Prince Regent the bad news, but there was no help for that.

Fifteen

ELLEN DIDN'T WANT TO come out and directly question Lady Ravenshire about the absence of Lord Ravenshire in today's activities. She'd mentioned that there had been some trouble with the sheep and he'd been attending them throughout the night.

Ellen felt guilty for having a wonderful night's sleep while Lord Ravenshire had dealt with such difficult challenges. Were the sheep all right now? She wanted to know, but who could she ask? Everyone was caught up in a game of lawn bowling on the south side of the back terrace.

There was no sign of Lord Ravenshire, and Ellen wished she could head to the barn without anyone noticing or caring. She couldn't concentrate or enjoy the game, and she didn't want to sit with Lady Ravenshire and the couple of older neighbor women who had stopped in for a visit as they sat in the shade of the terrace, enjoying their lemonade.

"I'm going for a walk," Ellen told Dinah. "I won't be long."

Dinah gave her a long look. "You're worried about Lord Ravenshire and his sheep, aren't you?"

"I feel unsettled, that's all," Ellen said. "Walking will do me good."

She walked about the gardens, then paused at the arbor that led to the rose garden. For some reason, she didn't want to explore it without Lord Ravenshire. She continued through the gardens, enjoying all the features and flowering bushes. She could spend hours out here, days, really.

Yes, her cottage garden was wonderful, but the gardens of Ravenshire were like an entirely different world. It was so peaceful, so beautiful, and she knew she'd never tire of the place, no matter how many times she visited. Although, if she were honest with herself, she probably wouldn't visit many more times. Surely, if Lady Ravenshire was this adamant in securing her son a bride by throwing a house party, it wouldn't be long before he obliged.

Once she reached the terrace again, she was surprised to learn from a maid cleaning up that the ladies had retired to their rooms for a couple of hours. "Some of the gentlemen went out riding," the maid said. "Would you care for some refreshment?"

"I'll have a glass of lemonade," Ellen said, "but I'm not hungry." After drinking some lemonade, she had a wild idea. She could go to the barn herself and check on the sheep. Maybe inquire after their well-being. Surely Mr. Smith would be around. Perhaps Lord Ravenshire would be there too.

Her pulse leapt at the thought of seeing him. Maybe she could be of assistance?

Instead of going inside, she detoured to the barn and found Mr. Smith coming out of it.

"Hello, miss," he said, taking off his hat.

"I heard there was trouble with the sheep," Ellen said. "Might I ask what happened?"

He put his hat back on. "We lost three last night to the fever. I don't think it has spread, though. We're keeping a close eye on them."

"Oh, goodness, I'm so sorry." Ellen felt a lump growing in her throat. How tragic. Lord Ravenshire must be devastated. "Is Lord Ravenshire inside?

"You just missed him, miss," Mr. Smith said. "The master returned to the house about thirty minutes ago."

"Thank you," Ellen said, turning and hurrying away before she could think more of her hasty actions. She entered by the back terrace again so that she didn't have to rely on a butler to let her into the front.

Perhaps Lord Ravenshire had gone riding with the men? Or perhaps he'd retired to his room. If not, the library? She headed there first. It might be presumptuous of her, but she had to see him if possible. She had to see how he was doing.

What she found was the library door closed, and no sound coming from within. She'd come this far so she knocked lightly on the door, then waited. Nothing. She knocked again, and then the voice she'd hoped to hear said, "Come in."

Ellen cracked open the door, slipped inside, and left the door ajar.

Lord Ravenshire was sitting at his desk, his head bowed over a paper. He was writing something—a letter—and his hair had fallen forward, obscuring his eyes.

"Lord Ravenshire," she said softly.

He looked up, surprise in his gaze. He stood, and it was clear how exhausted he was. Gone was the finely turned out marquess, or the teasing man in the barn. This man was despondent. Ellen's heart went out to him.

"Mr. Smith told me about the sheep," she said, crossing the room.

"You went to the barn?" he rasped.

She nodded. "I couldn't stand not knowing. When your mother said there had been trouble with the sheep, I was quite useless to everyone."

Lord Ravenshire's gaze seemed to be soaking her up.

She took another step forward. "I'm so very sorry, Lord Ravenshire."

"Call me Aaron."

She blinked. "Sir, I don't think that's wise . . ."

He walked around the desk and stopped in front of her. "A woman who cares about my sheep should be calling me Aaron."

His green eyes were dark, troubled, and possibly grieving.

"All right." She swallowed. "Then you should call me Ellen. It's only fair."

The edge of his mouth lifted, and he raised his hand. His fingers brushed her jaw. She couldn't move, couldn't think . . . what was he doing? His gaze was more intense than she'd ever seen it, and it was setting her chest afire. Would he . . . *kiss* her?

But he didn't kiss her. He dropped his hand and stepped away as if he'd just realized what he was doing. "It's over," he said.

Her heart nearly stopped.

"The project," he clarified.

The project, not their friendship.

"I received letters from two other breeders this morning, and they aren't having good results either. I'm writing the Prince Regent now."

"Oh." Ellen bit her lip. "I am so sorry. Are you sure? I mean, maybe you need more time."

"No." Lord Ravenshire scrubbed a hand through his hair, which made it even more tousled. "We've had plenty of time. The colder months will start shortly, and that will only stunt their growth more."

Ellen hated this. She hated that the project had failed, and she hated that Lord Ravenshire—Aaron—was so cut up over it. "Is there truly nothing to be done?"

He shook his head.

Ellen didn't know how it happened, or what her mind was thinking, but she suddenly moved forward, and wrapped her arms about his waist. It only took an instant and then his arms were about her, pulling her close. She was grateful he was returning the embrace, or she'd have another apology to offer.

She closed her eyes, feeling the beat of his heart against her cheek as she breathed in his scent of fresh air. He was bearing so much right now, yet he was still facing the duty of writing to the Prince Regent.

"Will the Prince Regent be so disappointed?" she whispered.

"He had very high hopes," his voice rumbled above her. "I hate to be the deliverer of bad news, but it has to be done. Merino sheep can be raised for mutton in England, but not for their pure wool—that will still have to be imported."

She nodded against his chest. He was so solid, warm, and his arms about her felt heavenly. Safe and sturdy.

"Ellen," he murmured and drew away.

She knew she was blushing fiercely, but he didn't completely let go of her. He grasped both of her hands.

"Ellen," he said again, "there is something you *can* do for me."

It wasn't even a question. "Anything," she breathed.

He smiled, dispelling the circles beneath his eyes. "Reconsider your decision to not marry a man with a title."

She stared at him. This was the last thing she'd expected him to ask. Her throat went tight, and she could hardly get a breath in. "Why?" she choked out.

His fingers tightened around hers. "Because out of all the women in this house, or in England, for that matter . . . in fact, in all the world, there's no one I'd rather have by my side than you. You don't have to host any dinners, or balls, or attend any social functions, unless you want to. You can spend as many hours in the rose garden as you want. Or in the barn with the lambs."

"You're not selling off the merino sheep?"

"No, they'll stay." His brow furrowed. "Wait, are you implying that *yes,* you'll reconsider if I keep the sheep?"

Ellen couldn't stop her smile. "I think I did. Did I?"

He chuckled, relief clear in his voice. Then his hands cradled her face. "If you did, might I ask you for one more consideration?"

"What's that?"

His thumbs brushed along her cheeks, and her skin prickled with awareness. "Marry me, dear Ellen."

She stared at him, and he only smiled.

Everything inside her buzzed with anticipation, delicious and sweet.

When his gaze dropped to her lips and he leaned down, she didn't move, didn't pull away. Ever so lightly, he brushed his mouth against hers.

Warmth sighed through her, reaching her very toes.

"What do you think?" he whispered.

"You are very persuasive," she whispered back. Her lips still burned with his touch, yearning for more of him.

"Am I?" he murmured. Those green eyes of his seemed to peer into her very center.

She nodded and perhaps it was presumptuous of her—again—but she lifted up on her toes and pressed her mouth against his.

He might have been surprised, but he recovered swiftly because he kissed her back.

Quite thoroughly.

Thankfully, the house was still quiet, and no one came into the library. Not that Ellen would have been compromised, because she was pretty sure that she'd just agreed to marry the marquess. Without any words, of course, but who needed words at a time like this?

Epilogue

"I THOUGHT I'D FIND you here," Aaron said, walking into the rose garden.

Ellen was in her usual haunt. Never mind that their wedding lunch was in less than an hour. All her relatives, and a couple of his cousins, had arrived to celebrate their wedding. They had been married that morning, and after the wedding lunch, they would travel to Scotland for a fortnight, where they could enjoy their new marriage, free of responsibilities and relatives.

At least Ellen had changed out of her wedding dress before traipsing through the gardens. Not that he'd mind if she hadn't. She was enchanting either way. And now she was his wife. A beautiful thought.

Ellen straightened from the rose plant she'd been using a pair of pruning shears on and smiled at him from beneath her bonnet.

"You're pruning?" he asked, trying to keep the incredulousness out of his tone.

"We'll be gone a full two weeks, and I don't want to return to find everything overrun." Her gaze strayed back to the cleared space beside the bush. "This little cutting needs plenty of sunlight."

Aaron crossed to her and took the pruning shears from

her hands. He set the shears on the stone bench that was also a new addition to the garden, at Ellen's insistence, of course. Then he turned to her and drew each of her palms to his lips, pressing kisses there. "We have gardeners. Three, in fact. And you told them yesterday how to take special care of your new rose bush."

It didn't look like a bush right now, just a few stems, but Ellen had assured him it would be a bush. It was the one from Aunt Margaret's London home that had been transferred to the cottage, and now here, at Ravenshire.

Ellen lifted her chin and closed her eyes. This was her signal for him to stop talking and kiss her.

So, he obliged. He found her lips warm, soft, and tasting faintly of roses. He smiled against her mouth.

"What?" she murmured.

"You are incorrigible, my dear, that is all."

She slid her hands up the lapels of his jacket, then over his shoulders, interlocking her hands behind his neck. "You knew who I was when you proposed."

"I did," he said, leaning down again. Kissing his fiancée was one thing, but now she was his wife, and—

"Aaron," she said with a gasp, drawing away. She was blushing deeper than any of her roses. "You're . . . we're . . . That's quite enough for now."

He grinned. "We're married now, my dear. We don't have to worry about being discovered or gossiped about or creating a scandal."

She trailed her hands down to his chest. "That might be the case, but I don't want to show up to the wedding lunch looking too disheveled." She touched a hand to her throat. "I'm blushing, aren't I?"

"Yes."

She grimaced, and he chuckled.

"You need to stay at least an arm's length from me, lest you are tempted to kiss me like that again." She moved out of his arms, but he caught her hand.

"I don't think an arm's length is going to stop my temptation."

She gazed at him with a coy expression. "Then I guess we should have chosen a closer location for our honeymoon."

Aaron's chest nearly caught fire. "If you had said that even one day earlier, I could have shifted all the arrangements." He tugged her hand, drawing her closer.

She stepped easily into his arms. Pressing against him, she tilted her head so that he could see every shade of blue in her eyes.

"Your mother is so looking forward to us visiting where she grew up," she said, "and I'd hate to disappoint her."

His other arm slid around her waist. "We can visit Scotland another time."

And before he knew it, he was stealing more kisses. He never thought he'd find a woman so perfect for him. He cherished her friendship, her wit, her quirks, and the way she melted completely in his arms until he wasn't sure where he ended and she began.

"Aaron," she whispered after a moment, "the sooner we get to lunch, the sooner we leave, and the sooner we arrive at the inn for the night."

He lifted his head and felt his grin push through. "Have I told you I love you, dear Ellen?"

"Only about thirty times per day."

"How about thirty-one? I love you."

She laughed and allowed one more kiss. "I love you too, but we must join the others now." She slipped her hand into his, then pulled him toward the arbor. Slowly, and with more than one stop to kiss again, they made it back to the house.

Inside, everyone was indeed waiting, but no one seemed to mind the delay. Cousin Dinah was all smiles, along with Aunt Margaret. Ellen's mother was all knowing looks.

His own mother had a smile of utter contentedness on her face, something he would never take for granted again. They both missed his brothers and father, but life needed to move on, and right now, it was sweet. Another thing Aaron wouldn't take for granted.

"Let me guess," Cousin Dinah said as she approached the both of them. "You went to check on the roses, correct, Ellen?"

Her smile was serene. "They are doing well, thanks for asking."

Cousin Dinah laughed. "You must be a patient man, Lord Ravenshire."

"Call me Aaron, remember, cousin?" he commented. "I think it's more that Ellen has to be patient with *me*."

Ellen turned to him and rested her hand on his arm. "I like your sheep."

Looking down at her, he was caught up in the sparkle of her blue eyes. "And they like you."

Ellen reached up to adjust his cravat, even though it didn't need adjusting. He captured her hand and pressed a kiss there.

"All right, you lovebirds," Dinah said. "We should begin the luncheon so the two of you can be on your way. I hope that by the time you return from your honeymoon, the both of you will be able to look at other people besides each other."

Aaron chuckled. "I'm looking at you now, Dinah."

She smirked. "Barely."

It was true, his gaze was once again drawn to Ellen. And if they weren't in a room full of the wedding guests, he'd kiss her again. She seemed to read his mind and squeezed his arm. "Let's eat, husband. My cousin is right."

"Lead the way, then, because I'm going where you go."

"Always the charmer," Ellen teased. "Come, then."

They settled in their places as guests of honor. The luncheon was superb—his mother had done an excellent job of creating the menu, and the cooks in executing it—but Aaron barely tasted anything. Dinah was right; it was true. He had a hard time looking away from Ellen. He couldn't quite believe that they were married, actually married. That she'd agreed to marry a titled man and that she seemed as obsessed with the merino sheep as he was. No, they weren't going to fulfill the dreams of the Prince Regent. Their wool wouldn't be considered top quality, but both Aaron and Ellen had become attached to the flock.

As the toasts were raised around the table, Ellen slipped her hand in his.

Aaron's heart had never felt lighter. Who would have thought he'd find a bride from among the wallflowers at a London ball?

"Are you going to make a counter toast?" Ellen whispered.

"I think I will." He released her hand and stood. "I'd like to toast to all of our guests here today. Thank you for attending, and thank you for not believing that Ellen and I were merely pretending to court." He looked down at Ellen and her upturned face and twinkling blue eyes. "We thought we were pretending, but it turned out that I was falling in love."

Ellen's cheeks pinked. "I was too."

Well. Forget their audience. He was going to kiss her anyway.

Aaron leaned down and kissed his wife.

A few of the guests gasped, but that was followed by clapping and laughter.

When Aaron broke off the kiss, Ellen rose to her feet and raised her glass. "To you all. And to a new life of love and happiness."

"And sheep," Dinah chimed in.

"And sheep," Ellen added. Then she tugged her new husband close and kissed him back.

The wedding luncheon had turned out to be a success after all.

Heather B. Moore is a USA Today bestselling author of more than seventy publications. Her historical novels and thrillers are written under the pen name H.B. Moore. She writes women's fiction, romance, and inspirational nonfiction under Heather B. Moore. This can all be confusing so her kids just call her Mom. Heather attended Cairo American College in Egypt, the Anglican School of Jerusalem in Israel, and earned a Bachelor of Science degree from Brigham Young University. Heather is represented by Dystel, Goderich, and Bourret. Heather's latest books include A Seaside Summer, Until Vienna, The Healing Summer, The Slow March of Light, and The Paper Daughters of Chinatown.

For book updates, sign up for Heather's email list:
hbmoore.com/contact
Website: HBMoore.com
Facebook: Fans of H. B. Moore
Blog: MyWritersLair.blogspot.com
Instagram: @authorhbmoore
Twitter: @HeatherBMoore

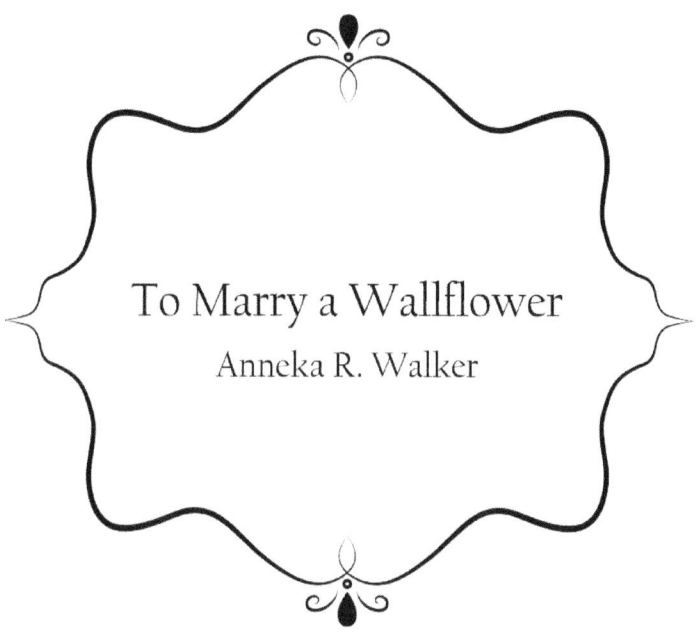

To Marry a Wallflower

Anneka R. Walker

Dedication

To the shy ones: may the right love make you brave.

One

London, England, 1804

LUKE HAD NEVER INTENDED to go to a gentleman's club and leave with a note of betrothal. Perhaps he should have left for Banbury as soon as the session of parliament had ended, but the lonely, empty walls of Newcliff Manor did not entice him home. Instead, he met his friend and neighbor, Lord Crawford, at White's for a drink. The club neared capacity, but they managed to secure a table in the back. Crawford had just begun to update Luke about his family, particularly his new wife, and his brother and sister, when a ruckus sounded near the door.

Crawford turned in his seat. "What is it now? A bet gone bad?"

Luke was nearly a head taller so it was easier for him to identify the source of the problem, and in doing so he recognized one of the men. "Some dandy is having a row with my father's friend Mr. Winters." He hadn't seen Mr. Winters since Father's funeral nearly four years ago. Guilt pricked his conscience. He should have sought the man sooner, if only to thank him. Mr. Winters had stayed with Luke the entirety of that dark night after his father's death and held Luke while he cried like a baby. That humble, broken moment was seared in his memory, as was the selfless friendship Mr. Winters had offered him. After all this time, Luke had no excuse for not calling on him and paying his gratitude.

"The dandy is Mr. Parker III." Crawford shook his head and his dark hair fell across his forehead. He swiped it to the side once more. "He might be well connected, but I question his membership here. If there was ever a hotheaded, obnoxious, ridiculous man, it is him. If you care for this Mr. Winters and want to rescue him before Mr. Parker verbally skewers him, I will gladly be your second."

Luke had only been friends with Crawford for two years, ever since Luke bought a summerhouse in Banbury near the earl's castle. They had become fast friends, and Luke had developed a great respect for Crawford's wisdom and opinion. "I don't know Mr. Winters as well as I ought to, but my father held him in high esteem. If this Mr. Parker is as bad as you say, then it is my duty to assist him."

Luke had never been one to jump into a fray, but this was his chance to return the service Mr. Winters had paid him. He pulled himself to his feet and marched to the front of the room. Crawford was quick to follow. By the time they weaved around a few other tables and reached Mr. Winters's side, two footmen were already escorting Mr. Parker from the room. Mr. Parker argued every step, but somehow the footmen managed to wrestle him away.

"What seems to be the problem?" Luke asked Mr. Winters.

Mr. Winters ran his hand over his nearly bald head and ruffled some of the black hair above his ears. "Lord Templeton, I am relieved to see you. You must help me."

Luke's title felt odd coming from Mr. Winters's lips, as if no time at all had lapsed since his father's death. A dozen pairs of eyes fell on them, and he pushed away the melancholy thoughts from his past. "Come sit down at our table, and we can talk more privately." He motioned Mr. Winters to the back of the room. Soon they were seated again, with Mr. Winters across from Luke and Crawford.

"I'm at my wits' end," Mr. Winters said, collapsing back against his seat. "My daughter has refused Mr. Parker's hand in marriage, and who could blame her? He is mean-spirited, and he would crush her delicate soul. No one ever prepares you for this part of being a father." He took out his handkerchief from his waistcoat pocket and mopped up a few beads of sweat that were forming on his brow.

"I am sure things will blow over," Luke assured him. Though he had no experience with this sort of thing, it felt like the right thing to say.

Mr. Winters shook his head. "That is what I thought, but then the rumors started. Mr. Parker and his mother have been telling everyone that my sweet Charlotte is an incurable flirt. Almost overnight, rumors have spread through the gossipmongers, and each one is worse than the last. We were quite snubbed at a card party last night, and I doubt we will receive any more invitations. My poor girl. She naturally possesses a more reserved nature, but no one would look at her twice now. I do not know how she will recover."

Crawford huffed. "That Mr. Parker is a real piece of work."

"I wish we had never met him," Mr. Winters said. "I arranged an interview with him this morning, begging him to stop, but he was so incensed, he could see no reason. Just before they dragged him out, he said to expect Charlotte's name to be in the Society papers come morning."

Luke folded his arms across his chest and pondered the situation. His father and Mr. Winters had been friends since their days at university, but Luke did not remember ever meeting Mr. Winters's daughter, likely because she had not been out yet in Society. At least not before his father's death. "Perhaps you have friends you can send her to until this has blown over?"

"If only that would be enough," Crawford said before Mr. Winters could respond. "Unfortunately, Mr. Parker isn't one to let grudges slide. The easiest solution might be to marry her to someone else. Did she have other suitors?"

"I am afraid not any who were as serious as Mr. Parker." Mr. Winters rubbed his eyes with his hands. "She does have a sizeable dowry I could advertise."

"You would just attract fortune hunters," Luke argued. "You do not want to sell your daughter to the first bidder." Although, such a method to marriage would surely simplify a lot of things. He had been trying to secure a wife for two years now, but the games of courtship were complicated. Just thinking about it made him tired.

Mr. Winters sighed. "You're right. Such an idea is ludicrous. She deserves someone as fine as you, Lord Templeton, and I should not make her settle for less."

As *him*? Luke would never have brought himself into the conversation as any sort of solution. But now that the idea was here, he couldn't help but contemplate it, ridiculous as it was. His brow furrowed. Having anyone in his house would be better than living with only the servants for company. And since Mr. Winters was a trustworthy man, his daughter could not be very different. His mind began to spin and his breathing quickened. What if it worked? What if this was the solution that he had been searching for?

"Templeton, what is it?" Crawford asked, his frown deepening. "Do you know someone who would marry her?"

Apprehension filled him and he swallowed. He couldn't believe he was considering this. "What about me? I have been in the market for a wife." He said it slowly, carefully, as if not fully committing to the absurd notion forming inside him.

Mr. Winters clutched Luke's arm. "I shouldn't ask it of you, but you would be doing me and my daughter the greatest honor. I promise you, you will not be disappointed with her. She is my greatest treasure."

Crawford blew out his breath in a low whistle. "Not every day does a man offer up his greatest treasure. But Templeton, you must be sure."

Luke's knees bounced under the table. Could he do it? He looked into Mr. Winters's desperate, hopeful eyes, and Luke wanted nothing more than to help him. He wanted to repay the debt earned on the hardest night of Luke's life. But this was more than a paltry act of service. This was a lifelong commitment. He wanted a wife, a family, and a house filled with joy again. Couldn't a marriage of convenience lead to that with time? His heart was in the right place, even if the idea seemed desperate.

A warm sense of peace filled him. His legs settled and his breathing evened. "I will do it."

Two

One week later—Banbury, Oxfordshire

HOLDING HER FAN LIKE a shield, Charlotte peered over the gilded silk at the man her father intended her to marry. His name was Lord Templeton, a baron if she could believe it, and he was a perfect stranger. The ball was a crush, but once her cousin Joan had pointed him out, Charlotte had been unable to keep her curious eyes from the back of his head.

"So that is him," she whispered. It was all the response she could muster.

Joan nodded, her golden curls bouncing. "Simply wait until he turns, and you will see that he is just as handsome as I said."

"But is he as kind as you said?" In truth, Joan had not said much about his character. All she was concerned about was his title, his fortune, and his appearance. How fortunate for her cousin that she only had to concern herself about those three things.

Joan scowled at Charlotte. "You worry too much. Why don't I have Mama announce that you have arrived early and introduce you?"

Charlotte furtively shook her head. She was not supposed to meet Lord Templeton for another two weeks, but Father had sent her ahead early with her aunt to prevent any further scandal. Such an idea was laughable. She hadn't done anything scandalous in her life. She had stayed safely in the background, content to observe others . . . until recently. However, the gossipmongers thrived on creating chaos from next to nothing, and that is exactly what had happened. Any plans she had for spinsterhood slipped through her fingers like fine sand. And since Charlotte had always done exactly as she was told, she would marry the man to satisfy her father's concern for her reputation, but she did not have to be happy about it.

Joan shrugged. "Very well, do it your way. Though, I do not see why you are prolonging the inevitable. I spent the entire summer last year trying to capture the baron's attention, and you don't even want to meet him."

Joan had never had reason to be jealous of Charlotte, since Joan never lacked for male attention, but it seemed she was now. "I will meet him at the appointed time when Father arrives. And you know this whole arrangement was not my idea," Charlotte said. "I am sorry if it has put out you or your mother."

"You have nothing to be sorry about. No one could have predicted Mr. Parker's behavior, or your subsequent betrothal. Besides, Lord Templeton is much too serious for me anyway. I could never get the man to tell me anything beyond trivialities. Now that you are practically engaged, I see he is perfect for you."

Because he was boring, he was perfect for her? She sighed. A serious demeanor was not so very bad. In fact, it would suit her own disposition well. Not that it mattered what her opinion was anymore. Whatever his personality, she would have to endure it, wouldn't she?

A man approached and Charlotte shrank behind her fan. She did not want a soul to know she was in town earlier than planned. When he quickly asked Joan if she would dance the next set, Charlotte breathed out in relief. She stepped back so they might pass her, then hugged the wall of the dance hall. When she still could not make out Lord Templeton's face, she shuffled down a few feet, almost in rhythm to the melodic strains of the violins, until his profile finally came into view.

He possessed handsome features, just as Joan had said, with unruly dark hair, styled in the popular Bedford Crop. It would be no great chore to gaze upon him for the rest of her life. She waited for a sense of satisfaction, but in truth, his appearance did little to tempt her. How could it when the greatest piece of information she had about him was that he was too busy to court a woman properly? He had essentially bought her with the same forethought one did when going to the market to purchase a pig. He laughed at something his friend, a taller man who was equally, if not even more handsome, had said. Did his friend support his strange methods of securing a wife?

A nudge at her arm caught Charlotte off guard. She turned to see Aunt Pratt, waiting with expectant blue eyes. All her features were most expressive, as was her dress and feathered turban.

"Well? Did I not tell you he was brooding and beautiful?"

Charlotte shifted her fan so her aunt could see her face and no one else. "He is not unpleasing to look at, but neither is he the most handsome man in the room."

Aunt Pratt's laugh carried over the music and several turned to look at them. Charlotte raised her fan a notch higher.

"You can no longer be particular, my dear niece, now, can you?"

"But I have done nothing wrong. In fact, it is I who has been wronged." She was not one to talk back to an older relation, but since her whole life had been turned upside down in the matter of a single night, she had to defend herself.

"You are right. I should never have encouraged him toward you. And Joan is to blame for her role as instructor. But you did listen to us, did you not?"

She had certainly listened. She was guilty of stepping away from the shadows and conversing politely. As such, the sin was laid at her own feet. If only Father would have been content to let her be a spinster, he would not have invited Aunt Pratt and Joan to stay with them for the London Season. Upon arrival, they had been charged with taking great care in securing Charlotte's future, since she had been quite inept at achieving the task herself. Such an invitation had led to Joan's extensive lessons on flirtations.

Perhaps Papa was right to have asked them to come. Her younger brother, Dennis, did not deserve to grow up to inherit an estate and the obligation of providing for his older sister. Charlotte's reserved nature had not secured her many suitors in the past, but neither had she been motivated to make an effort herself. It was far too frightening. Spinsterhood was a much safer alternative.

Somehow, she had managed to put aside her personal feelings, determined to do the best for Dennis and to please not just Papa but her relatives. Charlotte paid religious attention to Joan's lessons and forced herself to engage in more conversations. Something she learned must have carried over into her interactions with Mr. Parker.

That cursed man.

He was hardly tolerable, with his bright, overdressed attire and his conceited views. But she had learned the worst of it too late; he also possessed a terrible temper. She had not meant to give him the wrong impression. She had only been attempting to be pleasant. Her smiles possessed the same level of sweetness as when they were directed to any other person, and she had complimented him merely out of conversational habit.

Still, her behavior had earned her an unwanted proposal. She had gently turned him down, not realizing how incensed the man would be. His disappointment was followed by ugly rumors and Papa's irrational decision to marry her off to the first person he crossed. Truly, she could barely conceive how her future had fallen apart so quickly. Papa had left the house for barely an hour and had returned home with a most formidable announcement. Before she could truly digest the news, he had sent her away with her aunt and cousin to Mill Cottage in Banbury, along with a foreboding letter of betrothal.

She wondered which was worse: being engaged to the mean Mr. Parker, or a complete and utter stranger. She wanted to hide in a closet until this nightmare ended.

"You are a bit peaked, dear." Concern puckered Aunt Pratt's brow. "Try breathing through your nose. There is naught to do but make the best of the situation at hand."

Maybe it was the oppressive heat in the room, or perhaps the faster tempo of the music, but a wave of dizziness made her sway. Only one thought seemed to take purchase in her whirling thoughts. "I need to know more about him than just his appearance, Aunt. Then I can make the best of it, as you say."

"What more is there to know? He is rich and handsome."

"I thank you for postponing our introduction and allowing me to see him for myself first, but can you not wait until the appointed time of introduction so I might observe him longer? Please?" She would get on her knees if it made her plea more convincing.

Aunt Pratt's jaw worked on her objection, but remarkably, she fell silent. Aunt was similarly minded to Joan, and they both thought Charlotte's sudden arrangement to Lord Templeton was something to rejoice over. The only resistance she sensed from either of them was an underlying jealousy that it was not Joan who was betrothed to a baron. It should have been Joan. Charlotte was not an incorrigible flirt, as the rumors said, whereas Joan truly was.

"You know I cannot say no to you," Aunt Pratt said. "I could never say no to your mother either, God rest her soul. And lower that fan, for heaven's sake. Why would a woman with such pretty features hide herself?"

"I do not care for crowds." Charlotte kept her fan firmly in place. "And what if someone recognizes me?"

"We are not in London anymore, and since you arrived in Banbury only last night, the rumors have yet to catch up with you." Her aunt opened her own fan and began to beat air toward her face.

"True, but if I am to observe Lord Templeton without consequence, I fear I must stay hidden."

Aunt Pratt batted her words away with a swipe of her gloved hand. "Nonsense. We will stick to the plan and tell everyone that you are a different cousin who looks remarkably similar to your cousin Charlotte."

They had agreed to introduce her as Miss Lambe—a name attributed to her mother's family. It doubled as Charlotte's middle name as well, since at her birth, her parents had mimicked the British nobility, finding it fashionable to give her an extra name. It was a rare occasion to be referred to as such, and even now it would only be used as a precaution, since she was determined not to be introduced to a single person.

"I don't know how you can stand back here," Aunt said. "There is a decided lack of fresh air. I am going to move toward the terrace door. Do try to catch yourself a partner, or

I will feel very sorry indeed for not hurrying this introduction."

It would not serve her well to dance tonight, but she held her tongue.

Aunt took a few steps away, and as if she had read her mind said, "You know how I feel. No niece of mine will be a wallflower." And with that, she was gone.

Such a sentiment had started this whole mess in the first place, but she couldn't change who she was. Besides, if Charlotte had stayed safely in the shadows, she would not be in Banbury, spying on Lord Templeton. She wanted to blame her aunt and Joan for some of this, but in truth, she credited them for the dose of confidence she had received through Joan's lessons. Charlotte could no longer consider herself terrified of talking to new acquaintances, even if she would never be easy in large companies, and that was something to be grateful for.

Charlotte turned to search for Lord Templeton again. He was gone. She pivoted to check the other end of the room and came face-to-face with Lord Templeton's friend, the tall one she had seen him speaking with, and the one who claimed the title for the most handsome man in the room.

His wavy hair was black as night and his eyes a swirl of different shades of brown. A hint of stubble lined his angular jaw. The top of her head did not even reach the tip of his broad shoulders.

Never mind. Perhaps there was a new acquaintance or two who still terrified her because the thought of talking to this intimidating man made her tongue feel swollen in her mouth. And unfortunately, he seemed intent on conversing with her. She inched away from him. Thank heavens, propriety prohibited a conversation between them. Without a formal introduction by a mutual acquaintance of the master of ceremonies, who was nowhere in sight, him speaking to her would be quite impossible. He shifted uneasily and placed his back on the wall beside her. He turned his face away from her and spoke.

"I hear you are Miss Pratt's cousin."

The hand on her fan grew rigid. Did he expect her to respond? And to such a revealing question? Had Joan tattled and ruined Charlotte's hope to keep her identity a secret? She swallowed, unsure if she should speak to him, let alone be truthful. Her eyes darted around to assure that no one was watching. "I . . . I am."

He turned, his dark eyes connecting with hers for a single moment, her stomach fluttering in response, before he shifted back to his original position.

"What can you tell me about your mutual relation, a Miss Charlotte Winters?"

Charlotte exhaled in relief. Joan had told him a half-truth, which meant he thought she was Miss Lambe, not Miss Winters. Couples paraded in even lines, dancing in a lively reel, and small groups of people chattered away around them. They stood half hidden in shadows, and it seemed no one was aware of anything concerning her or this stranger next to her.

"What is it you want to know about her?"

"I . . . er—my friend is soon to be engaged to her. After my brief conversation with Miss Pratt earlier, I know this is not news to you, but my friend is still processing the development. He desires to know a bit more about her, but there is little time to correspond with her father before she arrives. You understand, do you not?"

"Cannot Miss Pratt enlighten you on her character?" How could she possibly tell him about herself? And what sort of man sent his friend to do his bidding? The same man who did not take the time to court a woman, that was who.

The tall man folded his arms across his chest, pulling his jacket tight around his lean shoulders, and again shifted away from her to further disguise their conversation. Even with this adjusted position, his nearness allowed his words to easily carry to her ears. "I tried Miss Pratt first and she sent me your way. I fear your cousin is much too engaged with pursuits of pleasure to take the time to relay such information."

Charlotte smirked behind her fan. He was likely right, but Joan was a romantic in more than one sense. This was her way of hurrying along the betrothal. She thought over the request for a moment before answering, and finally settled on a mutually beneficial idea.

"Perhaps I could tell you about her, if you would do me the same favor for Miss Winters." It felt odd referring to herself in that way. "I know she would like to learn more about the man she is to marry too."

He looked at her and his brown eyes set her stomach fluttering . . . again. "We have a deal."

Forcing herself to look away, she performed a quick search of the room. Her gaze landed on Lord Templeton once more. He was in conversation with a woman whose petite features and large eyes made her look doll-like. His gaze on the young woman was much too soft.

Swallowing back her apprehension, she faced the tall stranger once more. "What would you like to know?" The sooner he told her, the sooner she could ask her growing list, building in her mind by the second.

"Everything." He was no longer trying to hide their conversation. The earnestness in his expression could not possibly compare to the anxiousness she felt. "What is her character, her favorite pastimes, her hopes?"

She lowered the silk fan a smidge, but there was no way he could see her hopeful smile. This was exactly what she wanted to know too. "I will be generous in my answers, sir, if you will be equally glib."

He examined his right glove and pulled it tighter. "Do you take morning walks?"

Her brow furrowed. "Daily, sir." Or was he titled? She had no way of knowing the correct way to address him. She almost regretted her insistence in arriving late and missing so many introductions. Almost. But even though she did not know this man's name, he was closely connected to her future husband, and that was all that mattered.

"I do not know how familiar you are with the neighborhood in which your aunt lives," he began, "but if you walk north of the house, the road leads to a covered bridge over a wide stream. I will be there tomorrow morning at nine sharp. Bring your maid, or even Miss Pratt, if you are concerned about propriety, and I shall have a letter from Lord Templeton, composing a few things that might be of interest to Miss Winters."

"And I shall do the same in a letter, then. It will be a fair exchange."

He did not look at her again but nodded his head and walked away without a farewell.

Her eyes blinked rapidly to make sense of what she had just agreed to. As if securing an unpleasant reputation were not enough, now she was agreeing to meet a perfect stranger and to correspond with him. Her father was scrupulous in his manners and would be mortified. Charlotte was not a risk-taker, and her behavior had once been without fault. However, some risks were worth taking, and learning more about the man she was to marry was at the top of her list.

Three

MORNING LIGHT STREAMED THROUGH the study window and spilled over Luke's desk and the letter he was attempting to compose. It was easy enough to pen a physical description of himself, but anything more was nearly impossible. Mentioning his strengths felt boastful, and dwelling on his weaknesses was an even worse idea. He wanted to calm any nerves on his intended's behalf, but it was no easy task.

Honest.

He was honest. He dipped his pen in the ink and paused. Wait. Was it honest for him to go behind her back like this to receive information about her? No, but it wasn't exactly dishonest either. Surely, her cousin would explain the exchange of information, and Miss Winters would see it as a beneficial arrangement. He left the attribute on the page and continued.

Generous.

He did try to do all he could for his tenants and for his neighbors. Luckily, the neighborhood he had lived in for nearly two years made such efforts easy for him. At least if his future wife were disappointed with him, she would have a decent home and the hope for good friends to surround herself with.

He began to write the word *loving* and stopped after writing the L and the O, causing the ink to pool. Blast. He blotted at the spot. He could not very well say he was loving. What a dolt he was. Even if he wanted to explain to her that he would try to love her and to care for her, no matter if passion or attraction lay between them, he could not. That was not something someone explained in a letter. He went with a different quality instead.

Loyal.

He would be loyal to her, no matter what. The honor of the Templeton title demanded it, as did his conscience. He had come from a long line of men who were known for their fidelity to their wives, an unusual thing for Society, which he lived in, but Luke had been raised to want the same for his marriage. Though if the rumors of her flirtatious personality were true, then his wife would be the one he need worry about. He sighed and scrawled a few of his interests down.

Riding. Fencing. Chess. He almost added anything solitary, since all his activities had to be done on his own. He had friends, good friends. Lord Crawford not only lived close but had become his closest confidant. Lord Crawford's brother, Mr. Hadley, visited often and was a trusted friend, and another neighbor, Mr. Gunther, was becoming someone he enjoyed spending time with as well. They were all married though, and a man who lived alone had a very different sort of life. Would Miss Winters get along with their wives? Would any of her pastimes correlate with his? What did a reserved woman—if he could believe her father—mixed with a flirtatious woman enjoy doing?

He shook his head. All his imaginings had produced nothing. Luke hated the loneliness hovering over him, truly his greatest motivation to bind himself to Miss Winters. He had regretted and worried over his hasty decision ever since, but he was determined to honor his side of the agreement, no matter what.

He folded the parchment and closed it with a yellow

wafer instead of his usual seal. He pulled his watch fob out so he could see the time. Half past nine. Standing from his desk, he pushed his chair back and made his way to the door, tucking his letter in his waistcoat pocket as he did so. As loath as he was to deliver a letter all about himself, he was most excited to receive one about Miss Winters. His wait for a wife wouldn't be long, and the quiet corridors of Newcliff Manor would finally be filled with conversation and hopefully laughter and friendship.

Charlotte finished composing a letter to her brother, Dennis, before she dared begin one about herself. After sealing it, she tucked it into her reticule to frank when next in town. She sighed as she pulled the strings of her purse tight. It was easier to wish she was at home, playing dominoes with Dennis, than to think about her current predicament. She pulled a clean piece of parchment toward her, determined to do the one thing she at least could control about her frustrating situation. Most would frown heavily upon her decision to correspond with a strange man, and yet marrying a strange man was perfectly acceptable. She shook her head, pushing aside any guilt she felt for her decision. Her future would be a sight easier to endure once she knew a few things about her soon-to-be groom.

She dipped her pen in the ink and forced herself to write an entire page. There. Now to breech propriety again and actually meet the man on her morning walk. This was much harder to do than composing a letter. She would not even think about what her father would say about such an arrangement. It was quite beyond Charlotte's normal realm too, but she was not about to let her nerves get the better of her today.

After pulling the bell cord for her maid, she slipped the second letter into her reticule, as well as a painted silk fan not much longer than her palm. She didn't plan to use the fan on her walk, but it gave her comfort to have it just the same. Fans reminded her of her mother, and somehow, they made her feel safe.

When Minnie came in, she was already dressed for their walk, with a thin black cloak that reached her waist and her curly hair pinned back in a tight knot. "Can I get anythin' for you, miss?"

"Let me collect my spencer and we can leave," Charlotte said.

Her maid bobbed her head and waited patiently as Charlotte pulled on her cropped jacket and buttoned the front. Together, they walked through the house without running into Aunt Pratt or Joan. Both were late sleepers and were likely still abed. Even with this knowledge, Charlotte's relief came out in a deep exhale when the front door closed behind them.

"Are you all right, miss?" Minnie asked.

Charlotte chewed her lip for a moment, stewing about the best way to answer. "Minnie, there is something I feel I must tell you." She turned on the small steps to face the young woman who had traveled all the way to London with her.

Minnie's freckles were dark in the morning sun against her pale cheeks. They blended together when she scrunched her nose and brow in a curious manner. "What is it? Yer hands are shakin' something fierce."

Charlotte dropped her gaze and sure enough, her hands were trembling. She had not noticed. She tucked them behind her back and pushed a small smile to her lips to reassure her maid. "We might see someone on our walk. A man. I plan to speak to him, Minnie. And you must be discreet and tell no one of this."

"Yer father, miss . . . he would not like it."

Charlotte swallowed hard. "I know, and I promise to be brief. You must trust me and be loyal to my wishes."

"Yes, miss." Minnie was nineteen, Charlotte's same age, but sometimes Minnie seemed much older and wiser. This time, Charlotte had to trust her own instincts, though.

"If I tell him I am Miss Lambe, do not be alarmed. He does not know my true identity, and you must not correct him."

The slow nod that followed did not reassure Charlotte much, but she trusted Minnie more than anyone at her aunt's house. Minnie had been with her since her mother had died four years ago. Minnie was more than a maid. She was a piece of home, and her presence was as comforting as the fan in Charlotte's reticule.

"We can begin our walk now."

Minnie said nothing as they walked down the steps and the long lane to the end of the Pratts' drive. Charlotte was indeed nervous, but a small thrill of anticipation started in her chest. This stranger's offer intrigued her. She could barely wait to read the letter that would tell her all about Lord Templeton. Maybe it was the secret wish of every woman, but she dearly wanted to like her husband.

Four

LUKE WEAVED HIS WAY through his house, and a footman let him out the front door into the morning sunshine. The summer air was still cool at this hour, but the smell of the green grass and freshly trimmed shrubs met his nose, and at the same time, a sweet birdsong gave him a pleasant greeting. He had so many reasons to like Newcliff. He took one last glance at the impressive edifice and wondered why it still did not feel like home. Shaking his head, he moved toward his stables.

He had foolishly thought the purchase of Newcliff Manor as a summer home would be better than staying in a house full of memories of his dead parents. He had done so with the idea he would quickly fill it with a wife and children, and his new family would ease the sting of grief. When no wife had come along, and subsequently no children, the lonely nights had been harder than he had ever anticipated.

Within a few minutes, his stallion, Storm, was saddled, and Luke mounted. The ride to the covered bridge took only a few minutes, as it was on the corner of his estate. He'd always thought the wooden structure beautiful and had since learned that a local builder—who had grown up in Italy—had styled it off of the famous Italian architect Andrea Pallidio's designs. It had triangular trusses beneath it and cutout windows in the walls. It was only twelve feet long, as the stream beneath was not very wide nor deep, but it was a work of art and added a unique flair to his corner of the countryside.

He glanced across the bridge, and he caught no sight of Miss Winters's cousin. He could not believe he had forgotten to get her name. Then again, there had been no proper introduction. He was not so particular about such things despite his title and position, but most ladies were, and so he had been as careful as possible to not draw attention to them. Whether it had been enough, he could not say. Besides the lack of a name he had to call her by, she had showed him only her walnut curls and green eyes behind her silk fan, and his few glances had made it difficult to read her. Though, strangely enough, he could still see those same eyes behind his lids, as they had been unnervingly bright.

He dismounted and led Storm off the road to a copse of trees, where he tied his horse to the trunk of an oak. Storm's gray coat gleamed from a recent brushing, and Luke ran his hand down his horse's smooth nose. "Do you think she will come, boy? I was most presumptuous in my request. But can you blame me for wanting to know what I have signed myself up for?"

Storm tossed his head back and nickered.

"I know. It was rather desperate of me to agree to such a situation. If Mr. Winters had not been a close friend of Father's, I never would have agreed."

The horse stared at him blankly. Apparently even he did not think that was reason enough for such a rash action.

He stroked Storm's nose again. "You didn't see him. The man was desperate. Even more so than me. And I trust him, don't you?"

Again, his horse showed no response. Was Luke so lonely that he was speaking to a horse now?

"Sir?"

A soft, feminine voice sounded behind him.

He whirled around, heat extending to the back of his neck and ears. The woman he had met the night before at the ball was dressed today in a lavender cotton gown, dotted with a small flower of some sort, and she wore a tan spencer. Her head was lowered and her poke bonnet prevented him from getting a good look at her face. How long had she and her maid been standing there? And how much had they heard? A sudden desire to see what this cousin of Miss Winters looked like, without her face half shielded by a fan or a bonnet, stole away the embarrassment of having spoken aloud to his horse. A step or two across the grass did little to aid his view. If only he was shorter.

He had not come because of his curiosity about the woman in front of him, though, so he fished out his letter from his waistcoat pocket. "I must thank you for coming. I cannot imagine how uncomfortable my request must have made you." Perhaps that was why she would not look him in the eye.

"Not at all, sir. My cousin will be grateful for my efforts."

"As will my friend." He extended the letter to her.

She and her maid stepped off the road and closer to him to accept the letter.

Suddenly, her maid cried out and reached for her ankle.

Miss Winters's cousin curled her arm around the small woman. "Minnie, what happened?"

"'Tis my ankle." She lifted her foot off the ground, revealing the sole of her boot. It had come loose and hung from the toe in a precarious manner.

"No wonder you twisted it," Luke said, wondering how he could help. "I am afraid I know very little about cobbling to remedy it."

"You poor thing," her mistress said. "Does it hurt very badly?"

"Just a little, miss." Minnie, if he had heard right, took another step and nearly crumpled.

The woman rubbed her servant's back in small circles with surprising care. "We must turn back at once."

Luke shook his head. "She cannot walk on a sprained ankle. She will twist it again with those shoes." He pocketed his letter once more, stepped forward, and took the maid's elbow to help hold her up. "Have you ridden before?"

Minnie shook her head. "No, sir."

"Storm will see you home in a thrice."

The maid lowered her gaze. "On that big thing? I do not think I am brave enough."

"Minnie, you must," the woman said.

"No, miss. I've not the experience you've had. Walking suits me fine."

Miss Winters's cousin patted Minnie's back. "Think of it as an opportunity. When else would you have such a chance to ride so magnificent a beast?"

Minnie did not seem as impressed with Storm. "Oh, very well." She turned and nodded to Luke and tried to take a step forward. At this rate, they would be lucky to be home by dinner.

"Allow me?" He did not wait for an answer before swooping the maid up in his arms and carrying her to his mount. With a little maneuvering, he had her sitting sidesaddle. "This isn't made for a lady, but if you hold just here," he pointed to the pummel, "you should be just fine. I will lead you at a walk."

Minnie turned a little green behind her mess of freckles, but she nodded to him.

Miss Winters's cousin came up beside them and put her hand on Minnie's leg in an act of compassion. It was a gesture unfamiliar to him between a mistress and her servant. The simple kindness struck him. He had always tried to treat everyone as fellow human beings, but he so rarely saw such a similar mindset amongst the *ton*.

Miss Winters's cousin spoke softly to Minnie. "Once we are at my aunt's house, we will procure a wrap for your ankle and send for some new boots. And I think an order of chamomile tea and warm scones in the kitchen might be needed as well."

"Yes, miss." A small smile was all the maid could muster.

The woman sighed. "I am sorry, Minnie. Usually, it is my scrapes you are tending to, but this time, I will see you are quite spoiled."

Something softened in Minnie's features, and Luke took that as his cue to get his horse walking. After an initial jostle when they moved from the uneven grass to the road, Minnie seemed to relax. Miss Winters's cousin fell into step beside him, her bonnet completely obscuring her face from his.

"Here," Luke said, remembering his letter. He extended it again toward her.

"Oh, yes. I had already forgotten it." She took it, and after digging in a blue reticule that hung from her wrist, hastily produced a letter of her own.

He accepted the proffered paper and slipped it in his waistcoat pocket to read in the privacy of his study. Before he dropped his hand, he wondered if her partiality of her cousin would taint or bias her descriptions. He forced his hand to leave the letter alone. "Forgive my unorthodox methods, but I do not know your name to thank you."

"Lambe," she said rather quickly. Her eyes darted to meet his and he caught a glimpse of her perfect features: narrow nose, crimson budded lips, full cheeks . . . and, of course, her mesmerizing green eyes. She was a quiet beauty. "I mean, my name is *Miss* Lambe."

What name was he to give her? "I am Luke . . . Mr. Luke."

It was a half-truth, which felt more comfortable than an outright lie. Besides, Miss Lambe would soon learn his title if she stayed long in Society, so his ruse about asking for information for a friend did not bother him much. He knew nothing about Miss Lambe, but after watching her with her maid, he sensed a sympathetic nature. No doubt she would understand his reasoning with an arranged marriage on the table. "Before we reach your aunt's, was there anything else you wanted to ask me?" When she did not answer right away, he tried to clarify. "I meant, on behalf of your cousin. I want Miss Winters to be as comfortable as possible when she meets her intended."

Miss Lambe lifted her head once more. "There was one thing."

"Anything."

"When you speak to your horse, does he ever speak back?"

His mouth went dry. "Ah . . ." There was a teasing glint in her eye, and he suddenly questioned his impression of her. There was a hint of spirit he had not noticed before. But more importantly, what exactly had she overheard?

"Fear not, Mr. Luke. I did not hear whatever it was you confided in your animal."

She was a mind reader too, but at least she had missed his open discussion with his horse about how he had engaged himself to her cousin partially as an act of pity for her father. It wasn't exactly something he wanted bandied about. Though he did not take Miss Lambe to be a gossip.

"What about you, Mr. Luke? Is there anything else you would ask of me?"

He wished she would remove her confounded bonnet. It was hard to have a conversation, without being able to see her face. "I hope all my questions will be found here." He patted his waistcoat pocket.

"I hope so too."

They walked the rest of the way in companionable silence. It was odd to think that if he were not engaged, he might never have taken notice of this quiet woman beside him. Despite her efforts to keep to herself, after only a few interactions, he was intrigued by her. Not that it mattered now. He was committed to helping Mr. Winters and to securing himself a wife, so he did not allow himself to dwell on such a thought.

Once they were on the Pratts' property, Miss Lambe pointed to the front of the large cottage, a dark brown, two-story building with a flat face. It was only a few miles from his own estate, which would be an advantage for his future wife. She would not be far from her family.

"If you could take Minnie to the steps, I will find a footman to assist us through the house."

Luke did as Miss Lambe asked and moved Storm toward the front door. "I apologize to you both for this ordeal. I feel completely responsible."

"Do not worry yourself." Miss Lambe's words were soft, but not as careful as before. Perhaps she was feeling more at ease in his company. "You were a true gentleman, offering Minnie your horse as you did. We cannot thank you enough."

"A true gentleman?" He shook his head. "A true gentleman would not have asked you to meet him as I did."

She turned and gave him a glimpse of her bright eyes. There was a smile in her expression. "And a true lady would not have accepted."

Miss Lambe left his side and hurried to retrieve a footman. In a matter of moments, a capable footman whisked Minnie away in his arms, and all that was left was for Luke to say goodbye.

"Thank you, again," Miss Lambe said, her shy smile pulling free one of his own.

He mounted Storm and dipped his hat. "I bid you a good day." He maneuvered Storm back down the lane and nudged him into a canter. Thank goodness his house was not too far because he was eager to read his letter. When he arrived home, he handed his reins to a groom and jogged inside. He shed his hat and gloves and tossed them to the butler at the door. He was barely inside his study when he broke the seal on the letter and had it unfolded before the door even shut.

Dear Dennis,

Dennis? Who was Dennis? He continued reading.

Do you miss me as much as I miss you?

Luke's eyes narrowed. What was this? Had he intercepted a love letter? Was this from Miss Lambe, or Miss Winters?

I hardly had a chance to say goodbye. I hope you aren't angry with me. I am determined to make the best of my life here, and you must do the same. Study hard so that you might have the time to come to my wedding. I long to see you, even though it has only been a few days. Write to me as often as you can.

Yours,

Charlotte Winters

Luke pulled the paper tight between his hands. Was this proof of Mr. Parker's accusations? He had to know whether it was a love letter or just a note between dear friends. He could not make sense of it. His anger slowly diffused as confusion stole to the forefront of his mind. He collapsed back against the door and groaned. Of course she was in love with someone else. He hadn't even met her yet, and their marriage was already doomed.

Five

READING HER LETTER HAD to wait, but Charlotte's patience was growing thin. She had done her best to pamper Minnie and to see to her needs. It was not until her maid was perfectly comfortable, tucked in bed with her foot propped, that Charlotte was ready to explain the whole ordeal to her flustered aunt who had surely had a report already from the servants about the commotion. Charlotte slipped from Minnie's room, ignoring the letter in her reticule that was begging to be read, and made her way to the morning room, where both Aunt and Joan sat with their embroidery on their laps.

"Did you see I danced with Mr. Elliot twice, Mama? It is clear he is fond of me, but I do not know if he is quite rich enough." Joan emitted a heavy, dramatic sigh.

Charlotte slipped into the room and sat beside her cousin, hoping she would not be drawn into the conversation at hand.

"What do you think of Mr. Elliot?" Joan asked her.

Charlotte resisted a groan. "I can hardly say. I am not certain who Mr. Elliot is."

"Oh, never mind him," Aunt Pratt said. "We should be talking about you and your introduction to Lord Templeton.

We have accepted an invitation to a dinner party at his house at the end of next week."

"Yes, and Mama promised you would be there," Joan added, "so you must prepare yourself for an introduction. I can hardly contain my excitement for you. I wish I was meeting my intended."

"I could arrange something, dear," Aunt Pratt said, a mischievous glint winking in her eyes.

"Don't you dare, Mama. I will not need help catching a husband. I was merely showing Charlotte my support."

"That is very good of you." Aunt Pratt chuckled, and her eyes fell on Charlotte. "The dinner will be quite the thing. I daresay, if your cousin and I had not intervened and encouraged that horrid Mr. Parker, this great fortune would not be now laid at your feet. It has all happened as it was meant to. Fate has shown its true course. Now, do not frown. We will both be right there beside you at the dinner party. There is nothing at all to worry about."

"Thank you," she managed, her frown only deepening. Her relatives were very helpful, but sometimes too helpful. If she had not fallen prey to their advice in the first place, she would be home right now with her father and Dennis. This wasn't fate; it was the consequence of poor choices.

"Now, do tell us what happened this morning while I was still abed," Aunt said. "The servants say a gentleman rescued your maid, but so far I haven't spoken to anyone who saw him but the footman. Unfortunately, he is new and did not recognize the rider or the beast. You must tell me who it was so we can thank him."

Charlotte paused before answering. Hiding his identity was futile. Someone was bound to recognize him eventually. "It was Mr. Luke, and I did my best to thank him."

"Mr. Luke?" Joan frowned. "Do we know him, Mama?"

"I haven't the first clue who the man is." Aunt Pratt set aside her sewing and steepled her fingers to her lips. "We know everyone in Banbury. I wonder if he is visiting someone. But we would have known that too."

"I saw him at the ball," Charlotte admitted. "I thought he had spoken with you, Joan."

"I don't recall an introduction. Was he worthy of my notice?"

Mr. Luke was worthy of any woman's notice, but she did not want him discussed as Mr. Elliot or any of Joan's other conquests were. "I cannot say. Perhaps I was wrong about you two meeting. And I daresay he is staying with someone like Aunt said or you would recognize his name." Dare she mention his connection to Lord Templeton? She felt protective of Mr. Luke, but why? She did not even know him. But he had done Minnie a great service, and he had generously provided her a letter about her future intended. She was sure Joan would stake her claim on him, and something about that felt very wrong.

"We must find out who he is. Perhaps he will be at church tomorrow." The simple solution seemed to ease Aunt's mind, and she picked up her embroidery once more.

Charlotte said nothing to assure her. It was not Mr. Luke she should be thinking on, but Lord Templeton. Suddenly, all she could think about was her letter again. "It has been an exciting morning," Charlotte said, standing. "If you will excuse me, I might lay down for a bit."

"Go ahead, dear," Aunt said, and Joan shooed her away.

Charlotte kept her steps slow and ladylike until she reached the bend in the corridor. After that, she ran to her room and quickly closed the door behind her. She pulled out Mr. Luke's letter and unfolded it, her hands suddenly trembling.

It was short. Much too short. She glossed over his physical description, as she had seen him already, and went to the list of qualities. There was only a handful of them, and it seemed terribly vague. At least she knew he liked riding and chess. She put the letter to her stomach and tried not to cry. She wanted to know more. So much more.

Luke stepped into their small parish church, and his eyes raked over the attendees. He found Mrs. Pratt and her daughter in their usual spot. No Miss Lambe. Why had she not come? Was she ill? Was it because of her injured maid? She had been most concerned for her. He backed out of the church, knowing he could not sit through the service until he had answers. He had to find Miss Lambe and ask about this Dennis fellow, and this was the perfect opportunity while her aunt and cousin were preoccupied.

He turned and discovered Crawford was behind him with his wife. "Pardon me."

"The service is this way." Crawford pointed back inside the church.

"I forgot something." More particularly someone. "I will be back if I can." Perhaps he should have stayed at church. None of this behavior was like him. Maybe engaging himself to a stranger had pushed him over the edge of his sanity. Despite his mental berating, he mounted Storm and urged him into a gallop.

When he arrived at Mill Cottage, he was surprised to see Miss Lambe, sitting on the steps to the house.

He dismounted, but no groom hurried to take his horse. No matter. His business would be short. He grabbed the reins and approached Miss Lambe.

"Good day to you."

She stood and bobbed a curtsy, that darn bonnet back on her head. "How do you do, sir?"

"I was just passing by," he lied. "Are you not attending church today?"

She blew out her breath and nodded. "I was planning on attending, but my nerves got the better of me. I do not know many in the neighborhood, and a large group of strangers overwhelm me. I decided to worship right here on these steps instead."

He did not understand such fears, but he wanted to. "I am sorry. What helps in times like these?"

"I am not sure. I've always been comfortable at church. I think it's the entire trip that has me off-centered." Her cheeks pinked at her statement.

"I see." Suddenly his letter seemed not so important. He wanted to help Miss Lambe first. "Perhaps if you met a few more families." He thought about the dinner party coming up, but was not ready to reveal his identity. Not until he sorted out the letter. "Lord Templeton is holding a dinner party next Friday, and I believe you and your family have received an invitation." It was to be the night that he met Miss Winters, his future bride. He pushed away the wary thought, and added, "It will be a small party, and it will be easier to make a few acquaintances."

She ducked her head. "Perhaps." When she met his eyes again, she asked, "Why are *you* not at service?"

He had not planned how he would explain himself. "Actually, I was at church, but I left when I noticed you were not there." He cringed when he realized how his confession sounded. Sure enough, a pink blush grazed Miss Lambe's cheeks once more. He tried again. "I thought it might be my best opportunity to find you alone." Blast. He was making an idiot out of himself. "Because I had to ask about the letter you gave me." He said the last in a rush.

"What about the letter?"

"He reached into his waistcoat pocket and handed it to her. "Who is Dennis?"

Her face paled. Not even that wretched poke bonnet could hide the change in her pallor.

"I gave this to you by mistake," she said quickly.

"It was signed by Charlotte Winters. Is this her lover?"

"Her lover?" She choked and coughed into her arm. "You are greatly mistaken. Dennis is her younger brother."

"Brother?" The back of his ears burned. He *was* an idiot. "Forgive me. I had no idea."

A small laugh escaped. "It is understandable. I forgot I had the letter in my reticule. I had intended to send it . . . for my cousin."

"Let me do the honors, please."

"If you insist."

"I am almost afraid to ask for the real letter. I would hate to jump to conclusions about anything else . . . in Lord Templeton's behalf, of course. I fear my nerves are as unsettled as yours these days, though I cannot explain why."

She opened her reticule and pulled out the correct letter. "I understand more than you know. Here, take it."

He took the folded letter from her hands, already itching to open it. Before he could fall prey to his temptations, he tucked it away in his pocket. "How is your maid?"

"Better today. I told her to stay down, but I do not think she has the patience to remain there beyond tomorrow."

"I am happy to hear she is faring well."

"You cannot know how grateful I was to you and the lift you gave her."

The sincerity in her eyes pierced him, and he sensed once more his attraction to her. He cleared his throat and looked away. "If there is anything more I can do, please let me know."

"There is one thing..."

He brought his gaze back to her, his curiosity winning over his determination to control his thoughts. "Anything. What is it?"

"It's Lord Templeton's letter."

"And?"

"I took the liberty of opening it to ensure all was in order. You were a stranger to me, after all."

"I do not mind. Was there a problem?"

"It was so very brief. I wondered if there was anything you might add... for Miss Winters's sake."

It had been brief. Luke scratched his neck just under his collar, while attempting to not ruin his cravat. It had been much too hard to think of the few things he had already included, but how could he say no? "If you can find a way to meet me at the bridge tomorrow, I can bring another letter to you then."

"I will be there."

He fingered the reins on his horse. "I had better hurry back to the church. If I am lucky, I might catch the end of it."

Miss Lambe dipped a quick curtsy, and he tipped his hat. Once he was mounted again on Storm, his eyes were drawn back to her and her half-hidden face. What was it about this quiet woman that intrigued him so? He could not put his finger on it. He swallowed and pulled Storm back a few steps before circling toward the way he came.

Even after they were out of view of the house, Luke could still sense Miss Lambe, sitting on the porch steps. He did not like thinking that she was too afraid of his community. He had not lived there long, but he was surrounded by good people. Maybe because he vacillated between wanting to make Banbury his home and not knowing how, but he wanted Miss Lambe to find her place too. He should be thinking about Miss

Winters and how best to aid her transition. Unless, he could help them both.

He arrived just as church was getting out. Guilt trickled into his conscience. His mother, God rest her soul, would not be happy with him. Besides that, the vicar was his good friend. Instead of sticking around to try to come up with an explanation, he urged Storm toward home. He had a letter to read.

As soon as he was back in his study at Newcliff Manor, he opened it. The script was elegant, but not overdone. He wished he had it to compare to the letter to Dennis, but he hadn't been in the mindset to examine the penmanship. He went to the window where the light was better and read:

Lord Templeton,

In receipt of your request from your friend, Mr. Luke, I have included a few qualities and interests of my cousin, Miss Charlotte Winters. Miss Winters is similar size and appearance to myself. In fact, we share a remarkable resemblance to each other. It's uncanny, truly.

Miss Winters is quiet, but not because she lacks for things to say. She merely prefers smaller groups and a more intimate setting. Be patient with her and with time, I pray she will take to the intimidating role of baroness.

Miss Charlotte possesses no great talents to speak of, though she is passably good at the pianoforte and has a great appreciation for music in general. She loves to dance, when given the opportunity, and is most competitive when it comes to children's games. This is not because she lacks the intelligence for more complicated games, but because she has one younger brother who she loves to best.

I confess, there is a great deal of reservation on my cousin's part. However, she is a kind and sweet person. If you hear anything to the contrary—any unpleasant rumors—I assure you, it is absolutely false. If there is one thing I am quite certain of, it is that Miss Charlotte Winters is a good person who always tries her best.

Sincerely,

Miss Lambe

The words were like ribbons of knowledge to Luke, and he collected each beautiful piece of information about his future wife. After reading it through twice, he pocketed it once more. So he was to marry someone as lovely as Miss Lambe. The thought stirred him with anticipation. He could only hope his intended would have the same stunning green eyes. An image of the pianoforte filling his home with music and his future wife playing games with their future children seized him. Yes, this is what he needed. But dare he believe Miss Lambe's character reference? She seemed too generous in her opinions.

Mr. Winters had been quite sure he was handing Luke a wife on the precipice of tainting her reputation, so Luke could not believe the man's biased compliments of his daughter. There was one difference between the subdued Miss Lambe and his soon-to-be wife. Both might be beautiful and sweet-tempered, but there would be one drastic difference. He was marrying a flirt. Luke did not know the first thing about flirting. He'd have managed to find a wife on his own if that were the case.

Luke pulled out a sheet of parchment and penned a second letter. This one was easier to write, since he could imagine the woman he was addressing. And strangely enough, she did resemble Miss Lambe quite a bit.

Six

Charlotte finished painting the covered bridge on her paper brise fan with a silhouette of a couple, standing just inside it. She blew on the wet paint and set it aside to dry on the small desk in her bedroom. Once she had seen the darling bridge on her walk a few days back, she knew she had to capture it. She stared at her work, quite pleased, until she realized she had unknowingly made the silhouette to resemble the tall Mr. Luke and her much shorter self. "Oh, good heavens." Sometimes she became much too lost in her head when she was creating. Now she would not be able to take that fan anywhere.

She briskly rinsed her brushes in the glass of water, as if it would clear her confusing thoughts. Today she would not just be painting the scenery, but returning to it. And to him. She shook her head. No, she was going in anticipation of receiving another letter, not because she was seeing Mr. Luke again. She pulled out a small timepiece. A quarter to ten. Time to leave. Minnie's ankle was quite improved, but not enough for Charlotte to wish her to be on it and risk reinjury. She would simply have to meet Mr. Luke by herself. It would be a quick delivery of a note, and no more. And the contents of the letter would be worth any courage on Charlotte's part.

Grabbing her outer things, she hurried on her way. A

short ten minutes later, she was almost to the bridge, but there seemed to be some sort of commotion ahead. A wagon had overturned. Someone could be hurt. She picked up her skirts and ran the rest of the way. A farmer stood with his arms up to his horse, trying to calm him. From what she could see, there was no other person there, and the only damage was the spilled goods from the wagon.

"Are you all right?" she asked, keeping her voice even so not to further spook the horse.

The farmer took a hold of his mare's reins and rubbed her nose again and again. "T'was a bat from under the bridge. It flew right at my horse's face and scared the sense out of her."

Charlotte moved around the back of the wagon to assess what needed to be done. A barrel had rolled some feet away, and a bag of flour had come untied and spilled, as well as a bag of beans. Several smaller parcels were wrapped and still secure in their packaging but lay haphazardly in the weeds beside the road. She quickly moved to collect them, right as Mr. Luke rode up on his stallion.

"Mr. Carver, it looks as if you've met some trouble."

"Indeed, I have."

"Can I help you right your wagon?"

"I'd be much obliged."

Mr. Luke dismounted and took his jacket off, draping it on his saddle, then tossed aside his hat. His green pinstriped waistcoat matched the trees behind them. Between the two men, they struggled to lift the heavy wagon, their muscles straining until finally the wagon was righted. Charlotte was nearly mesmerized by the effort, but she blinked a few times and hurried to help. She placed her armful of parcels inside the wagon bed and bent down to collect the spilled beans. Mr. Carver loaded the barrel and Mr. Luke retied the flour. It took all three of them to recover the beans, but Mr. Carver was immensely grateful.

"I don't know what I would have done if you had not ridden by, your lor—"

Mr. Luke cut him off. "Think nothing of it. I'll have another bag of flour sent over. Now hurry home, or your wife will worry. I know her time is getting close."

"That it is. The flour will be much appreciated."

Mr. Luke waved him away. "No more of that. Be off with you."

Mr. Carver turned and bowed to Charlotte. "Thank you kindly, miss." He climbed onto his wagon seat and urged his horse on.

After the wagon had rolled out of earshot, Charlotte turned to Mr. Luke. "Are you always serving everyone? I have to say I am once again impressed."

"Anyone would do the same." Mr. Luke shrugged off her words. "In fact, you were here helping first."

Yes, but Mr. Luke had treated the poor farmer as if he were his dearest friend. "Like you said, anyone would have done the same." Though she knew the truth to be not quite as she said it. Many would have simply passed by.

"It seems that we never meet under usual circumstances."

She dusted her hands off on her dress. "It must be you. My life is fairly dull. Or at least it was."

"Are you implying that I make your life more exciting? I am not sure I have ever received such a compliment."

"Then you must be implying I possess an excessively generous nature, which would be correct." She was not normally one to banter with a man. His answering smile made her think that Joan's lessons must have paid off. It was too bad that she was once again practicing on the wrong man. Mr. Luke was just the messenger.

"Your cousins and aunt must benefit from this good nature of yours. Are you enjoying your stay at Mill Cottage, then?"

"I am. My father has always been protective of me, and I have not been allowed to visit on my own before."

"You seem quite fond of Miss Winters. Perhaps it will be even more enjoyable when she joins you too."

Charlotte groaned inwardly. She hated lying about her identity. "Yes, Miss Winters and I are quite similar, and we enjoy the same pastimes. Speaking of her, I assume you have my letter?"

"I do." He reached into his green waistcoat pocket and pulled out the folded parchment. He played with the paper for a moment. "You know, as unorthodox as this is, I do not regret our association. Neither does Lord Templeton. He appreciated the letter you wrote and is grateful for your help."

"He wants to know everything he can about her. I understand."

"Do you?"

She smiled sheepishly. "Wouldn't anyone want to know about the person they were to be married to for the rest of their life?"

"Yes, I suppose such a desire produces a few desperate feelings."

She thought of what she had written about herself and the ongoing desire she had to be wanted and appreciated. "Hopefully marriage produces some exciting feelings too." Though, any excited thought she possessed was accompanied by equal amounts of apprehension.

He held out the letter to her. "That is the hope." He cleared his throat. "Lord Templeton was only too happy to oblige you with this."

She accepted it and stared at the folded paper for a moment. "I cannot help but wonder what kind of man would agree to marry a stranger with so little time to think it over. I want to respect your friend, but this matter does not sit well with me."

Mr. Luke frowned. Had she offended him? He folded his arms across his chest and stared at the tree line. "I can see how such a decision would seem hasty from your perspective, but I hope Miss Winters will have more of an open mind."

An open mind? It was her turn to frown. Anyone would think she was doing remarkably well at making the best with her situation. Not knowing how to respond to such a rude comment, she gave him a small curtsy. "Good day, Mr. Luke. And thank you, for this." Her voice remained level despite his upsetting remarks. She thought he would be more sympathetic, and instead, she was made to feel like she was in the wrong.

Mr. Luke dipped his head to her and retrieved his hat. Nothing more was said between them, which was fine by her. He had seemed too good to be true anyway. Now she could see that Mr. Luke was indeed human, and somehow that knowledge made it easier to focus on Lord Templeton. She hurried back to the path to begin her walk home. When she was out of sight from the bridge, she pulled open her letter, determined to lose herself in whatever information she could about her future husband.

Dear Miss Winters,

You must forgive me. I have never corresponded with a lady before, and I was not sure how to begin. I thought the easiest method would be to make a list, but your cousin, Miss Lambe, thought you deserved better, and rightly so.

Charlotte chuckled, a bit of her displeasure fading, and resumed her reading.

In response to your letter, I must say I am happy to hear you have a brother. I have always wanted one myself. I hope you do not mind me sharing yours. I know a thing or two about young boys, and perhaps there will be something I can teach him or offer him in way of advice. I find the idea satisfies me greatly.

I don't talk of the loss of my family openly, but you should know—if you do not already—that you will not receive any close extended family members upon our marriage. Perhaps this is why the prospect of having not just a wife but a brother appeals to me. Since the death of my parents, I have not had anyone to spoil or be affectionate toward. I anticipate the day I can call someone family again.

I told you what sort of person I think I am, but it isn't easy or natural to describe myself. In truth, it is far easier to share the surface qualities, rather than anything personal. But since we are to be married, I hope for a much deeper relationship to develop between us someday. For that reason, I want to be forthright in my communication with you. Please be patient with me in my efforts and, no doubt, my failings.

Perhaps I have been too forward in telling you my hopes for a wife and family. First I revealed little, and now I feel as if I am baring my soul. I am not very good at this. However, if Miss Lambe is right, then you are a kind person, and I trust you will not judge me too harshly.

Sincerely,

Lord Templeton

Charlotte's heart hammered in her chest. Lord Templeton had surprised her. He was lonely and vulnerable. She had not seen that in her brief perusal of him. Had she judged him so very wrongly? Mr. Luke did not approve of her assessment of the man, but with these new, intimate details about the loss of his family, she felt conflicted. She traced his signature with her finger. She would share Dennis with him, no matter if she loved Lord Templeton or not. And she would thank Mr. Luke profusely for his part in this exchange, no matter how ill-mannered he found her. This letter made all the difference. It was the beginning of a connection that would not have existed otherwise.

Seven

THERE WAS NO POKE bonnet and no crowd to hide behind at the musical. With a week left until the dinner party, she had hoped to avoid any more public appearances until then. However, since Aunt Pratt had it on good authority that Lord Templeton was to be in attendance, of course Charlotte had to be as well. Aunt said it would ease her anxiety if she had just one more night of observation. She was likely right. Charlotte's avoidance of church had her aunt worried.

While Aunt Pratt and Joan greeted a friend, Charlotte avoided the introduction and slipped into a chair in the back row of the room. She knew Joan and her aunt would be annoyed with her choice of seat, but how could she sit elsewhere? Lord Templeton sat dead center of the room. He could see her if he turned his head, and she was not ready. Not yet. Oh, why had Aunt Pratt not let her stay home, this once? Now she would be forced to continue her ruse.

Charlotte opened her fan, a black silk, and held it up to her face, while making a slow, methodic motion with it. Three couples entered the room and she scooted over one chair, leaving an open seat on the end and setting her reticule beside her on the other side. It would be easier to save seats this way for her family. Her gaze quickly reverted back to Lord Templeton's head just as a woman sat down beside him. It was the same woman she had seen him with at the ball. He leaned down to whisper something in her ear, and from several rows away, Charlotte caught her giggle.

A knot formed in her stomach and she raised her fan, as if to avert the obvious fact that she was staring. Everything in the original letter testified that his friend was an upstanding man. Could he have misled her? Two other couples filed in beside Lord Templeton, and the conversation between him and the woman was no longer made in private whispers. Where was this woman's chaperone? Or were they perhaps family? But that was not possible. He had said in his letter that he had no one.

Charlotte glowered. She needed to speak with Joan. No, Joan would see no wrong in harmless flirting. But Mr. Luke might understand. How she wished he was here so she might ask him. She stood, unable to watch a moment longer and be tortured by her thoughts. She moved to the door and slipped into a small retirement room, papered in a muted green with two small sofas across from each other. Only one woman occupied the room, and she crossed to leave as Charlotte entered.

Charlotte fell into the seat nearest the door, her emotions getting the better of her. First, she was angry, and now tears stung her eyes. How could her father have done this to her? He had assured her that Lord Templeton was a good man, and she had thought that meant he was the exception to many and would take his marriage vows seriously. But her father was getting on in years, and perhaps he did not know the usual pursuits of young men these days. The very fact that he had betrothed her so quickly made her question his judgment. She had begged and pleaded for him to change his mind, but her father was two things: impeccably proper and incredibly stubborn.

She looked about the room for a clock but saw none. How long had she sat, stewing over what she could not change? Aunt Pratt would be put out if she had to miss any of the performances because she was searching for her wandering niece. Sighing, Charlotte stood and straightened her gown. She clutched her fan, her only weapon of protection in obscuring her identity, and forced herself to retrace her steps to the music hall.

Good heavens. The room was bursting with people. She stood on her toes. Was there not a single chair to be had? The first performer, a buxom woman with black hair and high cheekbones, moved to the front center of the room and clasped her hands together in preparation. Charlotte's gaze moved across the room again and landed on Aunt's turban, a dark wine color, and spotted Joan beside her. Joan turned and gave her a helpless look, as there were no open seats beside either of them. If Charlotte walked forward a bit, a gentleman would surely notice and offer her his seat, but she hated to inconvenience anyone. She shifted and craned her neck, her eye locating an open chair on the other side of the room right on the end.

What a stroke of fortune! Taking a deep breath, her skirts swished as she hurried to take it. A trill of notes from the pianoforte opened the song right as she sat down. Then a string of rapid staccato notes skipped out of the vocalist's mouth and with it went the pace of Charlotte's heart. She had not cared to see who was beside her, so intent was she on finding a seat at all. But somehow, she had sat down directly beside Mr. Luke!

She drew her fan to her face to cover her open mouth. She could still hear him condemning her for her judgmental thoughts from their last encounter. She thought they had become friends, but she was not so sure anymore. Now all she could think of was how embarrassed she was to have come and sat directly beside him.

When he met her gaze, his eyes widened. He stared at her, examining her with his marbled brown eyes. My, but he was handsome. Her cheeks warmed as the traitorous thought entered her mind. She forced her mouth to close at the same time he gave her a polite nod. He drew his attention back to the singer, and she forced herself to do the same.

She sighed audibly, letting the sound be lost in the impossibly high notes of the performer.

Mr. Luke leaned slightly toward her and she froze. "I hope the second letter was not too personal and will meet your cousin's expectations."

She sensed vulnerability in his voice and turned to catch his eye. He did not look at her, so she faced away again and whispered back. "I am sure it will be exactly what she hoped for."

At least, it had been at the time. Now she was confused again. Perhaps she would ask Mr. Luke about this woman who seemed to cling to Lord Templeton.

"Lord Templeton mentioned that Miss Winters is fond of music," Mr. Luke added. "It is a shame she is not in attendance tonight."

"Indeed," Charlotte found herself answering, "but sometimes the soprano voices are a bit too high for her taste." Tonight, the operatic notes were doing a number on her nerves. Her free hand was already twisting at the fabric of her dress, causing wrinkles she knew would remain once she stood again.

"Oh?"

Charlotte leaned an inch closer so not to bother the other patrons with her response. "She had a dog once whose howls were very similar and would keep her awake at night."

Mr. Luke started to chuckle but covered it with a cough. "I will make sure my hounds do not disrupt her sleep."

"You mean Lord Templeton's hounds?"

His smile slipped. "Of course. That is exactly what I meant."

"That is very kind, sir," Charlotte said. Besides his very pointed comment about her lack of open judgement, Mr. Luke was all kindness. Especially to worry about whether his friend's dogs would bother someone. More and more, she was hoping Lord Templeton would be exactly like his friend. She straightened, determined to let Mr. Luke enjoy his music. She lasted only a few moments before she began searching for Lord Templeton. Her blood drained from her face. He sat only a few seats down from them. Drat! What had she been thinking? It was not like her to be unobservant. What if he had overheard them? What if he saw her and later recognized her?

"Is something the matter?" Mr. Luke asked.

Where did she begin? She wanted to start with the very unfortunate fact that she was Miss Winters and about to be betrothed to a man she wanted nothing to do with. Should she at least ask him about the petite woman beside Lord Templeton? This was the perfect opportunity. The music softened and she waited for it to return to full volume before speaking again. "Does Lord Templeton hold a tendre for another woman?"

A smile pulled at his lips. "I should have clarified this when I—er, Lord Templeton—was worried about Dennis. The answer is no. Miss Winters can be assured that his heart is free." Mr. Luke looked at her then, his eyes connecting with hers and causing her breath to catch.

Why was he looking at her in such a manner? As if he were admiring her. Her breath came out in a nervous shudder. She wanted to know if Mr. Luke cared for anyone, but that was not the sort of question she should be wondering. She batted her fan to bring some air to her face and clear her senses. If she was not careful, she would find herself emotionally attached to the wrong man.

"It is right to worry over such things," he said, oblivious to the thoughts that wreaked havoc in her mind. "Lord Templeton is not normally a jealous man, but when it comes to his future wife, I imagine any man would be intensely so. I assume it is the same for a woman."

Charlotte appreciated Mr. Luke's attitude on the subject. "I would be." Her voice was barely above a whisper. "But not everyone feels the same. Especially with arranged nuptials."

Mr. Luke shrugged and pretended to listen to the impossibly high notes from their performer. "Arranged or not, marriage is in the sight of God and deserves one's utmost loyalty."

Loyalty. There was that word again. The same adjective had been attributed to Lord Templeton. She did not know if she could believe it of her future husband, but she believed Mr. Luke capable of such a virtue. She very much liked and agreed with his view of fidelity in marriage.

"Surely, Miss Lambe, you agree?" He barely moved his mouth, but she caught the question.

A man was asking her opinion on marriage? She had been forced into a betrothal, but never had she been asked her thoughts on the subject. To have the freedom to express herself brought a thrill to her chest. "Yes, Mr. Luke. I believe a married couple should cherish their promises to each other." It wasn't a speech, but the man sitting next to her was listening attentively and actually seemed to take note of what she said. She melted a little under his appreciative gaze.

The decrescendo of the final notes of the song settled the room. Some were drifting to sleep, while others were smiling peacefully. But not Charlotte. Her heart was thudding dangerously in her chest.

Eight

CHARLOTTE WOKE WITH THOUGHTS of the wrong man on her mind. There was only one thing to do about it. Distract herself. Which meant she needed to spend time with Joan. It was just her luck that her cousin had woken earlier than normal too.

"Joan, would you accompany me on my walk this morning? I feel that once Papa arrives and the betrothal is announced, we shall not have much time together." Charlotte didn't mind being alone, in fact, she ofttimes preferred it, but today she needed someone to ground her.

A yawn escaped Joan's mouth, and she slumped in her seat at the breakfast table. "You know this is far too early for me. Mama is not even awake yet, and my breakfast is half eaten. Perhaps if you wait a few hours, my limbs will be ready for such an excursion."

If Charlotte waited, she was certain Joan would feign a different excuse. She needed her cousin's company today, but she also needed exercise. She would go mad cooped up in the house all day. "I don't want to inconvenience you. I won't be gone long, and we shall spend some time together when I return."

"Yes, we will spend the entirety of the day together. Later. When I am fully awake."

Charlotte laughed at Joan's sleepy gaze and made her way outside. Without thinking, she found herself walking the road toward the bridge again. While she was routine in her walking habits, she usually preferred to try different routes and scenery. Something about the bridge drew her back toward it. When she neared it, she observed the charming structure and wondered if it was the romantic design or the uniqueness that garnered her attention. Stopping in the middle of the bridge, she gazed out over the small river and the shallow water running quickly over and around the many rocks scattered through its bed. Her gaze followed to the banks, where she caught sight of a horse nibbling on the grass.

A gray stallion.

Had she conjured it there because her thoughts had been so centered on its rider? She blinked a few times, but it did not disappear. Its saddle was absent, but it wore a bridle. She made her way quietly across the bridge toward it.

"Come here, good sir. Your master would not be pleased to find you have wandered away from him." The ears of the stallion perked and it lifted its head, but surprisingly it did not bolt. "Do you remember me?" A few steps closer and she could reach the bridle. "We haven't officially been introduced, but since your master is not so particular about such manners, perhaps you will be just as forgiving."

She extended her hand ever so slowly and closed her hand around the leather strap. She brought her free hand to his nose and ran it down the smooth short hair. "You must know that I was jealous of Minnie for getting to ride you. What a grand horse you are. I am no authority on the subject, but even I can appreciate how fine you are."

"When you speak to the horse, does he talk back?"

Charlotte's hand tightened on the bridle as she turned to see Mr. Luke, riding up on a brown mare.

"Please tell me you are not absconding with my stallion. I will not be surprised if he is partial to a pretty lady over myself, but I will miss him dearly." His hat was gone, and his hair was not as tidy as usual. The carefree look sat well on him. Directing the mare up beside her, he dismounted. He stepped toward her, his smile growing.

Charlotte returned the smile without hesitation. She should feel guilty for being happy to see Mr. Luke, but she assured herself that she was not betrothed yet, and it was acceptable to be pleased to see an acquaintance. "I did not steal your horse, I promise."

"I believe you. But if he spoke back to you, I cannot forgive him for that. There are not enough people in my life who actually converse with me, and it would be quite unfair. In fact, come to think of it, I am convinced my staff is the quietest in England."

"What about Lord Templeton? And surely you have other friends. You are an amiable man."

"Such compliments. It makes the paddock gates being left open and my horse escaping worthwhile. Yes, I do have some friends. You have no doubt noticed the area is friendly and warm, but as a bachelor, I do not enjoy the same sort of familiarity with my married friends. They have their wives and family, and I have neither."

"Then you and Lord Templeton are alike in that."

His smile dropped and a hollowness formed in his eyes. "Yes, we are much alike."

She found the horse's nose again and stroked it. "I am glad you have him, then, as this stallion is most tight-lipped."

His smile returned, smaller, yes, but she was glad for any glimpse of it. His words created the same sort of ache in her chest as she felt when she had read Lord Templeton's letter. She hated thinking of people being so alone in the world. She had lost her mother, but she had Papa, Dennis, and extended family. Even as shy as she was, she had never experienced the depth of loneliness that she caught in Mr. Luke's voice and expression.

"Yes, but Storm is still my companion in his own right." Mr. Luke reached up and scratched behind the beast's ears.

"The quiet ones hold their own." Charlotte watched Storm's long lashes blink shut. "We might not say much, but we know how to listen."

"Ah, now that is a beautiful trait, and one I value dearly." The stallion stepped closer to Mr. Luke and pushed Charlotte out of the way in the process.

She laughed. "I will resign him to you, since he has clearly shown his loyalty."

Mr. Luke stepped toward her and captured the bridle. In the process, he unintentionally wrapped his hand around hers. Warmth traveled from her hand all the way up Charlotte's arm and radiated through her entire body. His eyes met hers and she swore she saw a glimpse of longing there. But for what? Surely not her.

He released her hand, but the effort was slow and measured. He tore his gaze from hers and cleared his throat.

Retreating several steps, Charlotte said, "I should return before my aunt and cousin worry. I have promised to spend the day with Joan."

"Let me return the favor."

"What do you mean? You owe me nothing."

Mr. Luke grinned. "Ah, but you rescued my horse and kept him safe until I could find him. I insist you ride him home. I shall follow you, then take him home."

"Ride him?" She gazed in awe at Storm. "But he has no saddle."

"Are you experienced with riding?"

"Yes, but not on such a magnificent steed."

"Did you hear that, Storm? I would behave for such compliments." He turned back to her. "It will only take a moment and I can switch the saddles. It isn't a lady's seat, but I think if your maid can manage for such a short span, you can as well."

She shook her head in disbelief. For such a refined gentleman, he did turn a blind eye to things that would shock the *ton*. "It's too much of an inconvenience."

"I caught your looks of envy when your maid rode him last week. Surely you cannot pass up the opportunity."

To ride on a man's saddle and on such a horse was brave indeed. Maybe it was the change in the air, pushing her to try something new, or maybe it was the complete faith that Mr. Luke had in her ability to accomplish the task. Either way, she found herself nodding in agreement.

"You won't regret it."

True to Mr. Luke's word, he had the saddle changed in a matter of minutes. Instead of using a mounting block, she moved to Storm's side, and Mr. Luke scooped her into the saddle. She felt a rush as his hands met her middle, as he stood so near her. When he released her, she wondered if it was the unfamiliar horse and seat, or Mr. Luke's touch that had her heart racing. She had left the house eager to forget the man, and now her mind was full of nothing but him.

And worse, she had no desire to distract herself from her very confusing and wonderful thoughts. His words rang in her mind. *You won't regret it.* But would she regret thinking of him?

Nine

CHARLOTTE HAD ONLY ONE day until she met her future husband, and her nerves were tighter than the threads on Aunt's embroidery. Joan's steady stream of gossip was not helping either. What Charlotte needed was a long walk. And not to the bridge. No, she could not keep running into Mr. Luke.

The cottage was not far from town. If Joan was right about all the evenings out that she would have as the future baroness, Charlotte could use another pair of long gloves. She moved to the window and looked longingly at the gray clouds and the hazy afternoon.

She glanced at her aunt, who was holding on to Joan's every word. The two thrived off knowing everything about everyone. She opened her mouth to ask permission for a maid to accompany her, but she did so hate to inconvenience her Aunt Pratt's staff. If only Minnie was not still favoring her ankle. There was nothing to it. She would simply go on her own. Once she was known to the town and betrothed, there would be no going beneath anyone's notice. Besides, she could be there and back in half an hour.

When Joan took a breath, Charlotte jumped in. "Aunt, do you care if I take a walk?"

"A walk? But it looks as if it might rain."

If she was lucky. Charlotte loved the rain. "I won't be gone long."

"Oh, very well, but bring an umbrella."

Charlotte nodded and fled the room. She collected her bonnet, spencer, and reticule, but neglected to grab the umbrella. A little rain never hurt anyone. As soon as she was outside, she pushed off her bonnet and let it fall against her back. She tipped her head and breathed in the fresh air. It even smelled like rain.

And it was quiet too. Blessedly quiet. To think she had pestered Dennis to cease his incessant talking. His was nothing to her cousin. She would never complain about Dennis again. Once she was down the lane, she turned left, heading in the opposite direction of the bridge, toward town.

The milliner's brick storefront was not hard to find, since her aunt had mentioned several times the locations of various places. She had also repeated how fortunate Charlotte was to be moving to a town that had all the necessary shops and businesses, while still being so near the countryside. As Charlotte took a good look at the variety of storefronts and the various market stalls, she had to agree with her aunt. It was quaint, but functional.

The bell above the door dinged as she let herself into the milliner's. She went to the counter to order a pair of gloves but saw a ready-made pair about her size. Sliding off her own gloves, she slipped the new one over her left hand, pleased to find it fit perfectly. She quickly paid for her purchase and declined the wrappings, storing the new gloves in her reticule, which dangled from her wrist, and clutched her old ones in her hands.

A crack of thunder made the patroness behind the counter jump. Charlotte took in the dark clouds rolling quickly across the sky through the window and a little thrill of excitement hurried her steps to the door. She bid the shopkeeper goodbye and let herself out, a raindrop greeting her with a splatter on her cheek. She walked to the corner of the building and stopped.

The scent of a storm was stronger now, and the air grew thick around her. She and Dennis had spent many hours in the nursery window, counting the seconds between the flashes of lightning and the rumble of thunder. It had begun as a game to comfort him when he was scared after Mother had died, but it had turned into a cherished activity.

More drops of rain followed, racing each other to the ground. Instead of donning her gloves once more, she rolled them tightly so they would fit in her nearly full reticule. She extended her bare hands as the soft drips turned heavy against her palms. Drat! The storm had arrived far quicker than she anticipated. Tipping back her head, she tried to make sense of the clouds and if she dare make a run for home. As much as she loved a good, hard rain, she also respected the dangers of being caught in one for long.

Suddenly, two hands clasped her own. She brought her head down fast, more surprised by this than the sudden storm. Mr. Luke was the culprit, and he tugged on her hands, propelling her forward. He had come out of nowhere, and she was helpless but to follow as he pulled her inside a small alleyway, only a few feet from where she had stood. They stopped under a small eave, hanging over the side of the milliner's shop.

"I saw you when I came out of the tailor's and ran to your aid. This is all the protection I can offer you, I'm afraid."

If she had thought him kind before when he'd aided Minnie and the farmer, she was sure of it now. He was the epitome of a gentleman. Mr. Luke released one of her hands and brought his to her shoulder, tucking her tighter against the building and out of the rain. The gentle gesture unintentionally brought her closer to him. Her heart raced, her mind much too aware of the warmth of his hand around hers and the intimate feel of his near embrace.

"Th-thank you."

Mr. Luke met her gaze and she forgot to breathe for a moment. "I was not fast enough. You have to be soaked through."

She hadn't noticed a chill, but she knew the curls at her temples that Minnie had perfected that morning now strung in wet clumps against her cheeks. It was tempting to push them behind her ears, but her desire to prolong his touch outweighed her desire to move. "I don't mind a little rain."

"This is not a little rain."

"I suppose not."

He studied her features and his eyes went soft. Something shifted and he seemed to realize their close proximity for the first time. Suddenly, both of his hands released their hold on her, and he gave her a sheepish grin.

It was too late. He had affected her and she would not soon forget the sweet sensation in her middle. She stepped away from him, back into the rain, letting the heavy pattering mask her nervous laugh.

"What are you doing?" he asked.

"I told you, I don't mind the rain. Believe it or not, I even like it."

He frowned. "You are afraid of a few strangers at church, but you are fearless in a rainstorm. I do not understand you, Miss Lambe."

She laughed again, louder this time. "It's not so bad."

"But it isn't exactly pleasant."

"How can you believe that?" Since it was just the two of them, it was easier to be bold. She reached out and pinched the sleeve of his jacket, pulling him out into the rain too. "What do you think? Isn't it wonderful?"

He shook his head, his dry expression drawing another laugh from her. She let go of him and tipped her head back again as she had done when he had first discovered her. The water's steady stream danced on her closed lids, cheeks, and mouth. "I don't think you are trying hard enough to enjoy it." When she looked at him again, he had his hat in his hand and his head back.

"I am trying, for your sake. But what is it I am supposed to like?"

"Isn't it relaxing? The sounds, the smells, the feel of it?"

He tipped his head up and looked at her, a teasing glint in his eyes. "All I can think about is that you are going to catch a cold, and how sorry I will be when that happens."

She grinned and stepped back under the eave. Mr. Luke did the same, and he replaced his hat. Tiny rivulets of water ran down the sides of his face, and a drip formed on the tip of his nose. "If I grow ill, you mustn't blame yourself. Aunt Pratt told me to bring an umbrella, and I purposefully left it at home."

He shook his head. "I would have taken you for an obedient sort."

"I am very obedient," she said. "Except for when it comes to umbrellas."

"You will regret that, now that you are trapped here with me." He leaned his shoulder against the brick. "What is it about the rain that excites you so?"

She shrugged and mimicked his posture. "It's freeing—cleansing, even. And something about it makes me want to be myself."

"Yes, you do not have your fan out. You must be comfortable."

She gave him a smug smile. "I happen to like fans as much as I like the rain."

His shoulders shook with his laugh. "I believe it."

Just then a streak of lightning flashed across the sky very near them, and thunder roared directly afterward. Almost as an impulse, Mr. Luke reached for her, putting a protective arm around her shoulder. His eyes were on the sky, but hers were on him. The storm did not frighten her as much as the very real feelings she had for the man in front of her. Was it possible that heaven had intervened and sent her to meet Mr. Luke, not Lord Templeton?

Mr. Luke's concerned eyes turned to hers, and he immediately smiled. "Of course you are not worried at all that we were nearly struck by lightning."

Her smile was not as wide, but it was certain. "I feel safe here." She felt safe with him. The torrent of rain was like a massive cloak of water, hiding them from the view of anyone passing on the road. And though they were in a public setting, it felt as if they were the only ones in town. Mr. Luke held her gaze, and a warmth curled around her heart.

His eyes traveled to her mouth, and his sudden appraisal of her lips, with his so near hers, made her heart stutter. She felt the unmistakable pull between them. He was going to kiss her. She didn't blink or breathe or move. She'd never been kissed before, but it only took a moment to decide she wanted to share that first moment with Mr. Luke.

Suddenly he jerked back, breaking what had felt like a frozen moment in time. His eyes widened and he gave a sheepish, scared laugh. His hand released hers and his arm dropped away. She missed his touch almost immediately, but she wasn't cold. Every limb was filled with warmth at the thought that he had almost kissed her. And yet, her mind was racing, wondering why he had pulled away. He did not know she was Charlotte. It should have been her who had pulled away. She was the one who had quietly obeyed every order she had ever been given, and she should never have allowed herself to care for Mr. Luke. But a small part of her had begun to hope in that moment that this man had begun to care for her, and her fate of a loveless match would no longer be required.

"This rain isn't letting up anytime soon. With the lightning so close, we need to move inside." His breath was ragged, and he was no longer looking at her.

"Of course." She nodded, suddenly unsure of herself.

He motioned toward the street, and she stepped back into the rain, following him at a run. He motioned with his arm, and they turned toward the door of the milliner's. When they reached the door, Mr. Luke put his hand on the handle and paused. He turned to her, rain pouring down his face. "Before we go inside, I have to tell you something."

She wiped the streaming moisture from her eyes and nodded.

"I'm not Mr. Luke."

She didn't understand. "What do you mean?"

"Luke is my given name. I'm Lord Templeton."

Blood drained from her face, and she felt cold for the first time. "Lord Templeton? But you cannot be him." She shook her head as he nodded otherwise. "Then, are there two of you? Your friend . . . I saw him at the ball and again at the musical. He is shorter than you, and there was a woman with him, small with large eyes."

"You must mean Lord Crawford and his wife."

She swallowed back nausea rising in her throat. If Mr. Luke was Lord Templeton, then she had fallen in love with the right man. Instead of a rush of happiness, her stomach dropped, and she was sure she would retch. She had lied to him. He had lied to her. The only difference was he had not fallen in love at the same time. He couldn't have, because he hadn't wanted to kiss her as she had wanted him to. But what could be done? Her head was spinning so fast that she could not think straight.

The door swung open and it was the patroness of the shop. "Your lordship! Hurry inside. This storm is something terrible."

They were ushered into the room, lined with spools of ribbon and shelves of gloves and fabric. The kind woman pulled her toward a fire in a stove in the back room. Charlotte glanced back and knew at once that the man by the door would never be "his lordship" to her. He would always simply be Luke. He was shedding his wet jacket and apologizing for his puddle.

Charlotte needed to tell him the truth about her own identity, but she hated the thought of disappointing him. The worry made her feel self-conscious and incredibly foolish, and she found herself searching for her fan in her reticule. Her hands shook as she loosened the drawstrings. Luke deserved to know who she was before the dinner party on the morrow and their formal introduction. No matter how nervous she was, it was time to tell the truth.

And then she would demand an explanation.

Charlotte wanted to know why he had agreed to marry a perfect stranger.

And if he regretted his choice.

Ten

LUKE WAS A CAD. He could barely take his eyes off the sweet, feminine woman across the room. He hadn't meant to care for her. He had used her ill, and strict lines had to be drawn between them. He shook out the moisture from his hat and scowled at it. He was meeting his future wife on the morrow, and the banns would be read the following Sunday. Did he call things off and add further ruin to Miss Winters's reputation?

If only it were so simple. But he had too much honor for that. He would have to bury his feelings instead. If he had fallen so easily for Miss Lambe, there was a chance he could undo the damage just as quickly. It was a hairbrained notion, and it pained him to even think it, but it was the only thread of hope he had to hold on to.

He looked up and saw Miss Lambe's fan up by her face as Mrs. Jones, the proprietress, hurried to prepare some tea. His heart groaned for the hurt he must have caused her. She had to have known he was about to kiss her. Did she think him a liar and a fraud?

She would be right.

Worse though, she was sensitive, and he guessed that she would internalize her hurt. He hated to think he had wounded her. She didn't need him hovering about as she processed his misdeeds. He replaced his hat and quickly shoved his arms back in his jacket.

"Forgive me," he called toward the back room. "But I really must be off." Both Miss Lambe and Mrs. Jones turned toward him.

Mrs. Jones hurried in his direction. "But the devil is in that downpour, your lordship!"

He nodded absently, noticing Miss Lambe looking at the floor instead of him. "I will send a carriage to see your guest home."

Before he could change his mind, he let himself back out into the downpour. He trudged his way to the stables to collect his horse. Lightning or not, he was going home. For once he felt he deserved the unpleasant, solitary silence he would find there.

Once Charlotte was back at Mill Cottage and dressed in dry clothing, her aunt and cousin tumbled into her room.

"We thought you were lost somewhere on the property!" Aunt Pratt rushed to Charlotte and embraced her.

"You should not have scared us," Joan added, her arms crossing over her chest. "And to return in Lord Templeton's carriage before you've even been introduced . . . what will people say?"

Once Aunt released her, Charlotte took a towel to her hair, her insides twisting with the revelation that she still had not quite processed. "The only one I am worried about is Lord Templeton."

"What ever do you mean, child? And start from the beginning. I want to know how a walk led to all this." She motioned toward Charlotte's wet hair.

"I decided to walk to town and put in an order for a pair of gloves. I had no idea that I would run into Mr. Luke."

"*Two* men? Perhaps it is I who should have received lessons on how to catch a suitor from you." Joan shook her head in disbelief and sat on the edge of Charlotte's lavender quilt.

"It's not two men. Mr. Luke *is* Lord Templeton. They are the same person. He tricked me to get information on Miss Winters, just as I tricked him and told him I am Miss Lambe."

Aunt Pratt grimaced. "Good heavens. What a mess."

Joan paled. "Oh dear, I might have started this. He asked me briefly about you at the ball, and I pointed him your way. I swear I meant nothing by it. You must forgive me."

"I cannot be angry with anyone but myself," Charlotte said, though she did hope Joan would be more thoughtful in the future.

Aunt Pratt worried her hands. "But it is all sorted now, is it not?"

Charlotte set down her towel and slumped into the chair at her dressing table. "I am afraid not. I know who he is, but he does not know who I am."

"He will know soon enough," Joan said, her voice matter-of-fact.

"What will he think of me?" Charlotte could not even imagine. Would he go back on his agreement? She could honestly say she did not want him to, but he was a far superior person and capable of finding a much more sensible and prettier wife. Truly, with his title, appearance, and genuine kindness, he could have anyone he wanted. She would never understand why he wanted a wife unseen. No, tomorrow's introduction would not go well.

Joan came up beside her. "What you should be asking yourself is, what do you think of him?"

Charlotte did not have to think long. Luke was considerate and thoughtful. First, he'd helped Minnie, then the farmer. And she could not forget how he had pulled her out of the rain and sent his carriage back for her. She had never made a list of attributes she wanted in a husband, but she knew this was the sort of man she wanted for herself and as the father to her future children. Beyond that, he made her feel special. Noticed. "He is quite affable," she finally said, her cheeks warming, "and more handsome than I imagined."

"Did I not tell you?" Aunt gave Charlotte a knowing look. "I pride myself in being an excellent judge of character."

Charlotte did not bring up Mr. Parker, for he no longer mattered. "Lord Templeton is far too good for someone like me. When he discovers that I am the Charlotte he is betrothed to, he is sure to break things off."

"Don't worry too much," Aunt said, a sudden uncertainty entering her voice. "What is done, is done."

Her words gave Charlotte absolutely no comfort. "I suppose you are right." She loathed to think what her father would say about all this. "Please do not tell Papa. He will be so angry."

"Of course we won't, dear." Aunt came and set her hand on Charlotte's shoulder. "After all, I would be in as much trouble as you, for I encouraged this whole mess. It seems Joan and I do not make very good matchmakers."

The next day, Papa arrived in the late morning, just as he had said he would. His rim of black hair seemed thinner around the sides, his medium height and breadth more stooped than normal. Was it possible that this situation had put a strain on him as well?

He greeted his sister and niece first before turning to Charlotte. She waited for his soft cheeks to lightly wrinkle into a smile before falling into his arms. It was all she could do to hold back her tears. She couldn't let him know what had happened and how badly she had behaved, so she swallowed back the threatening moisture. She would not let him be even more disappointed in her than he already was.

"My girl, let me look at you." He pulled back and appraised her. "Has it only been two weeks? It feels like an eternity since you left. You're not still put out with me, are you?"

"Me? Put out with you? But it was I who upset you, when Mr. Parker made such an outrageous fuss."

"Nonsense. I hold Mr. Parker completely to blame for his poor manners. I meant about the engagement. Has the idea settled?"

She took a shaky breath. "Some."

"Good. I still feel it is best. Mr. Parker is still quite incensed. I tried to pay him off, but he seemed determined for everyone to know how brokenhearted he is." He held out his arm and Charlotte took it. They continued up the walk, with Aunt Pratt and Joan trailing some feet behind them. "Are you ready to meet your handsome young man tonight? At least, I think he is handsome, but who am I to say? I am just an old man, and you are a young lady. You will have to tell me what you make of him after dinner."

"Yes, Papa." She did think Luke handsome. Devastatingly so. But what mattered was what Lord Templeton thought of her. She was dreading every hour that passed closer to dinner.

That night, Charlotte sat in front of the mirror with her eyes closed as Joan dabbed cosmetics on Charlotte's brow and the outer corner of her eyes. "Are you sure this will make me look pretty? I have never worn more than a hint of rouge. Papa does not care for it."

Joan set down her brush and clapped. "Look for yourself!"

Charlotte opened her eyes and blinked a few times. The gloss on her lips and the rose in her cheeks truly added a little something extra. With her hair styled higher on her head as well, with curls cascading from the pins, she almost looked like a different person. Almost. There would be no fooling Lord Templeton, and she did not want to anyway. She needed to be honest with him as he had been with her.

"What is it? Do you not like it?" Joan asked.

"No, I love it. Thank you, Joan."

As Charlotte stood to leave, she picked up her reticule in one hand and her fan in the other. She hesitated and then with determination, she set her fan back on the dressing table. She would not hide. Tonight, she needed to be brave.

The carriage ride to Lord Templeton's estate took less than ten minutes, but it was long enough for Charlotte's stomach to knot in a ball of nerves.

"Here it is. Newcliff Manor." Her father parted the curtain on the window wider so Charlotte could lean across him and see for herself. Tall turrets and several chimneys crowned a manor of pale-yellow stone. The carriage stopped in front of a single wide door and a dozen steps. "Well, what do you think?"

Charlotte sat back in her seat while they waited for a footman to open the door. "It is impressive." And terrifying. To think she could be mistress here in a matter of weeks. She reached for her fan but remembered she did not have it.

Soon, they were all piled out of the carriage and inside the grand vestibule. The tile floor was like a chessboard of black and white colors, and large gilded portraits of beautiful people stared down on them from the long walls. Perhaps she would someday know the names of those in the paintings as well as she did her own. She swallowed hard when she heard the butler announce them to the drawing room of people on just the other side of the door.

"It is time," Papa said, pulling her forward on his arm.

"He will adore you, I am sure," Aunt Pratt said, though her voice still held an apparent tone of uncertainty.

One by one they entered the full room, holding half a dozen couples, and dipped a curtsy.

Luke approached Papa first, but his eyes were on her. She started to duck her head, but something about his gaze kept her from doing so. There was surprise and wonder behind that swirl of amber.

He finally broke their connection and looked to her father. "Good evening, Mr. Winters. I hope you had safe travels."

"Indeed, I did." Papa turned to her. "May I present Lord Templeton?"

Charlotte swallowed hard. "A pleasure, my lord." Charlotte curtsied, too flustered to feel the shame that had been eating at her since yesterday.

"Excellent." Papa turned back to Luke. "And this, as you surely have guessed, is my daughter, Miss Charlotte Winters."

"The pleasure is mine." Luke bowed, but though his body lowered, his eyes remained on hers. A curiosity nearly burned in his expression.

A footman came up beside Luke and whispered something. Luke gave a curt nod and the footman hurried away. "Dinner is ready."

No! Charlotte had not had a chance to explain yet. She stepped forward, but her father held her back. She narrowly missed stepping in front of the man she had mistaken for Luke.

"You must be nervous, dear," Papa said. "We must wait for the proper order to enter the dining room. Lord Templeton has esteemed guests here tonight. Why, did you not see Lord Crawford, with his wife on his arm? He is an *earl.* Soon you will be a baroness and such formalities cannot be ignored." She supposed that meant not masquerading as her nonexistent cousin, or pulling a baron into the rain.

"Of course." She shrank back as Aunt Pratt stepped in front of her with Joan and a gentleman she did not recognize.

"I simply have to introduce you both to Mr. Gilford," Aunt said.

Charlotte absently nodded to show she would accept the introduction to the short, pudgy-faced man, although she wanted nothing more than to melt into the walls and have the night over with.

Aunt motioned to the gentleman. "I present Mr. Gilford." As he bowed, Charlotte curtsied. "Mr. Gilford, this is my brother, Mr. Winters, and his daughter, Miss Winters."

Mr. Gilford seemed to have a ready smile, and his eyes flicked to Joan's. Surprisingly, her cousin seemed very much enamored. "Miss Pratt has told me so much about her favorite uncle and her lovely cousin. I am so pleased to meet you both."

"Yes, but perhaps we could get to know each other better over dinner." Papa gave him an impatient smile.

"Indeed, we can and should." Mr. Gilford laughed and moved aside so they could pass by him.

Charlotte entered the drawing room on her father's arm, surprised to see name cards. She had not thought this small party to be so formal, but at least she had a few family members in attendance. She traced the cards with her eyes until she found hers at the top of the table, seated on Luke's right. A footman stepped forward and pulled out her seat for her, right as her father took the seat opposite of hers. Lady

Crawford sat beside Papa and Lord Crawford down another seat. So much for formalities—not every day would you see a husband and wife so highly ranked sitting side by side in the middle of the table.

Luke gave her a cursory glance, uncertainty reflecting in his eyes that likely matched her own. He said nothing and launched into conversation with Papa. "Tell me, Mr. Winters, about your home in Gloucester."

She frowned. Why did he not ask her? Was he too angry? Disappointed? How she hoped it was not the latter. She could not bear it.

Her father loved to talk about their estate, and he launched into a tiresome list of facts such as the game on the property, the ideal weather, and his prized irises. She tried to think of something to add, but there was no good place to interrupt. Besides, what would she say? All she could think about was the need to explain her duplicity. And a public confession was not something she thought herself capable of.

The gentleman next to her cleared his throat. Mr. Gilford.

"What fortune I have to be seated by you, Miss Winters."

She gave him a weak smile in response.

"I know your cousin quite well, you know."

"Do you?"

"Since we were children." He said it as if Charlotte should have already known the story, but she had never even heard his name mentioned until this moment. Joan did not set her eyes on any one man when she could flirt with a dozen. Still, Mr. Gilford prattled on and dinner passed without a chance for her to say anything to Luke. She caught him staring at her once, but he quickly looked away. Was she so distasteful to him? How she wished that she had not pretended to be anyone else.

The women removed to the drawing room after dinner. Charlotte had not appreciated the room before, but with less people occupying the space, the details stood out to her. The bones of it were stunning, with thick, white trim and gold and white papered walls. The ceiling was taller than normal, and the fireplace, encased with large, white stones, stood as a grand centerpiece of the room. The decorations were minimal and more simplistic than she would have thought for a baron's household, but he was a bachelor without any family. It needed some color to warm it. Perhaps a painting above the mantle, and some new drapes and a few pillows, and books on the side table. It should feel like a home. Luke needed that after suffering through the loss of his family.

Charlotte caught herself. She had never desired to decorate a room before other than her own bedchamber, and she was presumptuous to think Luke would want her to change anything. The banns had not been read, and there was still a strong possibility that Luke might not want her as a wife. The thought stung and moisture filled her eyes.

Aunt Pratt and Joan circled around her, closing off the impressive view.

"Well? What did Lord Templeton say to you?" Joan asked.

"Nothing."

"I am not surprised." Aunt shook her head. "Mr. Gilford did not let him sneak in a single word. He monopolizes Joan's time every chance he gets. He is a good man, but surely he had to have noticed that Lord Templeton paid you special favor by setting your place next to his."

The men entered the room far more quickly than anyone anticipated. This was Charlotte's chance. Oh, but how she wished she had her fan. "I shall attempt to speak to him now." Both her aunt and Joan nodded. She slowly walked across the room, where her father remained in quiet conversation with Luke, and tried to keep her trembling hands still at her side. She looked at the two of them, deep in conversation. What were they speaking of now?

Father saw her and motioned her toward them. She came up alongside him and braced herself for yet another questioning look from Luke that she would have to do her best to interpret. She was surprised to see him look at her with some degree of affection. Was he not angry, then? Or disappointed? A small bud of hope began to take root.

"Charlotte, I was just telling Lord Templeton about your artistic talents."

She resisted a groan. "Papa, please don't." She did not need his bragging to add to what was already a tense situation.

"What sort of art interests you?" Lord Templeton asked. His voice was softer than usual, careful.

She could barely meet his eyes. "I have no real talent."

Papa shook his head. "She is incredible with watercolors and oils."

"My skills are marginal at best, Papa." She did not tell anyone about her attempts at art.

Luke seemed thoughtful. "What is your favorite subject to paint?"

She had not expected him to pursue the topic. When was he going to call her out and demand she explain her lies? She resisted a sigh. "Nature, my lord."

Papa nodded. "She has decorated several fans with her delicate strokes. You would be hard-pressed to not find a lady smitten by them. They are better than anything I have seen imported into the stores."

Charlotte reached over and tugged on her father's jacket sleeve. "Lord Templeton does not care about my silly pastimes." As soon as she said it, she knew she was wrong.

Luke had wanted to know everything about his future wife. But would it matter, now that it was her he was learning about?

"Do you have one of these fans on your person? I would like to see one."

She did not have one. She had left it behind. "No, I don't. Next time, perhaps."

His eyes flashed in confusion and seemed to dull. "Yes, next time."

What was it about her fan that had seemed to disappoint him? He had teased her about it already. He knew she adored her fans as much as she did a hard rain.

Papa put his arm around Charlotte. "We will leave Lord Templeton to speak to his other guests. We have quite monopolized his time tonight already."

We? Charlotte had hardly said a word to him. And she had so much she needed to say.

"There are a few I would like to greet and then, perhaps because I was remiss to make a few introductions earlier, would you favor me by meeting my friends?" His request was gently made.

"Of course, your lordship."

Lord Templeton dipped his head and retreated toward a man and wife, standing by the pianoforte, and Charlotte watched him greet them.

"He's a good man, dear." Papa squeezed her shoulder. "You will be cared for and so will my grandchildren. I could want for nothing else for my only daughter."

She tensed beneath his arm. "Then, he wants to proceed with the marriage after meeting me?"

"I am to return tomorrow morning to sign a few more papers, but the first of the banns are set to be read on Sunday."

He did not answer her question. Not exactly. She let Papa

direct her back toward Aunt Pratt and Joan. Somehow, becoming engaged to Luke like this almost felt harder than not knowing him at all. Tears sprung to the corners of her eyes.

Joan pulled her aside as soon as they reached them, leaving Papa to speak with Aunt Pratt. Joan shifted to block Charlotte from the others and dug into her reticule. She pulled out her handkerchief and handed it discreetly to Charlotte. "You cannot cry," she hissed. "Not here. You are to be a baroness, Charlotte. Something most of us can only dream about."

"Joan, I can't do it. Not like this."

"You can and you will. This dinner party is your first introduction to our society here. I might have gotten you into this mess, but I am going to get you out the same way."

Oh no. She knew where this was going. Charlotte furtively shook her head. Her tears of self-pity instantly dried with the fear of what Joan was about to recommend.

"You must, cousin. Look, he is coming our way to greet Mr. Gilford and his mother. Flirt with him, Charlotte. Rein him in like a master horsewoman. Then, when you know you've captured his interest, you can explain everything you want."

"I'm a wallflower, Joan. Not a flirt. I have learned my lesson."

Joan's expression made Charlotte feel like a small child, whose simple mind was incapable of understanding anything. "It's different this time. You want him to fall in love with you, do you not?"

Charlotte gritted her teeth in an attempt to resist Joan's well-meaning, often manipulative ways, but the temptation of what she'd said ruled out any logic in the end. "Oh, very well," she breathed. "I cannot believe I am desperate enough to do this. I hope I can remember the specifics."

"Of course you will. My lessons were quite memorable."

"That might be the problem. Mr. Parker comes to mind."

"Forget him. Now come, this is our opportunity." She linked her arm through Charlotte's and pulled her toward Mr. Gilford, Mr. Gilford's mother, and Luke.

"Mrs. Gilford," Joan said, stepping between the group and effectively cutting Luke and Charlotte off from the others. "Your dress, Mrs. Gilford! I must have the pattern and the name of your modiste."

Nerves sent Charlotte right into action. She drew Joan's character in her mind, prepared to imitate it. It was how she had succeeded in getting a proposal the first time, so it was worth trying on Luke.

She faced Luke and caught a scent of burgamot and sandalwood musk. "Lord Templeton, your cologne is quite nice."

"Pardon?"

She did not think she could repeat such a bold statement. "I can smell you." It was wonderful, and if she could just get a little closer to him, she could describe it too.

"I smell?" His brow furrowed. Oh dear. She was trying to compliment him, and he was taking it as an insult.

She tipped her head to the side and gazed up at him. "Indeed, you do." She wasn't going to hold back. Luke needed to know how she felt. She took a deep breath, filling herself with him and smiled. "It's heady and heavenly," she whispered, the truth easily sliding out, making her heart race. She tapped him lightly on the arm, a move she had practiced many times with Joan. "Did you wear that scent just for me?"

His cheeks reddened. "I . . . uh . . ."

Had she gone too far, or was he liking it? She gave her best coy smile. "I'm teasing you, Lord Templeton. Surely you are used to such compliments."

Luke's jaw tightened. "Not at all."

She batted her lashes and tried to look demure. "I daresay any woman would agree with me." Why was he studying her and not responding? "Your modesty is an admirable quality, but you mustn't be so serious, Lord Templeton."

"Such is my nature."

"Then I will have to tease a smile from you as often as I can." She reached up to tap his arm again but was surprised when he caught her hand.

She froze, but he did not release her. Her eyes widened beneath his penetrating gaze.

"Who are you?" he asked, a scowl tightening his lips.

Her act faded and with it her bold smile. She had not succeeded in hooking him. Instead, he had seen right through her behavior. Her mouth parted, ready to jump to her apology, sure tears would follow the explanation.

Suddenly, Joan whirled around, and Luke dropped her hand.

"How thoughtless of me, Mrs. Gilford, I will gladly introduce you to my cousin."

Charlotte barely heard the introduction and nearly forgot to curtsy. Flirting hadn't fixed anything. In fact, she was sure that her behavior had made Luke angrier than before.

Eleven

IF LUKE THOUGHT BEING unattached and lonely had been a burden, it was only because he was ignorant of the complications of relationships. Mr. Winters sat between him and Charlotte during Sunday service, but she might as well have been in a completely different church altogether. Luke had no idea what to say to her, or how to handle this situation. Maybe it would be simpler if he called this whole thing off.

And then the banns were read and their names were linked together. The words rang with finality. They might as well have been the actual marriage vows. Church had never been more uncomfortable. Luke shifted in his seat and tried to see Charlotte's reaction. Blasted bonnets. He shifted back, but he could not bring himself to relax. Either Charlotte was Miss Lambe with cosmetics and she had lied as he had, or Miss Lambe had understated her similarities in appearance to Charlotte. He had been convinced they were one and the same, but there were several slight differences that bothered him greatly. She had not carried a fan with her, and she had been openly flirtatious—so unlike the reserved Miss Lambe he knew. He massaged his right temple. He was second-guessing everything, and this was not the time to be confused. But how could he marry a woman if he was unsure of her identity?

When the service ended, the people filed out like ducks, waddling in their Sunday finery. He wished he could let loose his hounds to scare them out of the building a little faster. He was determined to speak with Charlotte and sort this out once and for all. Sunshine greeted them, and white, voluminous clouds dotted the sky like balls of cotton. He mumbled thanks to the vicar and stepped aside for Mr. Winters and Charlotte to do the same.

"Miss Winters," he said, extending his arm to her. "May I walk you to your carriage?" She tensed as if he would bite. Reluctantly, with a little encouragement from her father, she took his arm. They walked in silence for several steps, allowing a natural space to come between them and Mr. Winters. Her head was down, which reminded him of Miss Lambe. "I was hoping to ask you something."

Charlotte did not look at him. "Go ahead."

His frustration was mounting and he increased his pace. "It's regarding Miss Lambe."

"I wish Miss Lambe did not exist."

The loathing in her voice surprised him. "I am sorry to hear that. I was quite fond of her."

"You were?" Incredulity laced her tone, but she averted her gaze from him toward the line of carriages. "I am surprised. I'd think you'd be wary of her . . . of me."

"Confused, but not wary."

"It's all my fault. I did not want you to be disappointed at the party, and I should not have behaved as I did."

"But did you behave as Miss Winters or Miss Lambe? Because I have to know which one I am marrying."

Charlotte stopped walking and her eyes finally connected with his. He had not expected to see the tears there or the swollen lids. "Do you mean you did not know? I assumed you knew the moment you saw me. They are both my names.

Lambe was my mother's maiden name and is my middle name."

Air expelled from his lungs in a rush of relief. He had hoped for this. Wanted this. And if he was not so close to the situation, he probably would have figured it out without a second thought. But why hadn't she told him at the milliner's that night? Why had she persisted with the lie after he had come clean? He knew he cared for her, but this did not settle well.

"I'm sorry I lied. I wanted to explain, but there was never a chance." Tears streaked in rivulets down her cheeks.

This was his fault too. He had left the milliner's before she had had a chance to speak to him. Luke looked at her approaching father, and it killed him to have to postpone their conversation once more. "At the bridge. Tomorrow, same time as usual."

She ducked her head. "I'll be there."

He watched her walk away with her father, and he nearly kicked himself. Those tears had been because of him, and he had made no effort to console her. He would be a terrible husband at this rate. He tugged his hat down lower and made his way toward Storm. If he had the chance to do it all over again, he wasn't sure if he would do anything the same, except for one thing. He would've still agreed to marry Charlotte.

Crawford came up beside him and slapped Luke on the back. "I am not sure how you managed to make your betrothed cry so soon after meeting her, but all joking aside, I hope everything is all right."

"You saw it too?"

"Just a glimpse as I came nearer." Crawford eyed him. "You aren't regretting your decision?"

Luke shook his head. "Not at all, but I have made a mess of everything."

"How is that possible? You've only just met her."

A sigh escaped his lips. He hadn't wanted to tell anyone about his charade, but he trusted Crawford and desperately needed advice. After ensuring no one was near enough to overhear, he briefly relayed what had happened between him and Charlotte. "What do I do? Not every man is fortunate to have a connection with his wife, and if I wouldn't have charged into this the wrong way, I might have had one too."

"You need to tell her how much you care for her."

"Isn't it obvious?"

"To me, yes, but a woman needs to be told. The quiet, reserved ones especially rely on the security of a husband's affection. I married a wallflower, so I know."

Luke sighed. "I had forgotten how timid Lady Crawford was when she came to Banbury for that first visit."

"She was afraid of everyone, including me."

"So what advice do you have for me? You must know something that will help."

Crawford grinned. "Kiss her."

Easier said than done. Luke would like nothing better than to do just that, but he couldn't do so with tension thick between them. "I have to handle this situation with gentle hands. I cannot make a muddle of this a second time. I am going to speak to her tomorrow, but I will keep my hands to myself."

"Very well, but if you somehow find her cradled in your arms, the biggest mistake you could make is not taking advantage of the moment."

"You make it sound as if a kiss will fix everything."

"If only it was so simple." Crawford shook his head. "A kiss will seal the words you promise her. Don't take such an opportunity lightly."

His friend was married, which meant he was likely right.

But Luke had no intention of kissing Charlotte. Not yet. Neither of them were ready.

Charlotte leaned against her father's shoulder in their family carriage and tried not to cry.

"I know this is hard for you, dear, but you will adjust."

She did not respond. It wasn't Papa who needed the explanation, it was Luke. And she was afraid he would change his mind about their marriage. She didn't care anymore about her reputation. She cared that she had hurt her new friend. She cared that he was disappointed in her. And at the end of the day, she knew if he broke things off, her heart would break.

The next morning, Charlotte tied on her bonnet and put not one, but two fans in her reticule. She wouldn't need either one on her walk, but it made her feel better. She hesitated before pulling the cord for Minnie. Dare she attempt to meet Luke again on her own? Part of her wanted Minnie there for the same reason she wanted her fans, but Minnie was not going to be married to Luke, Charlotte was. It would be better to walk to the bridge alone.

Her aunt and Joan were used to her morning walks, and thankfully Papa had slept late. Charlotte slipped out of the house, welcoming the chill in the air and the clouds that matched her anxious mood. When she made it to the bridge, Luke was nowhere in sight. She stepped off the road toward the trees where she had met him that first time with Minnie. She plucked a leaf off a tree and twisted it in her gloved hands. She heard the stallion coming before she saw him or his rider. Sure enough, when she looked up, they were nearly to her.

Luke reined in his horse and dismounted. He nodded a greeting, his expression unreadable, and tied his horse to a tree.

She swallowed and found her voice. "How was your ride from Newcliff Manor? It is a short ways, is it not?"

Luke ran his hands down the side of his breeches. "Today it was long. I was up early and needed to clear my head."

The leaf in her hand fluttered to the ground, and her eyes followed it. "I imagine you have a great deal on your mind."

"At least I am no longer worrying about two different women. That has been a relief." He stood the span of his horse from her and did not seem eager to be near her.

"I feel terrible about that," she admitted.

"When you were dressed differently at the party, then acted differently, I knew not what to think."

Heat touched her cheeks at the remembrance of her blatant flirtations. "I wanted to make a good impression."

He stepped closer to her. "You made an excellent impression."

"I did?"

"As Miss Lambe and as Charlotte."

Her eyes widened. "I did?" she repeated.

He nodded. "It was hard to reconcile everything, and still is, in a way. I felt guilty when I started having feelings for Miss Lambe, and now I am engaged to her."

She gave a sheepish laugh, hardly believing what he was saying. "That is a problem I understand perfectly."

"Dare I presume you started caring for Mr. Luke?"

She reached into her reticule and pulled out one of her fans. Confessing her feelings was no easy thing. "Mr. Luke? Well, I . . . I . . ." She opened her fan and held it up by her face. Luke stared at it in a peculiar way. She beat it a few times, even though it was far too chilly to need any more breeze in the air.

"That fan."

"What about it?" She looked at it, only to realize she held the one she had painted with the bridge and the couple's silhouette. He stepped closer still, and the proximity and his inquisitive gaze made her back up.

"Is that supposed to be us?"

"It could be a remarkable coincidence..."

He followed her and she tripped on her dress as she attempted to take another step away. She felt herself falling, but Luke caught her before she made it very far. He pulled her up straight but did not release his arms around her. "Careful, whenever we are together, there is always some sort of mishap."

A rush of warmth filled her whole body. "It seems our entire acquaintance has been a bit of a mishap."

"The fan. Is it us?"

Her heart raced, but she was too nervous to lie. "Yes."

A smile grew on his face. "I had hoped I was not the only one who had felt something between us."

Her words came out a little breathless. "My father was desperate to marry me off, but you . . . you agreed for some reason I cannot understand."

Luke tightened his hold on her, probably worried that she would bolt. One hand fingered her dress at her waist, making it hard to remember to breathe. "Charlotte—may I call you Charlotte?"

She gave a quick nod.

"I agreed because your father was a good friend of my father's. I respected him and wanted to help him in my father's place. But mostly because I wanted a wife. I just had no idea that I would be getting love in the process."

She shook her head, hardly believing what she was hearing. "Are you sure you won't change your mind? I was sure that once you knew it was me, you would."

He reached up, brushing a curl off her face, and cupped her cheek. "You do yourself a great disservice. Once I knew it was you, there was no way I could change my mind."

"But we did everything wrong."

"I disagree. We did our best in a unique situation. And because we acted as we did, we got to know each other in a way we couldn't have otherwise." His smile was small, but caring. "But let's not lie to each other anymore, shall we?"

"Never." And she meant it. Relief and hope filled every inch of her.

Luke tipped his head and stared at her in a thoughtful way. "But you weren't lying when you said I smelled good, were you?"

Charlotte laughed. "No, I wasn't lying. I like everything about you, Luke." His given name slipped naturally from her tongue. "I tried not to, but you are so wonderful."

"And you are the same in my eyes. How did I get so lucky?"

"We are both lucky," she whispered. She wanted him to kiss her, but she was afraid he would and she would not know how to reciprocate, and even more afraid he wouldn't and he did not care enough about her. He spoke of love, but she needed to be sure.

His soft gaze fell to her mouth, and a breeze seemed to encircle them. "A friend told me that the best way to seal a declaration of affection is through a kiss. I would be remiss if I did not do the same."

She couldn't form words to respond.

His thumb grazed her bottom lip just before he leaned in and placed his mouth softly against hers. She let him kiss her for a moment before she had the courage to return it. It was sweeter than any scene she had ever painted and better than dancing in the rain. She brought her arms up around his neck, and he pulled her closer. All her reservations faded against the warmth of his kiss.

A few drops of moisture fell on her arms, but she did not

register them until more fell on her cheeks and nose. Luke pulled back, a grin on his face. "You can be yourself now. 'Tis raining."

She felt shy and brave at the same time. "I don't need rain to be myself any longer because I feel safe when I am with you."

His marbled brown eyes softened. "I promise to do better where that is concerned. My ride this morning was because I felt so guilty for making you cry. I always want to make you feel safe and cherished when we are together."

She stood on her tiptoes. "In return, I promise that you will never feel lonely again." And then she kissed him. What had started out as a horrible turn of events had turned into the most beautiful gift life had given her. Love was worth every act of courage and every mishap because it meant she was going to be with Luke forever.

Epilogue

CHARLOTTE LEANED BACK ON her hands and lifted her head so that the sun could make its way past her bonnet. When the effort proved insufficient, she untied her bonnet strings and laid the straw hat on the blanket between her and Joan. She was sure there was nothing lovelier than a picnic at Newcliff, and she wanted to savor every single ray of sunshine. She closed her eyes and thought about how perfect the last few weeks had been.

Even though they were quite engaged, Luke had insisted on courting her until their wedding. They had attended another musicale, one without an excessively high soprano, played chess, shuttlecock, and battledore, gone riding together several times, and Luke had even gifted her with a bouquet of plain fans for her to paint. Tonight, Dennis would arrive and then their courtship would end. She could hardly believe the wedding ceremony was on the morrow and all of this would be her home. She opened her eyes and studied the magnificent manor house. The surrealness left her uneasy. How was a quiet woman who disliked crowds going to make it as a baroness?

"What are you thinking about?" Luke asked, taking a seat on the small corner of the blanket on her other side. He had just gone to see Papa off, who was to ride to town for a few things before Dennis arrived. "Today is supposed to be relaxing, but you are not cooperating. I leave for a few moments, and I return to find you frowning at my house."

Aunt Pratt put a piece of cheese in her mouth. "No one could frown at Newcliff. What a notion, Lord Templeton."

"Indeed," Charlotte teased. "What a notion."

Luke chuckled and held his hand out to her. "I want to show you something. Will you walk with me for a moment?"

She nodded and he helped her to her feet. He did not release her hand and curled it under his arm. He led her toward the house, their pace slow. "For the record, I was most relaxed. The weather is lovely and the view even better."

Luke raised his brow. "And yet I so clearly caught your frown. You aren't nervous about tomorrow, are you?"

"Not about marrying you." Her cheeks colored. She was still not used to sharing her feelings so openly. Fortunately, Luke made it easy. They had both agreed to be honest with each other, no matter what. "My only concern is my ability to be a good baroness."

He squeezed her hand. "I am sure at times it will be hard for you. I can't make it rain every day, you know. You will have to be content staying by my side."

"All day long?" She laughed.

"How else am I supposed to steal a kiss when I want it?"

Heat filled her cheeks and her middle. They reached the house, and he let her in through a door off the veranda that led into the drawing room, preventing her from having to respond. "I hope you like my surprise." He pulled her to the fireplace and pointed above the mantle. There was her fan she had painted, with the bridge and their silhouettes. Somehow, he had procured a square frame for it and had it set elegantly against a dark matte.

"I thought it deserved a place of honor. I want this house to feel like it is both of ours."

She curled up against his side, and his arm came around her. "You make me feel as if I am some great artist."

"You are to me." He smiled down at her, and his marbled brown eyes seemed to sweep over her every feature. She caught his scent and leaned closer to savor it.

"I should ask what you are thinking, but I'd wager a guess," she said. With Luke, flirting came more and more naturally. It was nothing like Joan's lessons, but it was a product of trust and the easy flow of emotion between them.

"You'd guess that I want to kiss you?"

She grinned. "Was I right?"

"I think even my gardener or my cook could have guessed that." He chuckled, his face coming so near hers, his nose brushed her cheek. "And I would wager you would eagerly accept it." His breath teased her lips, and she could barely resist him long enough to answer.

"It seems you know me well." She scarcely finished her sentence before Luke covered her mouth with his own. Never would she have guessed that an unfortunate scandal and a hasty betrothal could lead to a beautiful romance. Charlotte returned Luke's kiss, never more grateful that her life had not turned out as she had planned.

Acknowledgments

I loved writing this story with Heather B. Moore and Jen Geigle Johnson! I hope you enjoyed it. I want to express my gratitude to my early readers: Mandy Biesinger, Emily Bradshaw, and Jill Warner. And special thanks to my family for their constant support and to my readers who keep me writing. As always, I must credit Heavenly Father for all my writer inspiration and for the opportunity to share another story with you.

Anneka R. Walker is an award-winning author, raised by a librarian and an English teacher-turned-judge. After being fed a steady diet of books, she decided to learn about writing. The result was a bachelor's degree in English and history. When she isn't dreaming up a happy ending for a story, she is busy living her own with her husband and adorable children.

Visit Anneka online: https://www.annekawalker.com/

More Timeless Regency Collections:

www.ingramcontent.com/pod-product-compliance
Lightning Source LLC
LaVergne TN
LVHW021759060526
838201LV00058B/3160